THE WIFE
WHO
RISKED
EVERYTHING

BOOKS BY ELLIE MIDWOOD

The Violinist of Auschwitz

The Girl Who Escaped from Auschwitz

The Girl in the Striped Dress

The Girl Who Survived

The Girl on the Platform

The White Rose Network

ELLIE MIDWOOD

THE WIFE WHO RISKED EVERYTHING

bookouture

Published by Bookouture in 2022

An imprint of Storyfire Ltd.
Carmelite House
50 Victoria Embankment
London EC4Y 0DZ

www.bookouture.com

ISBN: 978-1-80314-474-0
eBook ISBN: 978-1-80314-473-3

Dedicated to the heroic people of Ukraine. Before long, multiple books shall be written about your unimaginable bravery and sacrifices.

PROLOGUE

BERLIN. FEBRUARY 27, 1943

Something was terribly wrong. With her hand pressed against her chest, Margot watched the trucks pull to a stop along their narrow street, virtually sealing it. Through the fog of her breath on the glass, she saw the gray figures of SS men descend upon the snow-covered cobbles, slamming their jackboots onto the stones with blood-chilling finality. Moments later, they were inside the entrance to the building, their feet banging on the wooden stairs, their fists smashing into apartment doors.

Margot jumped at the sound of hissing behind her back— vicious, viper-like.

"Blast," she cursed quietly under her breath, groping for the burning ersatz coffee she had left on the stove. She grasped the handle with her bare hand and froze where she stood as the thunderous blows came again—raining on the front door of her apartment, this time.

"SS! Open up!"

Stunned and half-paralyzed, Margot wasn't aware of metal burning her skin until the pain caused her to scream and release her fingers. Hot liquid scalded the skin of her bare legs at the exact same time the butt of a rifle crashed into the lock of the front door.

"I'm coming!" Jumping over the puddle and waving her burned hand in the air, Margot rushed toward the door before they could break in and shoot her for not opening it fast enough. They'd done it to one of their neighbors already, during one of the previous round-ups, releasing a machine-gun round into her body right in the tub where she was showering, in front of her children.

"Aryan! Aryan!!" Margot shouted at the top of her lungs as she leapt away from the door, which was kicked open by the SS jackboot. She hastily took her identification paper from her pocket and held it up for the SS man to see.

Snatching it from her, he perused the document carefully, checked the name against the list and hurled it back into Margot's face. Any respect for a German woman flew out the window when the German woman was married to a Jew. This was nothing new. In the ten years that she and Jochen had been married, Margot had grown used to such attitudes. She caught her identification paper and stepped back, making way for more soldiers flooding the apartment.

"There's no one home," she said before they could start tearing the place apart in their search for inhabitants. "I'm alone here."

"Where's your husband?" the SS with the list demanded.

Margot looked at him. In his eyes was nothing but ice and death, and it occurred to Margot that only she stood between her husband and the man's machine gun.

ONE

BERLIN. AUTUMN 1935

Pins in her mouth, Margot kneeled in front of the velvet footstool—a suitable pedestal for UFA studios' rising star, Lida Baarová. She could very well understand Berlin's obsession with the Czech actress, who made up for her Slavic racial status with dark, sultry looks, lustrous locks and eyes in the depths of which one could drown—a veritable siren draped in burgundy silk. It pooled around Lida's satin pumps, one of which was tapping a nervous tattoo just before Margot's own eyes, which were red from strain and the blinding glare of the studio's mercury lamps. She shut them for a second, before threading another pin with utmost precision through the delicate material of Lida's gown.

"I'm not pinning it too low. Herr Wegener likes for the audience to catch a glimpse of his leading actress's ankle when she crosses her legs in front of the camera." Margot lifted her head, unsure if Lida had heard her.

The Hour of Temptation's leading star was staring at Margot with a blank look of utter incomprehension.

"Herr Wegener is your director," Margot clarified, speaking slower this time, secretly wondering if the rumors about Lida's mechanical learning of her lines without comprehending the German behind them were true.

Now that she thought about it, Margot hadn't once heard Lida speak to anyone on the set except for the studio-appointed speech specialist, who subjected his poor Czech student to regular torture in his attempt to make her sound like a native Berliner and who cursed like a fiend when, instead of crisp German consonants, soft Czech ones slipped from Lida's full lips.

When Lida finally uttered in her accented German, "I know who he is," it came out so soft and unsure, Margot felt an instant surge of sympathy for the actress. "It's just I don't think that I'm—"

The door to the dressing room flew open, cutting her short and causing Margot to stab her finger with the pin. Her sharp intake of breath was drowned by the producer's voice booming, "You're not ready still? Minister Goebbels is here and he has more important affairs to attend to than waiting for you to adjust the length of the dress that will be used only in the opening scene, which will be, in all probability, cut out from the film altogether during the editing." The wrathful glare of his black beady eyes fixed on Margot's finger in her mouth. "You pricked yourself? So clumsy. How did Wegener hire you in the first place?"

There was such outright maliciousness in his narrowed eyes, in that sneer Margot had grown to loathe with every fiber of her soul in the course of the past few months, it took all her effort not to throw something venomous in response and quit the blasted, poorly paid job on the spot.

"It's all my fault," Lida's faltering voice came in between their locked eyes. "I moved when I should have stand still."

"*Stood* still." To Margot's small triumph, the producer averted his gaze first, now fixing Lida with it. "Should have *stood* still." Rolling his eyes theatrically to the ceiling, he motioned to the women to follow him. "Take your sewing kit with you, Rosenberg." He spat out the Jewish name with such distaste that heat rose at once in Margot's cheeks—not out of shame, but out of sheer, cold hatred. "You'll be working on the set while Lida is rehearsing with Fröhlich."

Swallowing her pride, Margot worked for the next hour, crawling around on the set on her knees after Lida, stumbling over cables snaking around the floor and sweating profusely under the heat of the massive mercury lights aimed at her from all sides. When Director Wegener announced a break at long last, Margot finally straightened up, wincing as she unbent her back and rubbed some feeling into her aching knees. The sleeves of her white robe, studio staff uniform, were gray with dust. On her right stocking, already mended quite a few times, yet another hole was now showing.

In the corner, where Paul Wegener ordinarily took his coffee and an obligatory cigar during the break, Minister Goebbels was now sitting next to Lida, very close, with his crossed legs almost touching hers. He looked almost ridiculous next to the Czech beauty he was trying to woo, much too short, club-footed and it showed, with a chin that was too narrow and teeth too uneven and stained with nicotine. But he made up for it with the eloquence that had propelled him from an aspiring writer to the all-powerful Minister of Propaganda, the right-hand man of Hitler himself, the Gauleiter of Berlin who had the city at his mercy and, incredibly, all its women at his feet. Unlimited power and the sweet syrup of lies dripping off his lips had that effect on them. He hypnotized them into falling in love with him, much like he'd hypnotized the entire population of Germany into hating Jews, one of whom just happened to be Margot's husband.

Throwing a last glance at the abandoned set, she picked up her sewing kit and retreated back to the shadows, where she now belonged.

"That could have been you," a familiar voice sounded just behind her back. Margot didn't bother turning around. She knew it was Krüger, one of the picture's producers, and the most insufferable one. "That should have been your part. I wanted *you* to play the lead alongside Fröhlich, not that gypsy-looking Slav. With Wegener's vision and my money, we would have made you the biggest German star. An international star. Bigger than that bitch Marlene, who sold us out for Hollywood. And now, look at you, crawling on your knees like some lowly seamstress, wasting your God-given talent—" He seemed to almost choke in annoyance, then raked his hand through his hair, recovering himself somewhat. "It's not too late, Margot. With your looks, you could have the entire world at your feet."

He was so close, Margot could swear he leaned in and smelled the strands that had escaped her bun at the nape of her neck.

"Nobody told you to fire me, Ernst."

"I had no choice! Not after the Nuremberg Laws had been passed. You did it to yourself, Margot."

"Did what?" Half-turning over her shoulder, Margot measured him with her gaze. "Remained married to my husband?"

"Precisely."

"Since when is that a crime?"

"Since you're Aryan and he's a Jew. It's a race shame. You're effectively betraying your nation every day you remain married to him. And we can't have a UFA actress promoting *Rassenschande*, can we now?"

"I'm not promoting anything," Margot replied evenly. "I'm just trying to live my life."

"Are you telling me that you're choosing this"—he grasped her hand and brought her bruised fingers close to her face— "over that?"

She followed Krüger's gaze toward Goebbels kissing Lida's delicate palm with sheer adoration in his eyes.

Calmly, Margot extracted her hand from Ernst's, looked at him as though she was finding him perfectly amusing just then and walked away, shaking her head.

The question was ridiculous. Ernst would have realized it himself if he had met her Jochen in person. Having grown up during the post-war movement of German women's liberation in Weimar Berlin, Margot hadn't even thought of falling in love when she stood on the threshold of stardom not that long ago. Unlike her younger sister Gertrud, whose sole dream was to marry someone prominent or in a uniform, Margot had better things to do with her life than pursue any domestic bliss the new German Reich was promising. Neither did Jochen think of falling in love; he'd confessed that much, between giving directions to decorators following his set designs closely, and waving off the director and his ridiculous demands.

They'd met right here, in Babelsberg, at the staff canteen, not long before Hitler came to power. Jochen had jested with her effortlessly, invited her to the Romanisches Café—as a friend—and praised her determination to make a name for herself instead of turning into some Nazi bigwig's accessory, or worse, an SS breeding mare.

"Not a big admirer of the Party, I see?" Margot had teased.

"I'm Jewish," he had admitted with a barely discernable undertone of defiance about him that Margot had found impossibly admirable.

"Good for you."

"Is it though?" He had narrowed his amber eyes with mock sarcasm and snatched the recent issue of the anti-Semitic *Der Stürmer* from the newspaper waiter's silver tray. "Jewish fiends snatch blond Aryan maidens off the streets and molest them in some dark corners, you know. It's in the newspaper, so it must be true." As if to prove his point, he'd shown Margot the cartoon on the front page.

"Well, maybe some blond Aryan maidens don't mind being molested," she had teased back, and had then bitten her lip at her own audacity. There was some magnetism about him that Margot discovered to be positively impossible to ignore. He was handsome and seemingly unaware—or purposely negligent—of it. He had the face of an English nobleman, a bit too pale but sharp in all the right places, as though chiseled out of marble by a sculptor's hand, but not an ounce of the arrogance that usually went with such fortunate appearances. There was a perpetual wrinkle in between his brows that gave him the brooding look of someone constantly in thought, but under those golden slashes of brows, honey-colored eyes shone with mischief, crinkling in the corners each time he smiled. He raked back his enviously thick golden mane with his fingers instead of styling it, and in place of expensive suits, he wore sweaters thrown on top of shirts and didn't care one bit about the graphite staining his cuffs. An artist in the body of a professional athlete, full of good humor and perfectly placed sarcasm. Margot had kissed him first that very evening and lured him to her apartment on the Kurfürstendamm under the pretext of coffee.

"What do you know? It appears blond Aryan maidens are the perpetrators of the crime," he'd said the next morning, serving her coffee in bed—coffee they hadn't bothered with the night before. "I can't imagine what I shall do now that my reputation is ruined."

"I suppose I'll just have to make an honest man out of you and marry you."

It had been a joke, but somehow it wasn't and, just two months later, they were married. Now, Margot couldn't imagine how she had lived her life without him this entire time.

Would she choose Jochen over Goebbels' advances? Margot

almost laughed aloud as she recalled her former producer's question. *God, yes.* A thousand times over.

The same faint, amused grin was playing on Margot's face when she turned the key in the door of their apartment that evening and stepped inside, only to find herself in a veritable orangery. Bouquets of all sorts and colors covered the floor and every surface imaginable. The hallway was flooded with lilacs, roses, peonies and carnations, turning their ordinary Berlin apartment into a fragrant meadow. And in the middle of that fairy tale stood Margot's husband, smiling the smile that had made her fall in love with him three years ago, on the same set that had turned their dream into a nightmare.

"Jochen! What is this?"

"Flowers," he asserted with all seriousness, only the mischievous gleam in his golden eyes betraying his playful mood.

"Wherever did you get them from?"

"Gustav the florist," Jochen explained, embracing his wife and lifting her off her feet to plant a kiss on her mouth that sent her shivering with desire.

Margot had worked as a model for the Wertheim department store before Ernst Krüger had discovered her and signed her up for the UFA, but Jochen still towered over her with the impressive frame of a former professional athlete. He had abandoned competitive swimming after the UFA bosses discovered he had other talents too, only not as an actor but as a set decorator with an eye for expressionism. But then expressionism had gone out of fashion, together with the Weimar's democracy, and suddenly the famous Hans-Joachim Rosenberg had found himself on the street—along with every other professional who had the misfortune to be a Jew in a country suddenly infested with Brownshirts.

"He needed someone to decorate a new store he was opening on the Linden. Well, since it's a crime to be doing business with the likes of yours truly, I pretended that I did it out of boredom and he pretended that he didn't pay me in flowers."

Her arms resting on his shoulders, Margot lost herself in the liquid amber of Jochen's eyes and kissed him again, safe in the knowledge that, yes, she would choose him over anyone and anything, time and again. The adulation of the entire world didn't mean a thing; the love of only one man did, and that was all she needed to be happy.

TWO

BERLIN. AUTUMN 1935

The wan November sun wasn't yet up when the shrill sound of
the doorbell tore Margot out of her fitful slumber. Jochen stirred
next to her, threw the blanket off out of habit, but then paused
midway and looked at Margot. The torment in his eyes, still
veiled with sleep, nearly tore her heart in half. Just a few
months ago, he wouldn't let her as much as awaken before
placing a kiss of the tenderest affection on her shoulder. And
with a whisper—"Sleep, sleep, *Liebling*, I'll get that"—he would
send her back into dreamland.

But that was before they had to abandon their spacious,
beautifully paneled apartment on the bohemian Kurfürstendamm and move into East Berlin—the only arrangement they
could afford with their drastically reduced income.

That was before one official or the other made a habit of
conducting paper checks every other week, holding their
marriage certificate to the light with two fingers as one would a
dead rat before uttering, "You're still married then, hmm... You
are aware, Frau Rosenberg, that you don't have to go through
the pain of divorce proceedings." A pointed look, which Margot
invariably met with a blank stare. She'd grown used to these

men in suits. Before them, there were vacuum cleaner and insurance sellers; these men sold racial theories and Party ideology—same song, different words. "You can obtain an annulment if you only complete this form and submit it here, at the address listed on the bottom for your convenience." Margot never graced such suggestions with a response.

That was before Hans-Joachim Rosenberg had lost his German citizenship and become a Jew, a stateless person whose nationality had lapsed and who was now considered an illegal alien, a man without a homeland, an undocumented nobody with his fate hanging by a thread—a thread that could be cut on a whim by any of the new laws that the Nazi Party were churning out on an industrial scale.

And so it was Margot who threw the blankets off and snatched a robe from the foot of their narrow bed, saying, "Sleep, love. I'll get the door."

As she padded barefoot down the narrow, dingy corridor, floorboards stiff and cold as ice under her feet, Margot grimaced at the thought of this perverse new world order, in which a wife was the provider and protector and her husband was only alive because she refused to abandon him.

The doorbell screamed once again, right above Margot's ear, when she was already turning the lock—persistent and deafening. Yanking the door open, Margot was about to give the unwelcome visitor a piece of her mind, but choked on her indignation at the sight of a small, birdlike woman deliberately taking her arthritic finger off the doorbell.

"Ah, I thought you weren't home," the woman drawled in a syrupy, singsong voice. "Sleeping late?"

"It's not seven yet," Margot said weakly in her defense.

The woman, with gray hair smoothed with oil into a thin bun, scarcely reached Margot's shoulder, but Margot still felt herself cowering before her like she used to cower before Frau Böhler, her parents' building custodian, when she was a little girl. No child could be silent or invisible enough for Frau Böhler's liking and even the most well-behaved ones hadn't seemed to find themselves on the custodian's good side. Well-bred girl that she was, Margot had sincerely believed that if Frau Böhler witnessed one of Margot's good deeds, she would see that Margot was a good child, one who followed rules, who never made any trouble. The chance had presented itself when, upon her return from school, Margot had discovered some graffiti—*Kurt likes sausage in his mouth*—drawn in chalk on one of the staircase walls. Margot had stopped dutifully and, wetting her finger with spit, begun to remove the offending writing, the meaning of which she didn't understand at that tender age. As fate would have it, Frau Böhler's lover had come out for a smoke. Tugging on his atrocious cheap cigar, he'd watched little Margot erase the chalk—rather to her delight, it should be noted; he would surely report it to Frau Böhler, Margot had thought. Now, even the feared custodian would love her, the good child, the hard-working child, the conscientious child...

But the graffitied letters were much too big, her throat much too sore from the chalk dust she kept swallowing each time she wetted her little finger. Surely, no harm would come if she went home to eat her midday meal, change, and return thirty minutes later with a wet rag to remove the rest.

How devastating was the blow when Margot's mother had stormed into the kitchen, dragged Margot by the ear down two flights of stairs, past *in his mouth*, still visible on the wall, and positioned her squarely in front of Frau Böhler, who was standing in the door of her apartment with a malignant look of triumph all over her plump, red face.

The harder Margot cried, the more vehemently she denied any wrongdoing, the harder Margot's mother yanked at her ear.

"Apologize to Frau Böhler at once! For drawing *and* for lying!"

"I'm not lying!"

"Yes, you are! Frau Böhler's—" Her mother had stumbled, recovered herself quickly. "Frau Böhler's tenant saw you draw it!"

"I was erasing it, not drawing it!"

"Stop lying this instant!"

"I'm not lying!"

After that incident—which had broken something in Margot, snapped some naïve, childish belief in universal fairness—Margot had realized two things: that she would never trust in the authorities, and that even the closest family members could turn on an innocent person if that person was accused by someone holding power.

Since that day, she had never fully trusted her mother, nor her little sister Gertrud, who'd never missed a chance to tell on Margot in order to keep up the image of the favorite child. Since that day, she had grown progressively more defiant toward anyone in authority...

...Until this morning. Until Frau Fuchs, the landlady—so different in her appearance from Frau Böhler, and yet, so very similar in her manner, with those small, gleaming eyes like those of a vulture—brought the memories back with such force that Margot felt like a small, defenseless child once again.

"You know today's date, Frau Rosenberg?"

How was it possible for such a tiny, thin voice to reverberate with such power?

"Naturally, Frau Fuchs." Throwing a glance over her shoulder, Margot stepped over the threshold and pulled the door closed after herself. "It's December first."

"Your rent is due." Frau Fuchs smiled like a snake—a toothless, thin-lipped smile full of poison.

"I know, Frau Fuchs."

"Your December rent, that is."

"Yes." Margot passed her hand over her forehead. Beads of

sweat had broken out there despite the freezing temperatures outside.

"And I still haven't been paid for November."

"I apologize for the delay. I'll bring you the November and December rent money later today."

"I see Herr Rosenberg take the mail out of the mailbox every day at twelve."

Margot made no reply.

"He's not working, is he?"

"I said, I shall have your rent today."

"It must be difficult to pay your bills with only one salary."

"We're managing."

"If you're not, I can always move you to the attic. It's only one room and you'll have to use the outhouse instead of having your own private bathroom, but it's still better than—"

"I said, I'll bring it by later today!" Margot's cheeks were burning. She had long forgotten how it felt, being humiliated in this manner in front of so many ears, no doubt listening by their doors at this very moment. The walls were thin in Berlin's tenements and their inhabitants loved a new piece of juicy gossip.

But it wasn't the neighbors' opinion that made Margot clench her teeth as though in physical pain. She didn't give a brass tack if they heard her; she only hoped that Jochen didn't.

"See to it that you will. November *and* December." All traces of theatrical goodwill were gone from the landlady's bird-like, lined face. "I have a queue of good, hard-working tenants waiting for your apartment. I've been kind enough to let it to a Jewish household, but even my kindness has its limits."

"I'm not Jewish."

"Your husband is, and according to the Nuremberg Laws, if a husband is Jewish, the household is considered Jewish, Frau Rosenberg. You ought to subscribe to the *Beobachter* at least, if you don't fancy *Der Stürmer*. It would do you good to keep up to date with recent news."

"Whatever for?" Margot grumbled to Frau Fuchs' retreating back. "I have enough people *keeping me up to date with recent news.*"

Closing the door behind her, she discovered Jochen in his robe sitting on the edge of a stool in the kitchen. Judging by the desperate, haunted look in his eyes, he had heard every word.

"Margot, we haven't any money for rent?" His words came out in a strangled whisper.

Margot went to his side, taking his face in her hands and covering it in light, playful kisses. "What nonsense, love, really! Of course we do. It's just your silly wife isn't used to minding all our affairs and has forgotten to take the money out of the bank." The bank to which Jochen didn't belong any longer because he was a Jew. They were fortunate that at least Margot was "Aryan"; otherwise, they would have lost their joint account to the state altogether. Now, what used to be Herr and Frau Rosenberg's property was solely in Margot's name. "I shall go today, as soon as they open. Don't you fret about a thing!"

Jochen searched her face, studying her much too closely for Margot's liking, but he relaxed and broke into an uncertain grin after she gave him her brightest smile.

"You would tell me if we were in trouble, wouldn't you?" he probed gently.

"Of course I would."

"But we aren't?" He was still looking for reassurance.

"No. We aren't."

It was a good thing that he no longer had access to their bank account. It was an even better thing that Margot was such a brilliant actress.

THREE

Margot paused in front of the modern building with its gilded art-deco doors. There used to be a liveried doorman minding them, but after the Nazis seized power, he had quickly changed his livery to a brown uniform and was now some big shot in the local SA office. Nazis didn't care much for education or talent. German blood and fanatical loyalty was what mattered to them.

The doors, with their rays of Weimar-era suns, weren't all that heavy, but it still took Margot all her effort to push them open. This was her last resort. She'd roamed the city all morning, her mind feverishly at work, hoping to avoid coming here at all costs. Had Jochen not been at home, she would have gathered whatever UFA-issued gowns she had left and ventured to a seedy, dark street within walking distance from the Alexanderplatz to sell them to the same bearded fellow with tobacco-stained fingers into whose pockets most of her jewels had already disappeared.

Margot had sneaked them subtly, one by one, out of their apartment, so that Jochen wouldn't suspect anything. She knew her deception would have been uncovered if they still went out to the Horcher or the Romanisches, but those days were in the past. There were no fancy dinners to attend and so no reason for Margot to wrap herself in silk and fur stoles and pin her ash-blond hair with diamond studs.

Jochen would have been mortified if he had known. Only once did Margot mention the idea of selling her black fox coat, and she still remembered how well that had gone down. Jochen had paled, torn the fur out of her hands, stuffed it back into her closet that occupied nearly the entire wall in their old apartment (the one that also had marble floors and an elevator and whose staircases didn't emanate the stench of sour cabbage, stale cigarettes and urine), shoved its mirrored, sliding door closed and declared that he would hang himself before he would allow his wife to part with even one silk glove. And so, Margot began sneaking whatever wouldn't be missed whenever Jochen left for one odd job or the other. She had got away with it, and concealed their growing money troubles, until this morning and that blasted Frau Fuchs.

Her hand heavy on the polished wood of the handrail, Margot made her way, step by step, on the thick red runner nailed to the stairs by thick gilded rods, to the third floor. It was Sunday. They should be home at least till one or two before packing their silk-haired dachshunds into their Mercedes and driving to the Tiergarten for a walk and lunch. This had been their routine for as long as Margot could remember.

She fidgeted with her purse, raised her hand to the elegant brass knocker with the name Kasdorf under it, and lowered it once again without knocking—unable to commit—until the clicking of nails and barking betrayed her presence. There was nothing else for it now but to knock. Not that she had much choice, if she wished to keep a roof over their heads for at least another month.

"Quit your barking, you little beasts!"

Margot couldn't help but feel a mixture of shame and warmth fill her chest at the sound of the familiar voice on the other side of the door. It swung open and a young woman, the ropes of her long, almost black hair cascading down her white silk kimono, broke into a toothy, beaming smile. Anastasia Kasdorf, a half-Russian, half-German relative of the executed Romanovs, who had fled her homeland just before the Revolution and found her calling as an artist first in Paris and, later, in bohemian Weimar Berlin. It was here that Margot's father had fallen in love with her some ten years ago, stopping by her gallery to buy a painting he admired and discovering that he admired its creator even more.

Karl never divorced his wife—Margot's mother—from whom he'd been estranged long before Anastasia had come along. Now, he spent his days between two households: his own, where he and his wife slept in separate bedrooms, and Anastasia's apartment, which, Margot was well aware, he considered his real home.

"Margot! What a wonderful surprise!" Anastasia cried, sweeping Margot into a tight embrace and pulling her inside the apartment.

The air was clean and crisp, scented with citrus wood polish, freshly brewed coffee and Anastasia's French perfume. And all at once, Margot felt transported into a world of the not-so-distant past, when she, too, wore pajamas of white silk with delicate embroidery; when she, too, could employ a maid who waxed the floors and cherrywood cabinets once a week; and when she, too, could afford Chanel perfume—not only for special occasions, but just to enjoy its jasmine scent on a lazy Sunday afternoon.

"Please, forgive me for not calling—" Margot began, but Anastasia swept her apologies aside with a graceful wave of her hand.

"What nonsense! You're family. You and Jochen are always welcome here. How is he, by the way?" There was genuine concern in Anastasia's black eyes. An immigrant herself, she sympathized with everyone suffering from persecution and hadn't ceased speaking against the injustice, even though such speeches could now easily land one in prison.

"He's... managing," Margot said, pressing Anastasia's hand with all the gratitude she felt for her at that moment.

Her father's mistress or not, she was the only person whose questions about Jochen didn't start with an inevitable, "Are you still married to him?" That was the main reason why Margot had come to her and not her own mother. What a sad state of affairs that was.

"He doesn't have a work permit or any papers of that sort, but some old customers—who haven't emigrated, that is—still commission his work or recommend his services to friends who... you understand..." Margot left the words hanging in the air; a deliberate omission full of meaning. Covered by the cuff of her coat, her index finger kept picking at the cuticle of her thumb—a nervous habit she couldn't rid herself of.

"Can be trusted," Anastasia finished with a knowing nod.

"But mostly, he's a househusband now." Margot's lips trembled faintly as she tried her best to pull them into a semblance of a smile. "He doesn't complain though. And every evening I come home to a sparkling apartment and a hot dinner on the table. He doesn't say anything, but you can imagine how humiliating it must be for any man."

"Jochen is a good man. I'm sure he doesn't mind."

"Still..." Margot looked away, cringing inwardly.

"Still, if the tables turned and you were in that position, it is my profound conviction that you would have been grateful to him for standing by you and supporting you, just as he is grateful to you."

There was only a few months difference between them in age, but somehow Anastasia had become a mother figure to Margot, who knew just what to say and how to make everything better.

"And now, let me take that coat of yours before the dogs tear its hem to shreds. Remind me to book an appointment with the groomer to trim their nails. These little monsters, they've already destroyed my new rug! Your father is in the kitchen, reading. He had just had a batch of foreign newspapers delivered by that boy who works at the Adlon, so you know he won't notice if the sky drops on our heads while his nose is in his London press. Karl! Your daughter is here!" She shouted in the general direction of the kitchen, into which the dachshunds had disappeared, attracted by the mouthwatering scent of freshly baked bread rolls, eggs and sausage. "Kindly drop your glasses and give her a hug while I fix her something to eat."

Margot tried to protest as she was pulled into the spacious, sunlit room by her vivacious hostess, but all her efforts were thoroughly ignored.

"No, no, no, don't even shake your head at me," Anastasia said into the cabinet, from which she was fishing out another set of porcelain crockery. "Whenever a guest arrives, the host's first duty is to feed the said guest. It's an old Russian custom. It's not my problem that you've already eaten."

Margot hadn't, and she suspected that Anastasia had figured out that much but was much too gracious to say anything.

"Margarete!" Margot's father, indeed buried under mounds of foreign press, rose from his chair and spread his arms in a warm, if puzzled, welcome. "How are you, my dear girl? Has something happened?"

Karl wore a robe over his pajamas, and the still-tousled hair and a generally relaxed look on his face that was ordinarily creased with a careworn frown didn't escape Margot's attention. What a different man he was here; taller somehow, younger... happier.

"Does something need to happen for your own flesh and blood to visit you on a weekend?" Anastasia was upon him in a second, pretending playful indignation, to save Margot from embarrassment. Well, delaying it, if anything, until Margot gathered enough courage to ask for the money she so desperately needed. "She missed her father and didn't fancy visiting you at home with your harpy wife present. No offense." She held up her hand to Margot's benefit.

Margot couldn't help but burst with the grin of a conspirator. "None taken. She is a harpy—particularly lately."

"Pesters you about Jochen, eh?" Anastasia arched her expressive, wide brow.

"You don't know the half of it."

From Anastasia, another sweep of the hand. "Ignore her. Do you take cream with your coffee? Sugar? Me, neither. I like it dark and bitter, like my Slavic soul. Now, you know what you and Jochen need? To go out. No, hear me out. Your father and I, we're invited to a friend's party at his home in Grünewald. You ought to come. Karl, wouldn't it be just splendid if they came?"

"But of course!" Margot's father instantly joined in his mistress's enthusiasm.

"Without invitation?" Margot muttered, unsure.

"What invitation? You don't need an invitation. You're with us. Any friend of Stasia's"—he threw a glance full of unconcealed adoration at his Russian princess, calling her by her preferred nickname—"is his friend."

"Margot's not just a friend. She's family, just like Jochen," Anastasia added, placing a steaming cup in front of Margot, while Karl pushed a plate of bread rolls and eggs closer to her.

Under the table, Margot felt the wet cold noses of the pups nudging her ankle and, all at once, she indeed felt warm, welcome and at home in a way that she hadn't felt at her parents' house for years now; here, in the apartment of the woman who, according to Margot's mother, had ruined their family and was generally a whore and a bitch and a foreigner that had to be got rid of, just like the Führer had said.

The matter of money never had a chance to materialize. Just as discreetly as she fed starving Margot, Anastasia led her into her "boudoir," as she called it with a Parisian accent, held a new gorgeous evening gown adorned with pearls to Margot's frame ("It's much too small for me; I'd just get rid of it anyway, so do me a favor and take it off my hands, will you, Margot, love?") and slipped a thick wad of banknotes into Margot's pocket, all the while chirping about her latest exhibition and all the fun they would have at the Grünewald villa next week.

Margot gasped when, upon kissing her father and Anastasia goodbye, she stepped into the building's foyer and counted the money. It would not only pay their rent but see them through the entire winter.

She returned to the door, knocked, cried, "I forgot my gloves!" for her father's benefit and pulled Anastasia into a tight embrace. "I'll pay you back, every single pfennig," she whispered into the woman's ear.

"Pay me back what?" The Russian princess looked at her innocently. "I have not the faintest idea what you're talking about, dear. Now"—loudly—"here are your gloves, and don't forget next Friday." Lowering her voice once again. "There will be people there who can help Jochen with work."

Another gentle press of the hand, another friendly wink, and Margot felt her eyes swimming on the way home. Human kindness hadn't disappeared entirely, even in such a hell of a place as this new Germany.

FOUR

"*Ach!* Margot, do tell me this is my character's new dress!"

Margot's hand stopped just above the mannequin's shoulder she was about to drape with a chiffon scarf. Dressed in nothing but a very revealing, nude-tone negligée, Lida Baarová held Margot's own evening gown to her shoulders. The actress's face reflected such frank delight, Margot felt almost guilty at disappointing her.

"Afraid not." Gently but firmly, she took Anastasia's dress from Lida's hands. "It's mine. Not even mine, actually, but... something I borrowed for tonight. I shouldn't have left it hanging along with the other dresses, but it's silk; it would have wrinkled otherwise."

"Oh no, don't apologize, it was my mistake," Lida rushed to assure Margot, her black eyes, brilliant with admiration, still fixed on the gown. "I should have realized. Silver is not my color. I would have never pulled it off."

"You can pull off anything, you Greek goddess," Margot teased, hanging the dress behind the dressing-room's door. "I would kill to have your eyes and your gorgeous hair."

"But you're absolutely mad!" Lida regarded Margot in

astonishment. "You're a natural blond; it's all the rage right now."

Margot made no reply, only rolled her eyes expressively.

It was just as well that the poisonous remark she'd wanted to make hadn't left her lips, as the assistant director Hess stormed into the dressing room. Not in the least concerned with Lida's scrambling to cover herself up with a sheet of fabric—the nearest thing she could grab—he thrust a few drawings into Margot's hands.

"I need these costumes for next week's shoot," he said, and folded his arms across his chest. "Babelsberg Yuletide celebration is coming up."

"And?" Margot didn't grace him with a look, concentrating her attention on the drawings. They were almost identical to the ones that she had submitted: hers, the studio manager Klitzsch had torn in half with a sneer and announced, in front of the entire crew, that *there was too much Jewish gaudiness to them* before ordering *someone who is German to rework them entirely*. Judging by their current state, all "someone German" did was remove a tie from Lida's prospective suit and add a *völkish* motif to a dress that remained essentially the same. Just a few months ago, Margot would have exploded. Now, she only seethed with quiet disdain and left it at that.

"And, I have someone who's just dying to meet you."

"A representative of the Berlin Race office?" Margot asked in a deadpan tone, still sifting through the papers.

In her corner by the measuring table, Lida snorted under her breath.

Hess, however, only *tsk*-ed in apparent indignation. "No need to be so antagonistic, Margot. I'm only trying to help you, you know."

"How very kind of you," Margot replied in the same flat voice. "The trouble is, I don't think I'm invited to your Yuletide party."

Hess drew his gaze, full of theatrical suffering, to the ceiling. His expression was eloquent: it was the last thing he wished to concern himself with and here she was, being difficult as always. "Naturally, you're invited. You're German, aren't you?" He swung on his heel and was almost out of the door before he came to a sudden halt, as though remembering something. "Lida, Klitzsch saw your rushes yesterday. You need to gain some weight."

"But I'm heavier than Marlene Dietrich." The color draining instantly from her face, Lida pulled the cloth tighter around herself. "And her producers made her go on a diet..."

"We're not Hollywood, sweetheart. They like their women looking like stick figures. German women must project health, femininity and fertility. Granted, you're not German, per se," Hess made a dismissive gesture with his hand, cringing visibly, "but while you're under contract with the German film studio, you shall do as we say. Understood?"

"*Jawohl*, Herr Assistant Director Hess!" Unable to contain herself any longer, Margot slammed her heels together in a military fashion that would make any general proud. "I shall begin stuffing Lida's brassieres with cotton from Monday. I'll make her breasts so huge, they won't fit into a camera lens. Herr Klitzsch shall be very happy indeed."

Hess stared at her for a few moments, as if thinking of saying something, but then must have realized that Margot was beyond any help as he departed, slamming the door after himself.

"What an insufferable *Arschloch*." Margot shook her head and smiled when she saw Lida grinning at her in gratitude. Humiliation still showed in her cheeks in blotches of red, and her eyes were still swimming, but then Margot shoved a handful of crumpled paper into the mannequin's décolletage—"What do you think? Big enough for Herr Klitzsch?"—and Lida burst into laughter.

"Thank you, Margot," she said, blinking tears away, with her face directed at the ceiling, so as not to ruin her makeup. "You're a true friend." She let her improvised cover drop off her shoulders. "In fact, you're my only friend here, in Babelsberg."

It occurred to Margot then just how pathetic that was, that neither of them knew another friendly soul in an industry teeming with people who churned out one film about comradery and love after another, selling their lies to the unsuspecting public.

"Well, I say let's toast to our friendship," Margot declared in a bright voice, producing a flask from the pocket of her dress.

"Drinking at work?" Lida widened her eyes in mock amazement. "How very decadent of you!"

"I have to make it through the day without driving my tailoring scissors through anyone's eye, don't I?" Margot arched her brow after taking a healthy sip of brandy and handed the flask to Lida.

Without any hesitation, Lida also took a hearty swig and winced. "That's some vicious stuff you have there. Oh, my..." Nodding her thanks at Margot's offering of mint candies, Lida broke into another coy grin. "Something tells me you and I will have to have more fittings than usual from now on."

"You're always welcome here."

Lida's grateful smile faltered slightly when she eyed the stack of costume sketches on Margot's table. "Can I stay now or are you busy?"

"Not busy in the slightest. I've already begun tailoring the costumes I drew and submitted to the director."

"The ones that Klitzsch tore up?"

"The very same. They've scarcely changed them, so I'm very much on schedule." Margot looked up at Lida and tilted her head slightly. "Who are you trying to avoid at any rate?"

Lida hesitated before giving an uncertain shrug. "Minister Goebbels has been sending me flowers lately."

"*Ach*, the infamous Buck of Babelsberg is on the prowl again?" Margot teased, but receded at the look of concern creasing Lida's brow. "Don't fret, actresses are his weakness, but he won't pester you if you explain to him in no uncertain terms that you're not interested."

"It's not that." Lida was suddenly very interested in the worn linoleum under her feet. "He hasn't been pestering me, per se. It's just... Ugh." She passed her hand over her forehead, desperately groping for the right explanation, then remembered the makeup and cursed quietly under her breath in her native language. "Ignore me. You have enough of your own troubles to deal with. I'll sort my own out myself." With that, Lida perched on the edge of the measuring table swamped with scissors, rejected pieces of cloth, chalk and measuring tapes, and changed the subject. "So, where are you heading, all dressed up like a film star?"

"Frankly, I have not the faintest idea. Some event that my father's..." Margot stumbled, trying to find the right word, but then, seeing Lida swinging her long, shapely legs lightly, all girlish excitement and unconcealed enthusiasm, Margot felt a sudden urge to share everything with her. Lida wasn't Jewish, but she, too, was an émigré, a Slav snubbed by most of the UFA staff, and made fun of for her distinct accent behind her back by everyone, starting with the studio manager Klitzsch and ending with the stagehands. Who, if not Lida, would understand? "... My father's lady friend invited me and my husband along."

Everyone in Babelsberg knew that Margot's husband was Jewish. That was the reason why—right after the Nuremberg Laws had been passed, prohibiting all relationships between Aryans and Jews, but just stopping short of dissolving existing marriages—they had dropped *Margot* and replaced it with *Rosenberg*, until they ceased speaking to her altogether, which suited Margot just fine. Better to be ignored and left in peace than be constantly lectured about race shame and have to fend off unsolicited invitations to set her up with "someone suitable."

Everyone knew, but only Lida didn't even blink at the fact that someone in Berlin still invited Jews over.

"Your father's lady friend? I'm beginning to like you even more, Margot Rosenberg! And you two are... on friendly terms, I imagine?"

"Very friendly, yes. You would like her a lot. She's an émigré too."

"How splendid! From where?"

"Former Tsarist Russia."

"Nobility then?"

"Very much so. But she's so approachable, you'd never tell. A wild child of sorts. Very opinionated, too; has a lot to say about the ruling party..."

They were still chatting amicably when a studio staffer knocked politely on the door and inquired if Fräulein Baarová was available.

"Herr Minister Goebbels is here."

Despite the smile she threw over her shoulder on the way out, it occurred to Margot that Lida had a look of someone heading to the gallows.

FIVE

"It's quite amusing, isn't it?"

Lost in her thoughts and rather tired after a long day's work, Margot turned away from the taxicab's window, realizing that she'd missed what Jochen had been saying. "I'm sorry, what?"

"I was saying, it's quite amusing how one doesn't appreciate the small things until those little things are no more." He gestured vaguely around. "Traveling around in a warm cab instead of cramming ourselves into a U-Bahn train, for instance."

The well-bred man that he was, Jochen politely omitted to say why precisely the trains were so loathsome to him, just as they were detestable to Margot. The rush-hour crowds—thoroughly middle-class, white-collar commuters invariably armed with newspapers and leather satchels—weren't the ones that bothered the couple. It was the ones who came after them, drunk on cheap beer and stinking of it and stale sweat, their eyes bloodshot and breath putrid with slurred speeches copied almost word for word from the latest *Der Stürmer* about *those bloodsucking foreigners and snooty bourgeois spoiling it all for them, but that was all right,* der Führer *would show them all soon, he'd send them all to the reeducation camps yet and then life would he fine once again in Germany*—it was those crowds that made riding the train particularly intolerable. Lacking education, and good work as a direct result of it, they seemed to be mad at anyone who dared to wear a better coat than them, and picked fights with any "fairy man-whore" who dared to wear cologne on their train or offer his seat to a woman with a screaming baby at her breast, and then with any woman herself for daring to offer her breast to the child to quieten him. It all was so base, so very low and hateful and utterly revolting. Margot and Jochen didn't mind walking, her arm threaded through the crook of his, under one big umbrella, through sleet and mud and slippery cobbled streets, instead of descending to the bowels of human society and coming out at their stop dirtier somehow.

Now, as they rode in comfort through Grünewald, their legs warm and dry, tucked under a thick rug offered by a solicitous cabbie who even wore a uniform cap and who hadn't forgotten to lift it as he held the door open to Margot to help her inside, Jochen released a sigh of such deep torment, Margot felt something pinch inside her chest.

"This is the life that you deserve, Margot." His wistful gaze followed the amber shadows thrown by the tall lampposts, peered into the towering eyes of the French windows of the villas behind black wrought-iron fences. They had dreamt of buying one of those villas one day; had spent evenings with a glass of red wine on the floor in front of the fireplace in their old apartment, with Jochen sketching the furniture and the layout of their dream home and Margot gazing lovingly at him. Now, they couldn't afford to pay rent for a flat crawling with roaches and mice. The moisture dripping off the canopy of the trees over their heads and gliding down the taxicab window threw shadows over Jochen's face, making the streaks look like tears on his pale cheeks. "If it weren't for me—"

"Say another word and I'll punch you squarely on your handsome mouth."

Jochen stared at her with a mixture of amusement and something close to newfound respect. "Just where have you picked up such flavorful expressions, *gnädige Frau?*"

Margot responded with one of her famous one-shoulder shrugs. "The U-Bahn."

Through the rearview mirror, she saw the cabbie's widening, approving grin and for a few short hours everything was well again.

Tucked into the shadowy alley, the villa towered over the trees surrounding it, four stories high, crowned with small towers in the same red brick as the rest of the building and crawling with ivy—alien and mysterious in the diffuse golden light of the lamps. Elaborately crafted, the lamps themselves appeared to be transplants from some different place and even era, from the Ripper's London or a fog-shrouded American North, of which Margot had read extensively in Jochen's favorite novels.

The butler, attired in sharp tails, even turned out to be English. However, the crowd gathered inside was as multinational as Berlin used to be before the Nazis came to power and made *One Nation—One Country—One Führer* its motto.

When they had left their coats in the butler's gloved hands, Margot and Jochen stood in stunned wonder, gaping at the crowd shifting and whirling around them in its chaotic brilliance. The assault on all their senses was powerful: loud and impossible to resist, the sound of the saxophone and the piano sent waves of pleasant goosebumps all over Margot's exposed skin. Clouds of expensive perfume, leather and hints of citrus on the wood polished to mirrored perfection made her head swim. Tender and pink salmon melted on her tongue like butter —just one of the countless hors d'oeuvres carried around on trays by waiters in short, pristine white jackets piped with gold. Sleek and pleasantly cool to the touch, a glass of champagne sweated slightly in Margot's hand as her eyes drank it all in—the world without uniforms she had thought was no more; illusory and yet so very real.

"Margot, Jochen!"

From across the vast hall, Anastasia, dressed in black tails and a white silk shirt scandalously unbuttoned to reveal a hint of black lingerie covering her breasts, was gesticulating wildly at them as Margot's father stood by her side, a gentle smile playing on his face, slightly flushed from alcohol.

For a self-proclaimed misanthrope who preferred the company of her dachshunds to people, Anastasia had a rather uncanny ability to gather a crowd around herself. Either it was her striking looks or devil-may-care attitude, Margot couldn't quite tell, but she felt the same magnetic pull as she always did as she approached her now with Jochen in tow.

Anastasia made no bones about introducing Margot to the rather impressive crowd around her: "This is Margot, my step-daughter, and Jochen, my stepson-in-law."

"Are you quite certain they're not your siblings-in-law?"

Anastasia gave the joker a dirty look, but there was mischief in her eyes as she went on to say, "Flatter me all you want, you're still not getting a discount for my latest collection. I know you've been *dying* to sell it in your gallery. I have a certain life-style to support. I set the prices for my work—take them or leave them."

"Your Highness, you're slaughtering me in cold blood!" the man protested. "The inflation! The Wall Street crash—"

"Happened a long time ago and is no longer true," Anastasia countered, unimpressed. "Your excuses won't work. I saw you all salivating over my paintings, even though my biggest admirer wrote an entire essay about how bad they are."

"He's still after you, that poor sod?" The young man who

asked the question, accompanying it with a theatrical roll of mascaraed eyes, wore more powder than Margot, but, somehow, it suited him just as perfectly as those tailored tails fitted Anastasia herself.

"You're joking, right?" The gallerist arched a razor-sharp black brow. "He's been obsessed with Anastasia ever since her first exhibition here in Berlin."

"Who has?" Margot was growing curious in spite of herself. Somehow, among these artistic types, surrounded by liveried staff and with the champagne already gone to her head on an empty stomach, she forgot all about U-Bahns and the daily humiliations she had to suffer, surrendering herself to this fairy tale and its fantastic creatures.

"Oh, this yellow columnist who's secretly in love with me," Anastasia said, with a wink in Margot's father's direction. Judging by Karl's snort, the columnist had been the butt of their inside jokes for some time now.

"To be frank, the fellow's obsession with you *is* rather unhealthy," the gallerist said, assuming a pose of a psychiatrist on a nearby sofa. "I mean," he turned to Margot, "he attends literally every single one of Anastasia's early showings just to write how dreadful they are. You have to actually apply for these early showings, and he wastes hours of his life on an artist he supposedly despises with every fiber of his soul to write a several-page essay explaining why Anastasia is a terrible artist and how her works should be banned."

Even Jochen whistled at that, visibly impressed.

"I told Anastasia that she can easily blacklist him," the gallerist said.

"Why would I?" Anastasia shrugged, biting on a pickled cherry she fished out of her cocktail by its stem. "He's too amusing. Besides, every time he writes one of his essays, my sales go through the roof. One can't pay for this kind of publicity, so no, I am not blacklisting him. He's making me too much money."

"Doesn't it bother you though, the fact that he smears your work?" Jochen probed.

From Anastasia, another cold shrug. "Jochen, love, frankly, I don't give a rat's ass whether I'm liked by his type or not. I don't care whether I'm liked *at all* or not. Being liked doesn't pay my bills. I've lived through far too much to care about being liked. I care about cash. Cold, crisp cash. Because it's the cash that saw me through hunger and persecution; not my being a nice person."

And now Anastasia had invited Jochen here so that he could earn that cold, crisp cash that would get him out of the dark well, where she, former nobility, had nearly drowned. Margot looked at Anastasia, so artfully hiding her tremendous heart behind the veneer of a misanthrope and a nihilist, and felt the urge to find the columnist and spit in his self-important face.

"He writes all those things because he doesn't know you," she said quietly and through her teeth. "He doesn't know that you give half of all that money away."

"Margot, dear, what do I care? I do wish, though, that he would apply his talents otherwise. To something more constructive. Say, draw something that he would enjoy looking at, or write a novel."

"No, he can't," the gallerist countered from his couch, puffing on his fat, imported cigar. "You're a creative type, whereas he's a destructive one. People like him can only criticize. They cannot create. They're emotionally barren, no matter how they try to prove otherwise to the outside world. They scream to others about their passion, about how much they care, when, in fact, all they care about is themselves." He accompanied his words by a facial expression that was much more telling than his intentional, emphatic pause.

"*Ach*, leave him alone, Helmut. If telling everyone what a bitch I am gives him pleasure, then let him do so. No skin off my back."

"You're far too nice a person, Stasia." The mascaraed artist shook his brilliant blond head.

"I'm not nice in the slightest. I just love myself. That's the reason I survived through all that..." she gestured vaguely, indicating her past.

...*Without becoming embittered, broken,* Margot finished mentally what Anastasia had omitted. She was right about that, just like she was right about so many things, that enigmatic émigré with her crown of black hair, messy like thorns, around her high, white forehead. People who carry light inside them are incapable of hatred. People who carry darkness hope to spill it on everyone else just so they'll suffer the same way they suffer. To Margot, Anastasia shone as bright as a lighthouse among the dark waters surrounding them. Cold, black waves could crash over her all they wanted but they could never dim the light that attracted so many people, Margot's father and Margot herself included.

And Anastasia, unsuspecting of all the sentiments welling deep inside Margot's chest, was already taking her by the elbow with one hand and linking Jochen's arm with the other, excusing her way out of the circle as she steered the couple to the salon shrouded in clouds of cigar smoke.

"And now, down to business. The owner of the house is American," she began in an undertone, and without any unnecessary preamble, indicating the American with a thrust of her chin. "Has more money than he knows what to do with. Have you noticed ivy on the mansion's walls? He had it *transported* from his native state here, so he would feel properly at home." She arched her brows meaningfully. "As I said, more money than he knows what to do with. And just so happens that he's in dire need of a decorator."

A rather unremarkable man with bland features, he would have never caught Margot's attention had Anastasia not pointed him out to her. But when the American turned to hear one of his guests' remarks, and pulled forward, visibly interested, Margot saw the magnetic power of his narrowed gray eyes. It occurred to her then that the man was certainly *someone*. Before long, Margot was standing face to face with the millionaire as Anastasia made introductions.

"Call me John." He brushed away Anastasia's enumerations of his titles—something long and unpronounceable and including "the Third"—with an air of almost admirable negligence. "Is it true that you designed the sets for the last Mabuse film? The one that the Nazis banned before it had a chance to come out of the editing room?"

Jochen nodded, a bit at a loss. "I still have the sketches, if you should like to see them—"

"Why the sketches? I have a copy of the film." He jerked his thumb in the general direction of the back of the house. "Right there, in my projection room."

"I thought the Propaganda Ministry destroyed the negative?" Margot blinked at him in stunned amazement.

"Not before I got my hands on a copy." Hands thrust in pockets, John shrugged, wonderfully unconcerned. "I can see why they banned it. It does make quite a mockery of the Nazis. Funny stuff. We should watch it one evening. I'm sure you would enjoy it thoroughly," he said, bowing slightly to Margot and Anastasia.

"Give me anything expressionist and I'm there." Anastasia raised her champagne glass in a toast.

"Just a moment." Jochen was frowning, and refused to let the matter go. "But just how did you manage to procure a copy? I worked at Babelsberg at that time. Lang was just readying the negative for the first screening when the uniforms showed up and confiscated it on the Propaganda Ministry's orders."

"My good fellow," the American leaned toward him confidentially, "do you really think that Lang would make a film mocking the Nazis without making at least a few copies before

surrendering the negative to them? He's a shrewd little bastard.
As a Jew, or a baptized Jew, or a half-Jew—whatever he calls
himself these days—he knew that his days in Germany were
numbered. He also knew that the Nazis would most likely seize
his assets. He needed pocket money to start anew in his country
of choice. He calculated right that selling a film that made
Hitler into an idiot to people like yours truly would bring some
honest American cash without angering American studios,
blissfully unsuspecting of his little machinations. Technically,
he didn't do anything wrong. If anything, he saved a historical
picture for future generations, while flipping a major bird
goodbye to the Nazi government at the same time. I don't know
about you, but I admire such brass bal—" He quickly caught
himself. "Pardon me, ladies are present. I admire such... un-
apologetic boldness in a man. Now, that projection room of
mine, I want to have it made into a motion pictures theater, with
a sound system, chairs, everything as it should be. Money and
materials are not an object. When do you think you could
start?"

And just like that, almost as an afterthought to a lengthy
speech, Jochen suddenly found himself employed.

Later, Margot hugged him tightly, discreetly, in a dark
corner of a library into which no guests wandered, among the
intoxicating scents of old leather, paper dust from first editions,
journals from all over the world and banned books that had
narrowly escaped Goebbels' infamous pyre of 1933. There,
basked in the silvery moonlight that filtered through the
windows, they kissed, drunk on champagne and renewed hope,
and believed that everything could be well once again—because
of people who still cared for the others in a dog-eat-dog world
and openly proclaimed their respect for rebels and free spirits,
instead of hurling them into trucks to concentration camps.

When they returned to the smoking room, they found Anastasia at the center of a small group of men listening to her in

rapt attention. Brandy had replaced champagne in her hand and her eyes had acquired a hard, somewhat savage look about them. Margot had seen the same look of fiery, naked hatred in Anastasia's eyes whenever she purposely strolled into a Jewish store guarded by the Brownshirts and stared them down until they were the first to avert their eyes.

"The hypocrisy, that's what makes my skin crawl each time I hear them spew it from their podiums. And, no offense, Johnny, love, but your country is no better than my adopted one."

"Wait, wait, wait," their host laughed, waving a palm in front of his face. "The United States was one of the first countries that wanted to boycott the Games."

"Then why, in that case, are they readying their Olympic team for the Winter Games as we speak?" Anastasia pressed, slightly drunk, loud, and somehow even more charming in her uninhibited state. "I'll tell you why: as soon as the Germans promised you billboards all over the North, you Americans suddenly forgot all about Jewish persecution."

"You're vilifying capitalism too much for someone who has suffered from the Bolshevists." John laughed once again, but somewhat embarrassed this time.

"I'm not vilifying capitalism in the slightest!" Anastasia protested. "I love money. It gives me freedom to buy what I want, do what I want, and tell whoever I want to kindly piss off. Yes, I said piss off." She turned to a couple of young men who had burst into delighted heckles at such a colorful vocabulary coming from the Russian-German nobility. "In case you missed it the first time, I have suffered from the Bolshevist oppression. I have the right to curse all I want. Now," she turned back to her host, "before we were so rudely interrupted. I love capitalism, John, I truly do. But only until it turns to greed. I love capitalism because it gives me freedom to make as much as I can and give away as much as I can afford to the ones who need it. I know that you're a generous man as well; this is not about us. This is about those dirty moneybags who chose greed over morals. Who sold their conscience for German Reichsmarks—"

"Wait, no, Stasia, it's not the case—"

"Very much the case."

They were talking over each other now.

"Our government demanded that all persecution of minorities in Germany stopped and it did—"

"Oh, did it now?"

"Have you seen any more signs stating that Jews aren't welcome?" John asked.

Instead of a reply, Anastasia burst into cold, mocking laughter. "Signs? Oh, Johnny, my sweet, naïve child. You've just hired Jochen, haven't you?" Her laughter stopped abruptly; her hand, with an almost empty glass in it, was now pointing at Jochen, who, Margot saw, promptly lowered his eyes under everyone's curious gaze. "Do you know why? Because he can't find a job anywhere else. Go ahead, ask him if the persecution of Jews ended. Ask him if he can walk around freely, doing whatever he wants. Ask him if he risks going to a swimming pool or a tennis court. Or even to a café that he used to frequent and where the barman will recognize him and kick him out before he can even order his first drink. You ask your new decorator how good it is now for German Jews after you, Americans, interfered and made everything go away as though by magic."

Margot couldn't hear Anastasia's last sarcastic words behind the rush of blood that was pulsing in her ears. With unconcealed terror, she clasped Jochen's hand, just as cold and clammy and faintly shaking as hers, as the scene of a veritable apocalypse was unraveling before her eyes. It was idiotic, of course, feeling as though an abyss was cracking open under her feet, when Margot would have been the first one to laugh off the entire silly situation in the not-so-distant past. *A friend had a bit too much to drink and went into politics—it happens to the best of us. Let her sleep it off; she won't even remember it tomorrow.*

But now, something so insignificant, so positively absurd, threatened to turn their very lives upside down. Imploringly, Margot stared at Anastasia, whose righteous wrath knew no bounds.

"Don't you dare explain persecution to me, John. I lived through it. I know far too well what being a person without a land is. What it is to be unwanted, hunted! Have you ever had to sell your hair to pay for a room? Have you modeled naked for hours on end in a room full of art students to pay for your own lessons? Have you camped out in front of one embassy after another, trying to restore your papers? I was fortunate. The German embassy took mercy on me because of my father. But where should Jochen go? No, you tell me where. Palestine, perhaps?"

Margot was shaking. Jochen didn't need all this righteousness just now; it wouldn't change a thing. They'd grown immune to injustice. All they needed was the opportunity to work, to earn a living, no matter how illegal in the government's eyes, and now Anastasia was spoiling it all for them, souring their generous host's mood, and there wouldn't be any work to be had anymore, and who knew if his guests would go and denounce Jochen Rosenberg, a Jew, for trying to illegally obtain a job. And then it would be jail for him, or worse, that God-awful Dachau camp near Munich with which the SA loved to threaten all enemies of the state. Forced labor, beatings, who knew what else—

With lightning speed, hellish images of her husband being torn out of her arms and thrown into a truck flashed before Margot's eyes. Before she knew what she was doing—it was an animal's instinct, the prey's instinct to which they'd been reduced—Margot pulled at Jochen's hand, backing out of the room and tugging him after herself: to the safety of the darkness outside, where they could hide, where she could protect him still.

"Let's leave. Let's leave at once," she whispered, her voice suddenly robbed of all strength. They would walk until they found a taxicab. Or a U-Bahn station, whichever came first—it didn't matter any longer. They would run, run as far away as their legs would carry them.

SIX

When Margot arrived at the studio the following week, she found its skeletal staff immersed in a collective somber mood. Uncharacteristically ill-tempered, Director Wegener stalked about the set smoking and quarrelling with just about anyone who had the misfortune to cross his path.

"What are you doing with that film stock, you miserable oaf?"

Just then, it occurred to Margot that the young man with the shocked expression wasn't their usual cinematographer. Startled by Wegener's shout, he nearly dropped the film stock, but caught it after a few frantic manipulations. Holding it against his chest, he blinked at the director, who had descended upon him like a hawk.

"I'm asking you, what are you doing with that Kodak stock?"

The new cameraman opened and closed his mouth, made an uncertain motion toward the camera as though to state the obvious, then receded under the director's deathly glare and lowered his hands in surrender.

"Do you even know the difference between Kodak, Agfa

and Perutz stock? Of course, you don't. Have you even operated
the cinematographic camera before, what?"

"I..."

"I said, what?!"

"I have seen Herr Traut operate it."

Margot saw a vein bulge on Wegener's reddening face. He
was on the verge of exploding. However, at the last moment,
when the entire staff was preparing for the magisterial dressing-
down that was surely about to follow, Wegener only threw his
hands up, hissed a curse under his breath and stormed off the
set, kicking a wooden ladder on his way out.

"Where is Traut?" Margot asked no one in particular.

Most of the staff ignored her, as was their habit. Only
Heinz, the makeup man, whose love for juicy gossip
surpassed his Party loyalty, instantly broke into excited
whispers.

"Goebbels and his Promi people pulled all the good cinematographers from all the current productions to make a docu-
mentary about the Winter Games at Garmisch. We're left with
assistants and students for the time being."

Margot nodded her understanding as she watched the
assistant director explain patiently to the young cameraman on
the verge of tears the difference between the film stocks.

"We use Kodak only for the close-ups and so-called portrait
shooting as Kodak retains most of the shades and, therefore, a
character's expressions..."

"Is that what's got into Wegener then?" Margot whispered
at Heinz, making use of his chattiness.

"Oh, no." The makeup artist made a wry grimace. "Have
you noticed the absence of someone else?"

Margot looked around the set, struggling to see who was
missing. "The producer?"

Heinz rolled his eyes. "Whenever a producer is absent, it's a
blessing for a crew. We can film just fine without a producer.

Now, without a leading actress the task is more challenging."
He arched a meaningful brow.

It took a few moments for the meaning of those words to
dawn on Margot. "Lida? I assumed she was simply late."

"Wegener wishes that was the case." Heinz snorted with
disdain. "No, Margot, darling. Together with the best cinematographers, Dr. Goebbels requisitioned Fräulein Baarová as
well. Now we have to quickly reschedule the sequence of the
scenes to film whatever we can without her. Which, at this
point, means stills. We use Agfa for stills, architecture and such,
you muttonhead!" he shouted at the poor cameraman, causing a
tutting from the assistant director and, rather to his delight, snig-
gering from the rest of the crew. "Not Kodak. Even I know
that." He shook his head, his mood improving by the moment.
"Good for us, too. It appears, while they're shooting stills and
scenery"—He brought both hands to his mouth even though the
cameraman was well within hearing distance—"Perutz is what
you use for all that greenery outside, by the way!" Delighted
with his own joke, he turned back to Margot. "You and I shall
be temporarily out of work, Margot, darling. Enjoy your week
off. Or a month. Ta-ta!"

He was long gone and Margot still stood, stunned, as though
after a physical blow, in the shadows of the set, sensing an
ominous darkness close in on her like the lid of a coffin. Her
head was growing lighter by the moment and in the back of her
mind, like a demented alarm, one single thought was pounding:
out of work, out of work, out of work...

With a faint groan, Margot wiped her hands down her face.
She wanted to cry, but the tears wouldn't come; only something
black and acidic churned in the pit of her stomach.

Later that day, as she stood on the platform of a rat-infested U-
Bahn station, Margot vaguely recalled approaching the assistant

director, hearing his reassurances that they would summon everyone back as soon as the "Games business" had sorted itself out, asking her own stupid question about how precisely would they summon her—she didn't have a phone—and the assistant director turning away, already preoccupied with something that was much more important.

"Call the studio from a public phone; what's the big trouble?"

"When?"

"I don't know." Irritably, "Every morning?"

In the distance, the train whistled sharply. Margot hadn't told the assistant director that the public phone cost money; money that she didn't have now that she was out of work. From the depths of a tunnel, two glaring eyes of a steel beast appeared and, out of sheer madness—to the devil with it all—Margot stepped resolutely to the very edge of the platform, began leaning forward with her entire body of some desperate need... when a hand gripped her by the collar and yanked her forcefully back.

"Are you drunk?!" A voice roared above her ear, mixing with the squealing of the train coming to a halt and a shout of a conductor calling out the station's name and the next stop.

Still held by her collar like a dog, Margot turned toward a bear of a man in greasy worker's overalls and felt her lips quivering, stretching into an ugly grimace of utter despair. "I lost my job today..."

As though by miracle, the worker's features smoothed, relaxed into an expression of deepest sympathy. Releasing a handful of Margot's scarf and coat, he patted her awkwardly on the shoulder as the current of people swept around them, stuffing itself into an already packed train. "Don't you cry, old girl. This whole business, it's a bitch, the economics and the like. Things'll turn round still, you'll see. Is this your train?"

Through her film of tears, Margot regarded the crowded car dubiously but gathered herself and managed a nod.

Without any visible effort, the worker stepped inside and parted the commuters with his great paws like some East Berlin Moses parting the Red Sea. "Come 'ere, old girl. See, there's enough space for all of us—"

Whether it was those words or the tone in which he uttered them, the reaction they provoked in Margot was akin to someone cutting the thin thread that was holding everything inside her together. Muttering her thanks for his grubby hand-kerchief smelling of machine oil and faintly of iron, Margot wiped the streams of her tears and wept even harder at the thought that there was most certainly not enough space for all of them here. Not in Berlin; not in this new, Hitler's Germany.

Margot was on her hands and knees, scrubbing the floors, her eyes staring blankly into space. To preserve the electricity, only two candles provided the light for the entire hallway. Jochen was still out, selling charcoal sketches of Berlin to tourists near the Linden or Alexanderplatz. Portraits fetched more money, but they took longer to complete and sometimes the police—or worse, the Gestapo—arrived and demanded permits, which he, naturally, didn't have. Besides, it was much easier to gather his postcard-sized sketches and bolt at the warning whistle of a fellow black-market operator or a well-meaning prostitute without losing any profits than try to haul an unfinished life-size portrait he'd never be able to sell down the U-Bahn steps or through the narrow gaps between the Berlin tenement maze. Margot knew the deal. Jochen had told her about his escapades often enough, invariably laugh-ing, making them out to be harmless adventures, just so she wouldn't fret, wouldn't block his way out of the apartment and remind him that he couldn't possibly be arrested because it wouldn't be a simple arrest for trading without license; it would be something worse, much worse—because he was a Jew and Jews no longer had any rights as they weren't even citizens anymore, and therefore no one gave a rat's behind about what happened to them.

This was the first evening that Margot hadn't stopped her husband from gathering his drawings and heading out. Now, the guilt was eating her from the inside out, a vicious, ravenous worm that wouldn't still itself, no matter how hard she scrubbed the floors until her hands were raw and stinging, no matter how much she tried to feed it with explanations of how it was anyone's guess when they'd summon her back to the studio, if they would at all, and how the rent had to be paid and food bought, and how, out of them both, only Jochen could draw— else, it would be her shifting her weight from one frozen foot to the other, hoping for someone to buy at least one sketch before the police arrived and she'd head home, hungry, broke and disgusted with herself, just like Jochen had done countless nights before.

Somewhere, on the staircase, something crashed; drunken curses and shuffling were followed by the turn of a lock and a high-pitched dressing-down, replete with expletives that would make any sailor blush, with threats to *throw his no-good, stinking tail out into the street where he belonged; her mother was right; she ought to have listened to her; then, she'd end up a clerk's wife and not with some idiot plumber who fixed his clients' wives' pipes all right—*

The door was then slammed shut and Margot couldn't make out the rest; not that she had any desire to. To her, the return of the plumber neighbor for the night meant only one thing: the *Lokal* across the street where he got piss-drunk every evening after work had closed and Jochen still hadn't returned.

Margot scrubbed harder.

Through the paper-thin walls, the unappetizing stench of

fried fish had seeped and was now gone. Jochen was still out, in that indifferent, snow-shrouded Berlin night.

Margot changed the water, noticed that it was almost clear, but filled the bucket nevertheless and resumed her obsessive scrubbing.

Outside the window, the lights in the building opposite blinked out one by one. Only the red neon sign at the top floor, half-burned out but still discernable, advertised rooms by the hour. Somewhere on the second floor, the baby had finally stopped crying. Even the street dogs didn't bark any longer at the measured steps outside, echoing steel-like and cold off the mold-stained walls. The SA patrols, not regular police; by now, Margot could tell the difference. Regular police didn't wear iron-lined boots. Only Hitler's thugs did.

And Jochen was somewhere out there, a Jew without papers, fair game for them to stalk, to taunt, to kill at will.

In a sudden spasm of anguish, Margot hit the bucket with her elbow and gasped as cold water pooled around her, the neon sign on the building across coloring it blood-red. She looked at it in mute, helpless terror for some time, but then—the neighbors! They had nothing to pay for their ruined ceiling, let alone wallpaper. Margot threw herself on the pool of bloody water and began mopping it up and squeezing it into the bucket like a woman possessed.

It was quarter past one when Jochen returned at long last. Margot heard him from the sofa in the living room, where she was waiting for him, half-awake, jumping at every sound. He was shushing at someone who wasn't familiar with the layout of the room and therefore banging into things and apologizing in hushed whispers.

When Margot turned the light switch on, all four people froze where they stood, like criminals caught red-handed. Only

Jochen was grinning his silly, guilty smile that Margot missed to death and had been so very afraid she would never see again. His companions, Anastasia and John, were nudging one another silently, while the fourth person, looking suspiciously like a manservant, held in his arms appetizing-smelling dishes stacked to his chin.

"Margot, look who I ran into tonight," Jochen said sheepishly, gesturing with his thumb over his shoulder, looking like a dog expecting a thrashing. "I hope you're not too mad that I'm so late, but they kidnapped me—"

"Outright kidnapped him, right from the street!" John was the first one to recover himself. He stepped forward, though not without difficulty in such a narrow space, removed his hat and kissed Margot's hand, all gallantry. "I hope you will forgive us. The poor fellow was freezing half to death and starving, so I just had to bring him to dinner, even though he insisted that he was expected at home."

"There's a curfew," Margot heard herself saying, barely audibly. She placed her hand on her throat, still raw from tears and fear. "Curfew, for Jews…"

"Oh, Margot, you must hate me, you poor lamb!" It was Anastasia this time. Without any ceremony, she pushed John out of her way and pulled Margot into a tight, sisterly embrace, enveloping her in a cloud of her French perfume. "I behaved like such an idiot at that party! Alcohol doesn't agree with me, I fear; your father has been telling me this for some time, but did I listen?" She shook her head and the fur of her fox collar tickled Margot's cheek, sprinkled with melting snow, but still so very soft. "I should have come earlier, but I was too embarrassed to face you. Finally, your father gave me a metaphorical kick in the backside, and here I am! Ha-ha… well, I stopped at John's first—I don't quite remember what I said, but I imagined I owed him an apology as well—and we were actually in a taxicab on our way to your house when we saw this pretend

Gustav Klimt right under the lamppost of the Alexanderplatz U-Bahn."

"You haven't the faintest idea what she did," Jochen said, producing a thick wad of bills from his coat's pocket. "She climbed out from the cab and, before I could say a word, began calling me some strange Russian name I have never heard and asking me how I made it out of Russia, saying that she hadn't seen me for years and how she couldn't believe that one of Tsar Nicholas's favorite painters was now reduced to selling his sketches in the streets of Berlin and how they would cost a fortune once again."

"I wasn't even well into my speech about an American millionaire who'd buy them in an instant when some Herr Monocle descended on us, absolutely crazed, and bought the entire collection for four hundred Reichsmarks," Anastasia finished, positively beaming now.

"I would pay to see that show a second time!" John guffawed and, remembering something, turned to the manservant and gestured him forward. "Forgive me, please; it slipped my mind entirely! Your dinner, Frau Margot. After we kidnapped your husband with such blatant disregard to his own desires and the worries you had to endure, no doubt, he positively refused to eat. Asked me to pack whatever I wished to offer him, so he could bring it to you. Just so happened, I do have enough to feed both of you—"

"You have enough to feed all of Berlin," Anastasia said with a pointed look at him.

"I give to charity, so stop it with your glares." John turned back to Margot. "I fed Herr Joachim first and brought you—"

"—Half of your pantry, judging by the looks of it," Margot said, following the overtaxed manservant trying to navigate his way into their narrow kitchen. "Herr John, this is too much—"

"Nonsense. I have plenty to give and so I shall." John's eyes suddenly had a faraway look in them. "I already lost it all once when the market crashed. I know what it's like to have it all and to lose it all. If it weren't for the people who helped me start over, I wouldn't be where I am now. And the man who helped me the most, he wouldn't take a dollar back from me. Said, 'I already have enough to last me a lifetime. Maybe someday, you'll help someone who could use a friendly hand as well, eh?'" John winked at Jochen, clapped him on his back, bowed to Margot and Anastasia ceremoniously and went out, the manservant following him like a loyal shadow.

"That's what I wanted to apologize to him for," Anastasia said, throwing a glance at the front door John had left slightly ajar. "I didn't know that he was once in our shoes. Karl—I mean, your father—told me. Needless to say, I felt like an even bigger *Arschloch*."

"You're not an *Arschloch*." Margot discovered that she was smiling. "You're just a half-mad, passionate Slav with a pride rivaling only old Bismarck. The worst combination of two nations. Your parents should have never married."

Anastasia exploded in laughter, turning to leave. "They shall be saying that about your children!" she cried from the staircase. Someone called for her to shut her trap and she promptly advised them to shut theirs before she shut it for them. "Don't forget, you're starting tomorrow, Jochen!" Anastasia shouted as she reached the ground floor and headed out into the street.

Looking out the window, Margot saw John's car waiting, with the manservant holding the door open for the mad Russian princess. They drove off and the street was silent again. Beyond the window, the snow was falling softly, and, in the glass, Margot saw Jochen's reflection, his eyes gazing into hers.

"Come, eat," he called, tugging at her hand. "I brought you food. So much food, Margot. Even dessert!"

Margot wasn't hungry from all the nerves, but she followed him all the same. Her husband finally stood taller, with his shoulders squared, he finally felt like a man again, a man who could provide for his family, and it would have been the most dastardly thing to do, to refuse him the pleasure of seeing her enjoy the fruits of his labors.

Margot didn't object when Jochen flipped the switch on in the kitchen and only smiled as she saw his grin grow at the sight of her consuming her late-night dinner.

"Margot?"

"Mhm?" Her mouth was full. Her appetite had returned with a vengeance and she dropped the fork and picked up the leg of goose with two hands, sinking her teeth into its delicious, juicy meat.

"Do you think they'll truly say... what Stasia said?"

"About what?" she asked through the goose.

"About our children."

Margot stopped chewing abruptly.

"I know, I know, it's illegal for us to have children," Jochen began, stumbling over his own arguments. "They will arrest you and deport me to heavens know where, and the child—"

The rest he left unspoken. They would take the child and deport the newborn together with the father. No one needed more Jewish brats in the new German Reich. Margot knew it and swallowed with difficulty. The meat had suddenly lost all its taste. That was why they were so very careful. That's why a child was out of the question. And yet she looked into Jochen's eyes, reached for his hand and squeezed it with all the love she felt for him. "They will. When all of this over, they will."

SEVEN

BERLIN. SPRING 1936

With the spring thaw came hope. Everything seemed to be finally falling into place. Each day, Jochen left for work at John's villa with a valise in hand and a previously long-forgotten air of purpose about him. Each Saturday afternoon, he brought his weekly pay in a thick envelope, embarrassed to a degree about the amount of it, half-wondering if John was paying him more than he actually deserved. Things were beginning to look up. Before long, the idea of moving into a better building, a better neighborhood, started to creep into their dinner conversations.

When the Winter Olympics at Garmisch came to an end, the filming resumed, and Margot was back to wrapping Lida in silk and velvet—a personal present for Dr. Goebbels, signed *yours truly, Margarete Rosenberg*. The scandalous affair between the rising film star and the Reich's Propaganda Minister was no longer a secret. It was loud and clear on Lida's glowing face and the adoring smiles that were for Herr Minister only. It spilled itself from every bottle of Clicquot sent to Fräulein Baarová's dressing room, drowned in red roses and passionate notes in her high-ranking lover's handwriting.

Director Wegener disapproved but said nothing: the film's

budget had suddenly doubled, and he wouldn't be the one to question the reason.

Lida's fiancé, Gustav Fröhlich, definitely disapproved, but, just like Wegener, he kept his mouth shut, though for different reasons. Gustav was an actor as well and if he wished to continue to be one, it would have been utterly idiotic of him to pick fights with the man who could easily bring a swift end to his career.

Out of the entire film staff, Margot disapproved the most. Though, unlike her male colleagues, she actually had a spine. She held out for as long as she could; gritting her teeth in disgust whenever Goebbels' lips touched the back of Lida's hand; swallowing poisonous comments whenever Lida read her lover's notes to her in excited whispers, and tried her damnedest not to roll her eyes whenever the actress pressed the small square of paper to her heart and whispered, "He loves me, Margot. He truly does!"

He is incapable of love.

"He says he'll make me the biggest star of Berlin. Of the entire German Reich!"

He'll say anything for you to reject that offer from the American producers.

"He says he'll leave his wife for me."

It was then that Margot stabbed herself in the thumb with her small sewing scissors. "Blast!" she hissed, bringing the injured thumb to her lips. "Look, Lida. I know it's none of my business, but..." She sucked on her thumb again, as if in the hope that Lida would interrupt her in time, say something haughty and disdainful and make Margot lose all sympathy for her.

But Lida was listening closely, with her pretty head tilted slightly to the left, and Margot exhaled loudly, feeling the words surge to the surface, ready to break the dam.

"Dr. Goebbels is just as charming with women as he's ruthless with men," she began carefully.

"Is this about his politics? Oh, Margot, I know; I understand." Lida hid her face in her hands. "I disagree with many of the positions he takes," she proceeded through her fingers, her eyes still tightly shut. "We argued so much about it at Garmisch, and you know what? I think he saw reason. Whatever subjects he wouldn't even budge on before, we began to discuss little by little. He confessed to me that he'd never talked politics to women, Margot; that I'm the first woman that he—" She waved her hand in front of her face, breaking into embarrassed laughter, "No, no, I know how it all sounds. I hear myself and I know precisely what you think. *Naïve little girl, what are you thinking? Isn't it what all men have been saying to women from the dawn of time?* But it's different with him. He said..." The words caught in her throat. For an instant, Lida's eyes darkened even further, as though she, herself, was awed and slightly frightened by the power of them. "He said, if it's politics that stands between us, then to the devil with politics. He said he'd leave his family and retire from his post and we would go anyplace we want to and live like a regular couple and let the entire world go to hell for all he cared."

For a very long time, silence hung over the dressing room. Margot's thumb had stopped bleeding. She picked up the scissors once again, Lida's words weighing upon her like a dark cloud. The nerve of that swine! To be sure, it was a grand plan for him, a perfect exit from the stage on which a tragedy was in full swing. Let the world go to hell. The hell was already here, for men like Jochen, for Margot herself. He had destroyed enough lives. Now was the perfect time to retire, wasn't it?

But then it occurred to Margot that perhaps it was indeed a blessing in disguise. The Nazi Party had been in power for only a little over three years. It was anyone's guess how far they would go with their policies of ethnic cleansing and rearmament. Without Goebbels and his rousing speeches that had already hypnotized a reluctant population into shouting *Heil Hitler* and flying swastika flags from every window, the temporarily overlooked undesirables, the ones hiding in the shadows, still had a chance for survival.

And Lida was a good person. Truly a good person to her very core; not changed in the slightest by the promise of favors and fame, but, on the contrary, ready to challenge her lover at every step—by all accounts, a much better match for Goebbels than his wife, who, rumor had it, only married him to be closer to Hitler. Whereas Magda Goebbels only fueled her husband's hatred, Lida could cool it with the balm of her frank love and affection. After all, love and affection were contagious, just like hatred was.

Margot thought it all over and finally uttered, "I wish you all the best, Lida. I hope it all works out for you two."

All at once, Lida was upon her, all silky embraces and lipstick-smudged kisses. "Oh, Margot, how can you be so good? I know that you ought to hate him—"

"Oh, I hate him, all right," Margot grumbled into Lida's dark locks.

Lida only laughed and kissed her loudly on her cheek. "You have all the right to. He can be an ass sometimes and I never fail to tell him that. And I'll keep doing it; you'll see that I will!"

"I believe you. Just... be careful, Lida."

The smile slipped from Lida's face. "Why should I be careful?" she asked slowly, on guard for the first time.

"There's one person whom Minister Goebbels will always love more than you." Margot gave Lida a pointed look. "His Führer. And that Führer demands unconditional loyalty and doesn't like competition. I do believe that Dr. Goebbels loves you." It hurt Margot's heart to see how Lida's face lit up at those words. "But I also believe Hitler may not like it one bit."

"What does he care what we do in our own bedroom?" Lida muttered somewhat defensively.

A crooked smile broke on Margot's face. "Precisely the question I asked after the Nuremberg Laws had been passed."

All at once, Lida's face turned ashen as the realization dawned on her. "You don't think that because I'm not German... I mean... I haven't read the Laws; what do they say about Slavic people? Am I considered Slavic?" Her voice was rising in pitch, desperate, growing progressively more and more frantic. "Are Slavs considered Aryans if they're not Jewish?"

I don't know, Lida. All I know is that it's technically illegal for me to have sexual relations with my own husband. Why don't you go and ask Dr. Goebbels what that law says about Slavs?

The words stung the tip of Margot's tongue, but she bit at them, swallowed the bitterness and sarcasm and everything dark and vile that kept surging in her from time to time, ready to spill on someone unsuspecting. It wasn't Lida's fault that she'd fallen in love with such a despicable human being. Margot's own neighbor was married to a drunkard who kept pissing away all the meager money she made and beat her up on a daily basis. How was he better than Goebbels? A pig is a pig, only one wrote laws and the other one toasted them at the smoke-filled *Lokal* on the corner.

And so, Margot only shook her head and offered Lida all she could—a sympathetic smile and a warm squeeze with her injured hand. "I think as long as you're not Jewish, you should be just fine."

EIGHT

"I'm sorry, but this building is an Aryan-only establishment."

Margot stared at the building manager, having lost all faculty of speech for a moment. Just a week ago, he'd been so solicitous, all but dancing around Margot in the new prospective apartment—*"Just two U-Bahn stops from the new Olympic stadium, you'll be able to watch the Games right from the rooftop; we have a splendid veranda over there"*—patting the bald spot on the top of his head, reddish hair combed over it, with a white monogrammed handkerchief, licking his lips and eyeing Margot's patent leather handbag, the prestigious Wertheim department store written all over it. She'd casually mentioned that she preferred to pay cash and would rather pay not for one, but three months in advance. It was easier to pay quarterly instead of minding her expenses every month, wouldn't he agree?

He had agreed, of course. In fact, it was Margot's profound conviction that the building manager would agree to anything a handsome, well-dressed woman with a bag full of cash said.

It had been Jochen's idea to invest some of their savings into a few expensive wardrobe pieces. It wasn't vanity on his part, but pure, cold logic. Well-to-do people attracted less scrutiny. If they hoped to worm their way back into a middle-class Berlin society, they had to look the part. Who'd let an apartment to a couple in coats with frayed, oily cuffs bearing the faint U-Bahn stench of cheap tobacco, stale sweat and fried fish, instead of perfume from the shelves of the KaDeWe department store?

And now, in stunned disbelief, painfully aware of Jochen sitting stiffly in the chair next to her, Margot watched the very same building manager cross her application with a red pencil— a huge red X from one corner to another, so sharp it almost sliced the paper—and swipe it off his desk into wastebasket with a barely concealed look of disgust, as though it was a dead roach. Margot could swear she saw a trace of cold, malignant triumph in the manager's bespectacled eyes before he clasped his pudgy hands atop his office desk and smiled blandly at the couple in front of him.

"Is there anything else I can do for you?"

The question was like a final slap in the face. Next to Margot, Jochen was slowly rising to his feet, ghostly pale and even more achingly handsome to Margot's eyes just then, like some gothic knight in his black wool coat, black scarf with golden thread woven through it, groping for his black hat and leather gloves with his long, beautiful fingers of an artist.

But instead of standing herself, Margot only clawed at the chair's arms, feeling a surge of some dark force rising from the depths of her very being. It was primal and savage, that desire to protect her kin from the enemy; the instinct that overrode sense and logic and manners, and everything else that civilized society cherished. Margot's chest was heaving visibly now. "Now, excuse me, Herr—"

"Margot, let's go." Jochen was pulling at her sleeve almost imploringly, but Margot would have none of that.

"*I am* the renter," she said through grit teeth, her voice

dangerously low. "The application is in *my* name. *I am* Aryan. *I am* the one who'll be paying you rent."

"I understand this, Frau Rosenberg, but the problem is, you included your husband in the application and he's... well..."

"I'll repeat it one more time. The application is in my name. I'm the primary tenant. Now, what nonsense is this—"

"You see, according to the Nuremberg Laws, if a husband is Jewish, the household is considered Jewish regardless of the wife's racial status. So, it doesn't matter whose name the application is in. As long as you're married to him, you're considered Jewish in the eyes of the law. And even if the situation was reversed and, say, you were Jewish, and your husband Aryan, which would make the household Aryan, the building management still doesn't allow blended families in. As I've already said, it's an Aryan-only establishment."

"Margot, I'll wait for you outside," Jochen said softly and walked away. She could hear the echo of his new shoes, shined to mirrored perfection by a boy outside the taxicab stand, as Jochen hurried away from the manager's desk in the direction of the exit—as if he couldn't wait to get away from the humiliation.

The spark in the look the building manager threw at her retreating husband didn't escape Margot's attention. She narrowed her eyes, a slow, disgusted grin creasing her lips. "Does this give you pleasure?"

"I beg your pardon?" The manager blinked, feigning ignorance.

"Does it make you feel more like a man?"

The manager reddened. "I'm afraid I don't understand..."

"You understand perfectly well." Margot leaned back in her armchair, clasping her own hands this time. There was nothing else to lose. "You—bald, small, with your weak chin and your bad eyes, with your potbelly." She kept striking at him, letting her eyes roam over his form, just like he had ogled her a week ago when he thought she wasn't watching. "Army rejects like you make perfect Party functionaries. Perfect little clerks, little cogs that keep the machine running smoothly. The only reason why you were allowed whatever minuscule power you have now is because more ugly little men like you were so jealous of men like my husband that you just had to think of something to reduce them to nothing, as this was the only way you could elevate yourselves. Men—real men, who aren't threatened by anything—they don't bear hate in their hearts. They give instead of taking; they love instead of hating; they help instead of taking pleasure in humiliating others. Do you know what my husband would have done if the roles were reversed and you came to him and I was sitting right here, next to you, in this very chair?"

The manager reddened even more. The idea appealed to him; that much was obvious. It occurred to Margot that he never, not once, had a chance with a woman like her, but instead of pity, she despised him even more.

"He would have closed his eyes to your racial status and approved the application, knowing that the management would be none the wiser. But you're not him. You'll never be like him." Closing her eyes momentarily, Margot tossed her head to regain her composure, feeling a pang of guilt in spite of herself. "I'm sorry about what I said about your looks. In truth, none of this matters to me, to many women like me. I would have easily fallen in love with you if you were half the man my husband is. I fell in love with his talent, his inexhaustible imagination, his kindness, his intelligence, the way he always puts other people first; not because he's tall and handsome and would have been a poster man for your blasted SS, no matter how ironic it seems. Your very core is rotten and that's why you're still alone." Margot smirked at the instinctive gesture with which he covered his bare finger where a wedding ring was supposed to be. "Enjoy your Party. It'll be the only mistress you'll have for the rest of your miserable life."

Unhurriedly, Margot gathered her handbag, her gloves and her scarf and headed for the door without a single look back.

"I should report you to the Gestapo for what you just said," the manager gasped faintly behind her back, unable to fully recover himself.

"Go right ahead," Margot threw over her shoulder, laughing scornfully. "You'll only prove me right."

"You do realize how much easier your life would be if you divorced him, don't you?" Maria Kaltenbach asked.

Margot stared silently at her mother's collection of porcelain figurines, her finger twisting the fringe of her new scarf. It was a mistake coming here; Margot had known it long before she stepped through the door. That was why, instinctively, she had kept her coat on, only unbuttoning it but not removing it altogether, as she sat across from her mother in the living room that remained the same as she remembered it as a little girl, frozen in time, stuck in its ways—just like Margot's mother herself.

"You had such a brilliant career ahead of you," Maria continued, shaking her head with the distant, stern expression of a teacher disappointed with a student. She should have been a schoolmarm, it had occurred to Margot on multiple occasions. Maria certainly took great pleasure in lecturing, and did it with the air of a person with an unshakable certainty in her way being the only way. No one else was allowed their opinion.

"Brilliant career?" Margot repeated dully. Any desire for an argument had long been extinguished in her. The sun would sooner rise in the west than Maria change her views. "You never approved of my career choice."

Her sister Gertrud's "career choice" of becoming an SS man's wife was much more to Maria's liking—a fact that

Margot's mother never missed an opportunity to rub in her daughter's face.

"That's right, I didn't. But at least you had some prospects ahead of you. Now, you have nothing and all because of that Jew."

Margot bristled. "His name is Jochen."

Maria's only response was a negligent sweep of a hand.

"Will you help us or not? All I'm asking is for you to submit a rental application in your name to one of the apartments that we considered before settling on the one we've been denied. We have the money." After digging in her bag, Margot produced a thick wad of bills. "I'll give you three months' rent upfront, right this instant."

Maria pulled away from Margot's money as though it was contaminated with plague. "Are you quite mad? You're asking me to break the law, no less! My own daughter, insulting me in such a manner in my own house."

Margot sighed, suddenly very tired. "I'm not asking you to break anything. I only need your name on one idiotic paper is all. *Vati* will co-sign it if needed."

"Naturally, he would," was her mother's poisonous reply. "Your father just loves everything that isn't proper or moral, or even legal for that matter. Why don't you ask that broad of his to sign it for you? *Ach.* That's right. I forgot." She smiled sweetly and viciously. "She's a foreigner also."

That was the end of it.

Without another word, Margot put her money away and rose to her feet.

"Where are you going to go? Mm? Don't you walk away from me when I'm talking to you, Margarete! You'll end up homeless soon; you mark my words! Or worse, in jail—and all for that damned Jew! If he had just a drop of good conscience, he would leave you himself, or better yet, hang himself so he wouldn't give you any more trouble."

Margot was already at the door, turning the knob. But instead of hot tears, only a dull ache was now somewhere low in the pit of her stomach. She'd grown a very thick skin over the years. She'd grown immune to insults and verbal assaults and even injustice.

"The Olympics are coming, and you won't even be able to fly an Olympic flag from your window!" Her mother's voice echoed along the staircase as Margot took one step at a time, not bothering to turn around. "The shame! Everyone shall fly their flags but you! And everyone shall look at your window and know why!"

Somewhere on the second floor, a door creaked; a face appeared in the opening, bearing the expression of someone for whom such squabbles represented the peak of excitement. All at once, the entire situation seemed so positively ridiculous, so incredibly absurd, that Margot burst out laughing.

"Has it ever occurred to you, Mother, that we have no desire to fly your idiotic flag?" Margot shouted in the general direction of her mother, laughing even harder. "The flag! The Hitler salute we're not allowed to give! I'd rather chop my hand off with a butcher's knife than give it. They think they're depriving us, ha! Take your flag and shove it for all I, *and my husband*, care."

Above, Maria gasped audibly, only adding to Margot's amusement. There must have been something so wild and positively witchy about her laughter—or the statement—that the second-floor neighbor swiftly withdrew, visibly frightened, and pulled the door shut after herself. Margot heard the rustling of the chain being moved into position. She shrugged, unconcerned, still grinning to herself. Good. Let them fear her. Being feared was better than being despised and hunted and, heavens knew, she refused to be the helpless prey. The more they pushed, the harder she shoved back. If her mother was right and Margot indeed ended up in jail, so be it. She'd rather go down fighting to the last than submit to them with a meek head bowed low.

"So, rent an apartment in your name only; what's the big problem?" Anastasia asked, sinking her teeth into an apple.

Margot blinked at her like an owl, unable to form any coherent words for a few moments.

After the fiasco with her mother, it was only logical to head someplace where she was welcome for a change. The sun was already sinking past Grünewald, setting the tops of the ever-greens on emerald fire. Margot hadn't come here so much for help as for a talk and a glass of the brandy she knew her father would definitely have somewhere in a cupboard. Anastasia herself was more of a vodka person. She drank it like a princess, from a small crystal shot glass that she held with two fingers, and didn't even cringe afterwards. Margot knew that Jochen respected her immensely for that. He, himself, wouldn't drink the vicious stuff even if his life depended on it.

"Just in my name?" Margot repeated slowly, tasting the thought that had oddly never occurred to her personally.

Anastasia only shrugged with one shoulder, chewing on the juicy green apple, her thick black mane draped over her silk cream pajamas, which, it was Margot's profound suspicion, she had been wearing since the morning. Or the afternoon, when she ordinarily woke up. Her studio, remodeled from one of the bedrooms, didn't care one way or another when Anastasia graced it at long last with her presence, and Anastasia, according to her own confession, preferred to paint at dusk, or, better still, at night. That's when the demons of the past came and haunted her and could only be cast away if she confided them to the canvas, caught behind the bars of her brushstrokes. She drew their ugly, burning eyes, their monstrous teeth and sharp claws, and all the night terrors from which they'd crawled. *Degenerate art*, the new German Reich declared. Anastasia shrugged, unfazed, and sold them to the rich foreigners who, unlike Minister Goebbels and his people, knew talent when they saw it.

"Well, *da*," Anastasia said, mixing German with Russian—a habit Margot's father adored and Margot, too, found positively delightful. "How do you think my family rented lodgings in Berlin when we first came here and were still considered refugees? It was only in my father's name, since he's the only German among us. Mama and I, we just lived there until our papers were processed. And back in Paris, it was funnier still; we had no legal status altogether. So, we had to rent for cash from those who were subletting their apartments to people like us. Paperless. Land-less. Undocumented. Unwanted. Refugees," she finished with a crooked grin, punctuating every word. "There's always a way for people like us, Margot, my dove. Just go to the management and fill out the form for yourself only. Who cares if you bring a lover to live with you afterwards? They won't check his papers. It's your apartment. You can bring whoever you want there."

"But it says that I'm married. In my passport." Margot began digging in her bag.

"So what?" Anastasia chuckled, as if she was finding Margot incredibly funny just then. "You're so German, with your papers and whatnot. Tell them your no-good Jewish husband has run off and you can't find him to divorce him. They'll sympathize, trust me. And lay it on real thick while you're at it; tell them how he lured you into marriage and how the Führer has opened your eyes and how that pitiful rat has run off with your jewels and how you don't know how to rid yourself of his name now that he's gone. Tell them you've already hired a lawyer who promised to bring the case before the judge who will grant you a divorce without your husband's presence, but it takes a long time, and, in the meantime, you live in a shack with communist scum and so on. They'll sign your lease so fast, you won't be able to finish your teary-eyed story. You're an actress, Margot. So, act."

Margot thought for a moment. She *was* a good actress.

Just a few days later, she had a signed lease on her hands.

Old friends rarely sought Margot out nowadays. Most of them, the "Aryans," went to absurd lengths to avoid any association with her and even crossed the street to dodge the embarrassing business of having to say hello to the wife of a Jew. So, it was all the more surprising when one of the stagehands at Babelsberg informed Margot that a friend was waiting for her outside the vast warehouse housing the set.

"A friend?" Margot repeated, lifting her head from her Singer sewing machine.

"That's what he said." The stagehand indifferently scratched at the stubble on his neck.

"Did he give a name?"

"Just a Reichsmark for my troubles. Must be a Jewish fellow, the poor sod. Only they choose to stay nameless nowadays, and only they have the decency to give a working man some *Geld* to buy himself beer after a long day." With that, the man was gone. Supposedly, back to his duties; in fact, to smoke one crudely rolled cigarette after another in the company of his comrades and gossip about the old days, when the unions had paid double for the extra hours they put in and the directors hadn't been so demanding.

The "poor sod," in the stagehand's terms, was indeed Jewish. And not just a dear old friend, but a colleague in fact; a former senior lab technician who'd worked on such cinematic masterpieces as *Nibelungen*, *The Cabinet of Dr. Caligari* and, just before he was dismissed, on *Blue Angel*, which had exploded in box offices all over the world and sent Marlene

Dietrich's star into the stratosphere. Directors used to worship him. Cinematographers used to demand that only he, personally, develop their precious films. He was the man who could save an overexposed or underexposed shot. He had the touch of a true genius, and could turn an ordinary roll of film into living, breathing magic. He *was* the man, and that damnable business all but tore Margot's heart in half.

"Adam! How happy I am to see you!" She threw her arms around his neck, burying her face in the folds of his scarf, avoiding looking at him too closely. It wasn't that he'd aged, but rather he looked like a man with a terminal illness who tried to conceal the grimace of constant pain behind a faint smile. But his sunken cheeks, his receding temples, his hollow eyes behind steel-framed glasses, without hope, without their former luster, betrayed him all the same.

"And I'm even happier to see you, my beautiful Margot." After kissing her warmly on her cheek, Adam held her in his outstretched arms and Margot didn't like the pained look in his gaze one bit. He had known her as a rising star. Now, she must look like a veritable scarecrow, pale and overworked, no makeup, straight hair in a messy bun, the white robe of a seamstress, instead of a silk gown, hanging on her much-too-thin frame.

Suddenly embarrassed, Margot wormed her way out of his arms and rubbed at her eyes, stinging and likely red with strain. "Beautiful, my foot."

"I was surprised they didn't fire you as well."

"Yes, well... Wegener felt sorry for me."

"He wanted you to star in his movie."

"He wanted you to develop it for him."

Both went silent, haunted eyes trained on the set that wasn't theirs any longer.

"I'm a seamstress now."

"Yes. Jochen told me."

Margot looked at Adam in surprise. "You've seen him then?"

"I just came from your apartment. He said you're moving, so I guess I caught you in time." Adam gestured vaguely toward the Babelsberg gates, his smile quivering. "I was wondering whether they'd let me in."

Margot rubbed at her chest. In the past few years, she had learned to suppress her tears—else, she would cry her eyes out altogether—but now they felt as if they were buried somewhere just behind her ribcage, churning and burning like acid. "I'm so sorry, Adam."

"Oh, no, don't be." He feigned cheerfulness, almost success-fully. "They did let me through. The fellow remembered my ugly mug from the old days. Anyway." Adam slapped his thighs, changing the subject abruptly. It was getting too torturous for both of them. "I came to talk to you about something."

Margot was all attention now. "Are you looking for work?" She probed gently when she saw Adam hesitating. The subject was embarrassing for him, it appeared; he didn't quite know where to begin. "Jochen is working for this American busi-nessman—"

"Oh yes, he told me all about that too." Adam waved his hand with his hat in it. "It's not about work. There isn't any work for me in this country—legal work at any rate. Not that I want to stay here longer than I can help it," he continued, suddenly disgusted. "As a matter of fact, I got my visa for the United States approved a couple of months ago. Just finished paying all of the taxes that I apparently owed this government for the upcoming year"—his laughter was cold, cynical, slicing through Margot's very skin—"and now I'm finally free to go. I've bought a ticket for the first brass tack that is sailing for New York and, if I'm entirely frank with you, I can't wait to wave this damned hole of a country goodbye and forget it like a bad dream."

"I don't blame you."

"Hitler and his cronies will." Adam's smile was a grimace now, all bare teeth—a cornered animal bleeding to death. "They're trying to get rid of us all through their new fancy policy of forced immigration. But as soon as we're out of the country, that clubfoot Goebbels will be the first one to start screaming: 'Didn't we tell you all? Jews are no patriots! After Germany gave them so much, they abandoned it like the rats that they are and are now headed for greener pastures to leech off of them and their nations. People without a land. Parasites who only survive on a body of a host nation.' And our good fellow Germans will nod and eat it up with a spoon."

"There are Germans who don't eat it up with a spoon."

"Don't get offended, Margot. You know I don't mean you." Adam sighed, almost in exasperation, took his glasses off and pressed on his eyes before replacing his spectacles. His gaze was of someone going through mortal agony. "Margot, I came to speak to you because your husband won't see reason. He needs to leave too. The sooner, the better. Get the visa while they're still giving them out and get the hell out of here before it's too late."

Margot's face clouded over.

"The trouble is, he won't go without you," Adam continued.

"Naturally, he won't. We're husband and wife."

"You could change that."

Margot crossed her arms over her chest. "What are you saying?"

"I'm saying, you ought to be the responsible spouse and divorce him."

Margot's laughter echoed vacantly around the deserted street. "You know, Adam, out of all people I expected to hear this from—"

"Margot, it's for his own good."

"Kicking him out like a dog is for Jochen's own good?" Margot demanded, suddenly outraged.

"No, but saving his life is," Adam stated gravely.

"Nothing is threatening his life."

Adam made no reply, only raised a mocking eyebrow.

"I'm more than able to protect him, Adam."

"Really?" Adam looked somewhere at the horizon and puffed out his cheeks, releasing a voluminous breath. "What will you do when someday—and mark my words, that day shall come—the Gestapo come for him?"

Margot said nothing. Her eyes did.

"You're one obstinate woman, Margot, I have to give you that much." Adam replaced his fedora on his head. "All the best of luck to you and Jochen. You'll need it. I'm not saying it out of malice."

"I know."

"Promise me you'll at least think of emigrating. Both of you. If you don't want him to go alone."

"That much I can promise."

"That's good enough for me to calm my conscience. I did all I could."

"Thank you, Adam. For caring. And all the best luck to you too." A faint semblance of a smile warmed Margot's face. "I bet they'll fight for your services there, in Hollywood."

"Hardly. There are too many of us there already. But thanks all the same."

"Goodbye, Adam."

"Goodbye, Margot."

As she watched him go, an unbearable, stinging pain flooded Margot's lungs with every breath. But, once again, her eyes were dry and clear, all the hurt tucked neatly inside until the day would come to unleash it on the ones who had caused it.

NINE

BERLIN. SUMMER 1936

The Olympics were in full swing. Colorful Olympic banners and international flags had replaced crimson swastikas, and somehow Berlin was its old self again—bohemian, multinational, a bit decadent—a metropolis where everything was possible (Had not Jesse Owens, a black athlete with a dazzling smile, just set a new world record, besting Hitler's "Aryan" supermen? Had not some mad American just grabbed Leni Riefenstahl herself and stolen a kiss from the Reich's most celebrated director right in front of tens of thousands of spectators?) and everything was allowed.

Of course, no one sold cocaine or opium in the open like in the good old Weimar days, but the signs *Jews are not welcome* and *Aryan business only* had indeed come down, just as John had predicted they would. But what amazed Margot even further was the absence of the vile anti-Semitic caricature sheet *Der Stürmer* behind the glass of the newspaper stand she and Jochen frequented in their new neighborhood. While Jochen was getting his usual papers and a few international ones that were temporarily allowed to be sold for the tourists' benefit ("One had to grab the goods while they were coming," was his logic), Margot searched the several stands from top to bottom. *Der Stürmer* was gone. Now, instead of a swarthy, big-nosed Jew carrying a bag of money on his back—a typical *Stürmer* front-page affair—Jesse Owens was smiling on the front page of the Berlin special Olympic edition. And Berliners—the same Berliners who used to consume the hateful racial propaganda with a hearty appetite—were now just as enthusiastically admiring Owens and his athletic triumphs.

"Psst."

Ever since she had turned twelve and suddenly become very attractive to the opposite sex, Margot had made it a point of honor to ignore catcalls, along with whistles, unwanted compliments, and offers to buy her a drink. But this man, dressed rather oddly in a trench coat in the middle of a sweltering afternoon, displayed the insistent characteristic of those who'd never been taught to respect the simple word "no." After his repeated attempts to attract Margot's attention had failed, he reached out and touched her wrist.

"I thought you were looking for this," he said in a hushed tone, pulling Margot behind the newspaper stand with one hand and tugging at his trench coat to open it.

Suspecting the worst, Margot squeezed her eyes shut and was just about to scream for help when the man's hot breath, thick with tobacco and stale beer vapors, hit her nostrils.

"*Der Stürmer*. The latest issue, just published this very morning. Don't fret, my good woman, I'm the SA."

When Margot finally risked opening her eyes—he was still holding fast onto her wrist—the man motioned his head toward the paper, its corner just creeping from under his coat. Not a sexual predator then. Just some SA muttonhead. Which wasn't, essentially, much better.

"We've gone underground, just like back in the twenties." His pockmarked face stretched into a grin. "Officially, we had to take it off circulation. International press, tolerance, brotherhood among nations and all that rot." He rolled his eyes in apparent disgust. "I'm almost all sold out. But there are a few copies left and I saw you searching for it... You know, I tell you what." He looked Margot up and down, and suddenly, she wasn't all that sure that he wasn't a sexual predator in addition to being in the SA. The Nazi macho culture bred them just like rabbits. Proving one's virility by getting into a brawl or forcing themselves onto anyone in a skirt was something of a given among these men.

"Jochen!" Her husband's name came out in a frantic squeak despite Margot's efforts to remain unperturbed and dignified. But the Brownshirt was standing much too close to her now and, for an instant, Margot had all but forgotten that her husband was Jewish and bringing him face to face with an SA man was an utterly idiotic thing to do—

"—Promise to pass it to a family member or a friend or anyone like-minded." At the same time, the SA man finished his request, and stepped away from Margot at once after her sudden outburst.

In a second, Jochen's firm, warm palm was upon her bare shoulder. Instinctively, Margot backed into the protection of her husband's embrace and clasped at his hand with hers, wrapping it around herself like a protective shield. Frantically, she was thinking of a way out of the situation, but her mouth had grown dry all of a sudden, without a single word finding its way out.

For a few moments, two men silently assessed each other— Jochen full of relaxed strength, his gaze inquiring in a friendly way; the SA man suspicious at first, but growing progressively more amiable as he took in Jochen's golden hair, impressive height and, Margot saw when she shifted her gaze from one to another, the complete absence of fear in his amber eyes.

As though recognizing an equal, the Brownshirt raised his arm in a salute and even smiled as he slammed the heels of his civilian shoes together. "*Heil Hitler!*"

"*Heil Hitler*, comrade," Jochen replied, saluting the man with such natural ease, Margot almost fell over with shock.

"I was just telling your"—the SA man promptly noticed the wedding rings on their hands—"your wife here that I still had a few copies of the paper left."

It was Jochen's perfect nonchalance that helped Margot recover herself. "He has *Der Stürmer*," she hastily said, with a smile full of hidden meaning directed at Jochen. "That's why I called you."

"*Ach!* And I thought someone was robbing you by the way that you screamed." Jochen laughed heartily with the Brown-shirt, who looked like he found it to be a perfect joke.

"I've already told your wife that I'll give her this issue for free if she hands it to someone... of our kind. You understand." The SA man was all benevolence now.

"Oh, you can count on us! It'll be doing the rounds, all right," Jochen assured him and, to Margot's further astonishment, clapped the Nazi square on his shoulder.

The SA man not only didn't take any offense, but seemed mightily pleased with such familiarity. "Say," he began in a conspiratorial whisper, handing Jochen the paper, which the latter promptly folded and hid in his light linen jacket, "are you in the SA as well? No. Wait, don't tell me. Not the SS?"

Jochen only continued to smile mysteriously.

The SA man's eyes fell upon Jochen's gold wristwatch—a present from John ("Just got it from my father for my birthday and what do I want with my fortieth damned wristwatch? Take it off my hands, do me a big one."), then at the tickets for the Olympic stadium peeking from Jochen's breast pocket—another present from Jochen's generous employer ("You go, children; I'm busy elsewhere this weekend."), front seats, among all the Nazi bigwigs and their businessmen. Suddenly, the SA man's expression grew very long and his face seemed pale. He pulled himself up visibly, arms along the seams. "The Party?" His words were a strangled whisper now. Beads of sweat broke out on his sunburnt forehead.

Jochen only leaned closer to the man and took the button of his coat into his fingers. "What's your name, soldier?"

"Press, Herr—" He stumbled upon the rank and swallowed hard.

"Parteigenosse," Jochen offered, playing with the button. "I'll make sure that people above learn about your hard work, Press."

The SA man pulled himself even straighter. "Thank you... Parteigenosse."

"At ease, my good fellow. Keep up the good work."

Having patted Press on his cheek, Jochen strolled away with the most unconcerned of airs. Only his eyes, when Margot looked into them, were glittering with feverish fire.

"What in Hades did you just do?!" she hissed at him when they were far enough away from the newspaper stand.

Jochen shrugged and laughed vacantly. "Couldn't resist showing at least one of them how it feels being made to feel small."

"We can still turn around," Margot said as they made their way forward. Uniforms of increasingly high rank were replacing colorful dresses and light civilian jackets the further they went. Just a few more steps, and black-clad SS adjutants would replace civilian ushers. "Go to a lunch instead. Or the Wannsee... The lake will be all but deserted now."

But Jochen only tossed his head, his jaws pressed obstinately together. "I want to see the Games."

He didn't have to explain himself. His face said it all: *I have just as much right, as a German, to be here, as these self-impor-tant dungheaps with Party pins. While I still can, I shall sit among them and drink that fizzy brown official drink of the*

Games and smoke my cigar and root for my team and kiss my wife when they win, without fear of being arrested for race defilement.

Margot didn't question him further; only looked at him with infinite admiration for his bravery, no matter how suicidal it seemed.

This time, it was Jochen who handed the tickets to an usher in a black SS uniform and tall jackboots. His hands were perfectly steady.

Still lightheaded with nerves, Margot apologized and thanked her way through a throng of Reichstag members, industrial magnates and Party officials, all rising as she passed them by, bowing their fat, gleaming heads gallantly.

She and Jochen hadn't had a chance to settle properly when a typical Party Golden Pheasant—brown uniform and round belly, all business as it should be—transferred a fat cigar from the corner of his mouth and into his left palm and reached over Margot to pump Jochen's hand.

"What do you think of this weather, eh? Perfect weather today; Führer weather!" he offered by means of introduction, following it up with his name, which Margot was sure she'd seen a few times on the front page of the *Beobachter*. His face was also familiar, round and gleaming with health, with a few broken vessels around his nostrils and the overall expression of an overfed cat.

"Joachim Rosenberg," Jochen introduced himself and, before the benevolent grin of the pheasant could turn into a frown of suspicion, added, "like Minister Rosenberg."

The pheasant's face brightened at once. "*Ach!* You and Alfred are related then?"

"We could be," Jochen replied with a smile. "My paternal grandparents were transplants from the Baltics as well, so it's a possibility. I wouldn't venture to say for sure, of course..." He trailed off.

Margot stared at him, stupefied. After the stunt he'd pulled with the SA man, Jochen's desire to test fate had only intensified, judging by how splendidly he was spinning his tales to the Reichstag member, no less.

"Similarly, I'm Adolf," the pheasant said, once again reaching for Jochen's hand. If things progressed at this speed, they would soon start referring to each other with the familiar "du," it occurred to Margot. "Like the Führer."

The men laughed, and women joined them.

"Why, you ought to compare your genealogical trees!" the pheasant's wife—or a lady friend—ventured at once, her wide, blue eyes brimming with enthusiasm. "You could be distant cousins for all we know! *Bubi*," she said, touching the pheasant's sleeve, "is Alfred here today? We absolutely ought to find him!"

"No, I haven't seen him. He would have stopped to say hello. Rosenberg, I didn't catch your rank." The Party bigwig turned back to Jochen, rather to Margot's alarm. "I want to mention you to Alfred next time I see him. With his obsession with genealogy, he'll know whether you are related or not for sure."

Both men chuckled at the shared joke, as if Minister Rosenberg wasn't one of the biggest bigots in the entire Nazi Party and didn't push the question of race and blood into every possible new law.

"I don't hold one, I'm afraid," Jochen said with the same devil-may-care look about him—a man with nothing to hide and nothing to fear whatsoever.

"You don't? I could have sworn... with your height and looks? I could bet you were in the SS."

Jochen only spread his arms in a helpless gesture, his amusement growing by the second.

"What is it that you do then?"

"I'm a decorator."

"Government orders?"

"Private sector mostly. Grünewald."

"You scoundrel, you!" Reaching over Margot's back, the pheasant slapped Jochen's back as though the two had been best friends for years. "Grünewald. Now I see why you snub the SS. Decorating Grünewald's villas pays better!"

"That it does!"

Little by little, the tension in Margot's back began to dissipate. The sun was warm on her shoulders and the men's banter was no longer threatening but amusing. The pheasant had a personal adjutant at his beck and call; before long, bottles of Coke were sweating in Margot's and Jochen's hands. The athletes were warming up on the field as the camera crews ran to and fro, checking the equipment and deciding on a better shot. The two couples toasted a German victory. Ice-cold Coke burned Margot's throat deliciously. She realized just how dry her mouth had been from the nerves.

A murmur of voices reached them from the back. Reichsmarschall Göring was advancing forward, his decorated marshal's baton raised in the salute. Everyone rose to their feet, arms stretched forward in a Hitler salute. Instantly full of rebellion, Margot turned to Jochen. She'd sworn that she'd never give that blasted salute, that she would chop her own arm off with a meat clever before it would happen—

But then Jochen looked at her impishly, nudged her in her side and lifted his arm first. Raising her own arm with great reluctance, she kept searching Jochen's face and saw that, even though he was keeping it perfectly straight, his shoulders were shaking with barely contained chuckles.

She wondered how he could laugh in this nest of vipers, playing along and chatting with the familiarity of an equal? But as it always was with Jochen, his emotions were so contagious, Margot felt a fit of giggles overcoming her as well. They were playing a fine trick on the Nazis, and if that was not the bluntest form of resistance in this new Germany, she didn't know what was.

"Thank you for coming with me, Margot," he whispered in her ear, the cheers of the crowd nearly drowning out his words.

"What do you mean, coming with you?"

"Because even if you had refused to come, I would have gone myself anyway."

His sudden confession took her by surprise. Margot realized that there was something so important about this situation for Jochen—something life-and-death—though she couldn't understand it. Perhaps she never would. She wasn't the one being persecuted. She suffered from staying married to a Jew, to be sure, but unlike Jochen, she did have a choice; she could get out of her "unpleasant situation," as so many of her fellow Germans called it, easily. He couldn't escape his.

"Jochen, why?"

"Because I needed to discover something about myself today."

"Did you?"

He nodded confidently, a mysterious grin back on his face. "If I couldn't go through with it, if I lost the nerve at the last moment, I would have packed my suitcase and gone to... hell, Mexico, for all I care, just like Adam suggested, because a brave woman like you can't have a coward for a husband."

Margot bit into her lip, which was suddenly trembling with emotion, but for a different reason. Brave? Recalling the earlier episode with the SA man, she wasn't so sure that she was brave at all. It was all fun and games, cursing the Nazis from the comfort of their home, but look at how quickly her spirit had deserted her when she came face to face with one of them. "I'm not brave. Apparently, the first thing I do when in trouble is call your name."

"That was different."

"Different how?"

"You were afraid for yourself, as a woman. If it was me who was in danger, you would have mauled that poor devil with your bare hands."

Margot couldn't imagine how she would possibly achieve that, but she let Jochen believe it, if he wished.

In front of them, the Olympic committee representatives were gathering around the microphones together with Göring, ready to announce the opening of today's Games. Any late-comers were apologizing their way to their seats, when one of the couples attracted Margot's attention. Instantly, a cold sweat broke out on her temple and palms. The young blond woman—she was the first one to stop in her tracks right in front of Jochen and Margot—turned deathly pale, just like the SS officer following right behind her.

"Gertrud?" Her sister's name almost stuck in Margot's throat.

"Margarete?" Gertrud was staring at her as one would at a relative long dead and buried who had suddenly come to life.

But it was Gertrud's husband, Kurt, who worried Margot much more, and particularly in the presence of their current company.

As though on cue, Kurt's usually stony face turned to a grimace full of icy scorn. "Fancy seeing you here." Slowly, he shifted his eyes from Margot to Jochen.

"Why, we can say the same." Jochen smiled pleasantly but didn't go as far as to offer his brother-in-law his hand.

Kurt's face was slowly blotching with angry red patches.

Next to Margot, the pheasant was growing interested. "You know each other?"

"Yes," Margot said loudly and clearly before anyone could say a word. "This is my sister, Gertrud, and her husband, Kurt. Gertrud, Kurt, you must know our good friends, Adolf and Anna." Swiftly kissing Gertrud on both cheeks, Margot pushed her in the direction of the cheerful pheasant and his escort.

Kurt was still blinking at her in utter stupefaction—his Jew-loving sister-in-law and her Jew husband, on first-name terms with one of his superiors?—when Margot enclosed him in the embrace of a king cobra.

"You say one word or try to make a scandal, I'll burn your house to the ground, with you in it," she hissed in his ear and noticed with great satisfaction how Kurt struggled to pull away from her. For an instant, their eyes locked. Margot couldn't say what he saw in hers, but whatever it was, he moved away from her.

He saluted Adolf rigidly, and took his place a few seats away. Not once did he look back in Margot's direction. Nor did he say a word.

By the end of the day, Margot realized that she had discovered something about herself too. As though reading her thoughts, Jochen grinned at her like a fellow conspirator. After all, he had turned out to be right. She would have mauled anyone for him with her bare hands.

TEN

WINTER 1936–1937

It was that festive time of the year again, when the world seemed wreathed in tinsel and bright lights. In the display windows of the Wertheim and KaDeWe department stores, towers of boxes wrapped in colorful paper and tied with vibrant ribbons advertised bestselling gifts: a small miniature army, complete with tanks and planes, for boys; realistic dolls, who could be fed from the bottle and wet their nappies, for girls.

"What is the bestselling gift this year for girls"—Jochen asked the salesgirl in the store, grinning as he wrapped his arm around Margot's shoulders—"who are slightly more adult?"

Beaming brighter than the headlights of an upcoming train, the salesgirl instantly produced a red and white monstrosity from under the counter. "A new goose-roasting pan, extra deep!" Well-rehearsed and frequently uttered lines flowed beautifully from her lips. "The ultimate necessity for every German housewife. It will not only produce the juiciest Christmas goose for your entire family, but can be utilized to cook stuffed duck, chicken, fish and bell peppers! Imagination is your only limit. Feed your entire family using only one pan! Its thick enamel cover allows you to cook side dishes together with the main course at the same time. And, our limited-time offer, it comes with a cookbook that includes more than three hundred recipes and illustrations; while supplies last."

"No! A free cookbook?" Jochen's eyes snapped open in theatrical enthusiasm. "You simply have to wrap it up right this instant. You do deliver, don't you? It's a bit too heavy to carry all the way home."

"Of course we do. Just leave your address, and we'll have it delivered within two days." Beaming another thousand-watt smile, the salesgirl went to fetch a delivery form.

Even though she suspected that it was nothing but a trick of some sort, Margot nevertheless gave Jochen a death glare sufficient to reduce a less resilient man to ashes. "You put that under the tree for me and I'll bash your head in with it," she said to him softly and sweetly.

Jochen almost choked in mock indignation. "I was hoping you would put it under the tree for *me*! Out of us two, you're the only one holding an official job. Which makes *me* the housewife."

"You do have a job. With John." Margot nudged him lovingly in the ribs. "Whatever are you getting this ridiculous thing for? I couldn't roast a goose to save my life. You want me to tailor you a suit, I can tailor and sew an entire suit. But cook a goose?"

Jochen kissed her on her temple. "We'll need it for something."

"For what?"

"You'll see."

With a sigh, Margot surrendered and almost managed a watery smile at the salesgirl's congratulations on acquiring such a wonderful cooking machine.

. . .

In between the tram tracks, bundled-up sellers fluffed up their trees—an improvised winter garden made up entirely of ever-greens, just as uniform in shape and size as the SA men patrolling the streets. With the Olympics finished, everything was uniformed once again in Germany: the trees, the *Hakenkreuz* flags flying from the windows, the BDM girls and *Hitlerjugend* boys shaking their collection boxes on every corner. Even the new concierge in their building wore a uniform now.

Not the concierge, the *Blockleiter*, Margot mentally corrected herself as they crossed the decorated lobby under the piercing gaze of his beady eyes.

They had had a run-in with him already, on his first day on the job. He had stopped them with a hand gesture and demanded to see their identification. Margot hadn't argued then —he was new, didn't know his tenants yet, and particularly Jochen, who was away for work for days on end—she could understand it all very well. But then, after perusing her passport closely, the *Blockleiter* had demanded to see Jochen's. The dialogue that had followed still festered in Margot's memory:

"He doesn't live here; he's only visiting," Margot had said.

"As a Party official, I still need to know who visits the tenants."

"There's no law against having guests in my own apartment."

"No, of course not, but—"

"There's nothing against it in my lease either."

"No, but it's my duty to keep household card indexes, survey all comings and goings, and to ensure that other laws are being followed by everyone occupying the premises."

"Such as?"

"Such as, no Jews in the building's vicinity."

"Does he look like a Jew to you?"

"No, but..."

"Well then, quit harassing us and mind your own business. If you must know, he's a married man and we're having an affair; that's why he won't give you his name, because people like you report just about anything. Satisfied?"

Whether he was truly satisfied or not was anyone's guess, but she knew the *Blockleiter* marked their comings and goings each time they passed him and made no secret about it.

"Jochen, what is this all about?" Margot called from behind the closed bathroom door.

It was Christmas Eve and she had been in the middle of arranging cold cuts in the kitchen when Jochen had danced in, smelling of frost, his eyes twinkling with mirth and excitement. He had a surprise for her, but he needed to bring it in; if she could just go into the bathroom and wait there...

"Just wait!" he called back. "Don't come out yet, I need another minute!"

"If it's that goose pan you're arranging under the tree—" Margot began in a threatening tone, but then remembered that the pan had been delivered a few days ago and was presently collecting dust inside the oven they hadn't once used since moving in.

She listened to the sounds of fussing and murmurs, until finally Jochen came to fetch her. He was still in his overcoat, with his scarf hanging half undone around his neck. He must have been sweating under all of those layers of clothing; Margot felt the heat radiating from his body as he stood behind her and put his hands over her eyes, careful not to smudge her makeup.

"One more step... and another one..."

With her hands outstretched in front of her, Margot discovered that she was giggling. No matter how many years they had been married, he could always make her heart flutter, just as he had on their very first date. He was full of surprises, her husband, and she wouldn't trade him for anyone or anything in the world.

"... And another one... almost there..."

There was a certain irony in the fact that Jochen always made such a big deal about Christmas despite the entire outside world screaming in his face about his Jewishness. He was technically a Protestant, baptized at birth by his parents—themselves Jews baptized into Protestantism later in life, but still— and knew virtually nothing of Jewish lifestyle or traditions. The Rosenberg family was fully assimilated. All the holidays they celebrated were Christian. Jochen had gone to Sunday school, for heaven's sake; something that neither Margot nor her sister could boast of. It was Jochen who decorated their tree every year and sang "Silent Night" in his beautiful voice. And yet, in the eyes of this new hateful Germany, he was still a Jew, an alien element, a predator preying on blond German girls.

At that moment, he took his hands away and Margot was glad that he did, so he couldn't feel the hot, bitter tears suddenly springing to her eyes at the unfairness of it all. In front of her stood a mysterious box.

"Merry Christmas, Margot."

His voice caressed her neck as warmly as if he had touched her skin.

"What is it?" She could swear something moved inside the box.

"I can't give you a child yet, but..."

Margot couldn't see his face but could sense him smiling behind her back.

"...I figured I'd give you the next best thing."

With a giddy feeling of wonder, of a holiday miracle slowly unraveling its multicolored wings in her chest, Margot squatted in front of the box with several holes in it and pulled at a big golden bow at its top. In another instant, she lifted the top off and out sprang a puppy of a rich mahogany color with big liquid eyes and then it was all wet nose and warm tongue all over her face, excited whines, a squirming body in her hands and a tail that wouldn't stop wagging.

"He's an Irish setter," Jochen explained, rubbing the pup's ear with obvious affection. "One of John's friends, whose wife's greenhouse I'm remodeling, offered me a puppy—not as a payment, as a present," he quickly added. "His dog just had a litter. They're breeding them for hunting, but he says they make great family dogs as well."

"Oh, Jochen, you're the absolute best husband in the whole world!" Margot still couldn't get her face away from the squirming furball even to kiss her husband.

"You like this little fellow then?"

"Like him? Oh, I love him, I love him already, so very much!"

"I'm glad to hear that, because otherwise I'd have to return that big goose pan back to the store instead of making it into his new dog bowl."

Margot looked at him, realization dawning on her. "Is that why you bought it? You've been planning it all along, you crafty fox, you!" Margot swatted him with one hand, the other one holding the puppy firmly against her heart.

"You have discovered my plot."

Margot leaned into him, closed her eyes and felt such over-whelming love for him and his puppy and John's friend and John's friend's dog, it was making her chest swell.

"What do you want to name him?" Jochen asked later as they watched their new puppy wolfing down his Christmas meal out of his new red and white pan, his long ears buried halfway in the food. "Our little *Mischling*, first-degree."

Even the Nuremberg Laws' slur for a mixed-blood child somehow lost its hateful meaning when applied to the pup.

Margot looked at Jochen, a wry grin on her face that reflected on his.

"Goose!" they said in unison and laughed.

Oblivious to everything around him, the newly baptized Goose kept chomping on his meal, his entire body shaking with delight.

ELEVEN

FEBRUARY 1937

The first blow came unexpectedly, on the first of February. It was still dark when Margot arrived at Babelsberg's film studio. With the yellow glare of the gatekeeper's light as her only source of illumination, she rummaged through her handbag in search of her pass as the man inside the booth sipped his coffee with a bored expression. However, instead of returning it after marking the time of Margot's arrival, he frowned at the name, checked it against some new journal Margot had never seen before, picked up the phone while holding a finger in the air —*wait a minute, Frau Rosenberg*—and grumbled solemnly at some instructions on the other end.

Impatient and growing colder, Margot began to tap her foot on the frozen ground. She hadn't slept well; Goose was making good progress with his house training, but Jochen and Margot still alternated nights when one of them had to get up, get dressed and take the pup outside. Most of the time, he did his business quickly and fell back asleep right after Margot wiped his paws clean. On some nights, though, Goose was too warm and snug in Margot's and Jochen's bed; he blinked at them sleepily when either husband or wife put the leash on him and, when taken outside, stood on the cold ground, miserable and yawning, sitting down instead of relieving himself after countless requests and nudging Margot's hand with his wet nose as he pulled the leash back toward the building. To avoid any accidents, whoever's night it was had to get up in another two hours and try the entire routine again, sometimes also without any effect, just to wake up to a puddle in the middle of the living room and Goose sitting by the front door with a guilty expression in his big, liquid puppy eyes.

Last night was just that kind of night, and while Margot had all sorts of patience for Goose, she had none left for this paper-checking nonsense. Just as she was about to knock on the glass and demand her pass back—she didn't have a car, unlike the studio bigwigs, and it was a long way from the gates to the studio itself—the gatekeeper finally put the phone down and, looking Margot in the eyes, calmly cut her pass in two.

"Just what do you think you're—"

"I'm sorry, Frau Rosenberg, but your employment with the UFA has been terminated, effective immediately."

For a moment, Margot lost all faculty of speech. A new kind of cold began to seep under her coat, under her skin, turning her very blood to ice.

"No. There must have been some mistake..." Her voice was still strong despite the inner tremble that was just beginning somewhere in her core. "I've been working here for years—"

"That may be so," the guard interrupted her, searching for something on his desk, "but according to the new German Civil Service Law dated..." He finally fished out the needed article and squinted at the date. "Oh yes, here it is. Dated January 26, 1937, your employment has been terminated."

"What new law?" Margot's question sounded more like the scream of a wounded animal.

"The law that requires the resignation of any civil servant married to a Jew," the guard explained and looked at her through the glass as though she was a curiosity of some sort. "Why would you? You're a very handsome woman. I'm sure you would have no trouble securing a German husband—"

"Oh, go hang yourself!" Margot shouted at his stunned face, thoroughly enraged and mortally offended.

She swung round and headed off—the further out of that cursed place, the better. It was bad enough she had to put up with her mother's lectures, but she would drop dead before she would allow some greenhorn just out of *Hitlerjugend* to teach her about blood and race and marriage.

On the train, she held it together. Losing a job wasn't the end of the world. Jochen still had his, no matter how illegal. They had managed to save up, squirrel away as much money as they could for a rainy day. All in cash, strategically tucked away in hidden places all over the apartment. It went without saying that it would have been safer to keep it in the bank, but then how would Margot explain such cash deposits to the authorities? Back in the Weimar days, the bankers hadn't cared where the money came from. Now, "reliable" Nazis had replaced them and, all of a sudden, each pfennig had to be accounted for, taxed properly, traced from the employer to the employee with truly impressive Nazi bureaucracy. As for Jochen, he wasn't even a citizen any longer. If he tried to show his face at a bank, they'd laugh at him, in the best-case scenario. In the worst, they would report him to the men in ill-fitting suits, or order a doorman to give him a few kicks on his backside before throwing him out in the street.

Laughing at the absurdity of all this, Margot wiped her hands down her face. There was no mirth in her laughter.

In the street, she held her head high. Looking at her, no one would know that a part of her world had just come crashing down. She was strong. She was resilient. They were doing everything in their powers to wear her down, to break her with these new laws and regulations, but she had steel inside her. She wouldn't cry. She wouldn't let them win.

Baring all her teeth in a brilliant smile, Margot chirped a bright, "Good morning" to the *Blockleiter*.

"*Heil Hitler*," he grumbled back and marked something in his ledger.

But it was when she pushed the door open to her apartment and felt the first warm touch of a squirming, wiggling body against her legs; saw those brilliant brown eyes full of infinite love; heard Goose's excited whines and barking; and felt his paws clawing at her as though in disbelief that she was back, finally back, all his own, *Mommy, Mommy, Mommy*, did Margot allow herself to collapse on the floor and let Goose lick the tears off her face with his soft puppy tongue.

"Goose, oh Goosie," Margot repeated, hugging him and kissing his snout, his eyes and the top of his silky red head. "What are we going to do now?"

Faced with such an important question, Goose tilted his head to one side and, after a final few licks of Margot's face, he disappeared into the bedroom.

Margot was still sitting in a heap on the floor, her back pressed against the door, when Goose returned with a bright red ball in his mouth, tail wagging, a satisfied doggie grin on his face. Margot couldn't help but smile as he dropped the ball in her lap and wagged his tail questioningly.

"I asked you what we should do, and you decided that we should remedy the situation by playing fetch," Margot said, picking up the ball and turning it in her hand this way and that. Goose's tail began to wag faster. "All right then."

Margot threw the ball.

Goose had an innate talent for making Margot smile in the darkest of times.

So did Jochen, who didn't betray himself even with the tiniest muscle twitch in reaction to the news that Margot stunned him with that very evening; he only narrowed his eyes at their pup theatrically.

"Now tell me, kindly, Herr Goose: whoever did you bribe at Babelsberg to get your mom fired and have her all to yourself while I'm toiling, like a right idiot, at work, for days on end?"

Just hours ago, Margot felt like her life was just about over. Now, as Jochen's lighthearted reassurance wrapped around her like the softest of embraces, she felt the tight spring inside slowly uncoiling. In the midst of this Nazi-imposed madness, she had somehow forgotten that she wasn't alone. There were two of them against the entire hostile world and, together, they'd get through anything.

They said misfortunes never came singly and, just a few days later, the bitter meaning of the saying manifested itself to Margot in the form of two men.

"Gestapo," they announced plainly, flashing their identification. "We need to search the premises."

Struggling with holding the ends of her robe together in one hand and Goose's collar in the other, Margot moved out of their way, still too stunned to speak. It was much too early; Jochen had just left for work, not twenty minutes ago. She wasn't dressed and felt vulnerable, embarrassed. It was one of their tactics, to catch one off guard; in her mind, Margot was aware of that, but it didn't lessen the overpowering sensation of being exposed, and feeling vaguely guilty of something.

"Can you tell me what you're searching for?" she asked, her voice suddenly hoarse. "I'd love to cooperate, but it would be easier for me to do so if you told me what you're looking for in particular."

The men ignored her with an astonishing arrogance. One of them was already in the bedroom, where the bed was unmade. The second, who must have been in charge, it occurred to

Margot, marched straight into the living room and began pulling one book after another from the bookshelf, shaking them and dropping them carelessly on the floor.

In Margot's hand, Goose—ordinarily the friendliest dog in the world—was going mad with barking. His fur stood up rigidly along his spine, and he was scratching the floor with his claws in his futile attempts to lunge at the intruders.

"You live alone here?" the younger Gestapo called from the bedroom.

"Yes," Margot replied after a short pause.

A triumphant, malicious sneer on his face, the Gestapo appeared in the bedroom door, holding a few hangers with Jochen's shirts in the crook of his finger. Without saying another word, he dropped them on the floor and returned to the bedroom. Margot saw him attack the dresser with a renewed vigor. Her cheeks turned crimson when he began pulling fist-fuls of her lingerie from the drawers, shaking it, just like his colleague was shaking the books, before discarding the intimate items on the floor.

"Now look what we have here!"

Swinging round, Margot felt all blood drain away from her face as the second Gestapo counted the money he had discovered between the pages of one of the books.

"I don't trust banks," Margot blurted out and attempted a weak smile. "After that market crash..."

The second Gestapo counted the bills and wrote the amount into his small black book, leaving the cash on the side of the table. "Do you have a receipt for all that cash, Frau Rosenberg?"

"It's... from different people." Margot's heart was hammering so hard in her chest, she felt as though someone was hitting her with a fist from inside her ribcage.

The Gestapo arched a mistrustful brow.

"My father and... his lady friend..." Margot wetted her lips,

THE WIFE WHO RISKED EVERYTHING   97

on the verge of desperation. "They've been helping me with money. It came from them."

"Mhm." The very tone of his voice implied just how insulted he was with such amateurish lies.

"This yours too?" The first Gestapo again, sneering as he used his handkerchief to hold Jochen's underwear in front of Margot's face as though it was a dead rat. "And these?" After dropping the underwear on the floor and kicking it unceremoniously into the corner, he proceeded to pull out suspenders, socks and cotton undershirts from the drawer. To Margot's horror, another wad of money fell out of one of the socks.

"I'll be damned; your father must be a financier or something!" the second Gestapo drawled, counting more bills that had fallen out of books.

Margot's head began to pound. She didn't know where to look. There were just two of them, but they were everywhere, turning her entire life upside down; opening photograph frames and throwing the memories on the floor, stepping on them—walking all over her pride.

"I've just lost my job," she tried to explain to their uninterested backs. "My family has been trying to tide me over."

They were in the kitchen now, rummaging through the cabinets; nodding to each other at the two empty cups still on the table. "Where's your husband, Frau Rosenberg?"

"I don't know."

"You don't know?"

"No."

"This your wedding picture?"

"Yes."

"If I show it to the *Blockleiter* downstairs, will he recognize him?"

A cold serpent of hatred twitched in the pit of Margot's stomach. The *Blockleiter*. Of course. That's who must have reported them.

The Gestapo nodded knowingly, taking her silence for an answer. "You've been living here illegally with your husband."

"Since when is it illegal to live under one roof with one's husband?" Margot muttered with what was left of her defenses.

"Since it's an Aryan-only building, and you lied on your rental application and brought a Jew here. Not only that, according to the report we received, you've been displaying an astonishing lack of political reliability. You've never, not once, responded to the *Blockleiter*'s, or any other tenants', greetings with the appropriate *Heil Hitler*. You aren't subscribing to any of the Party newspapers."

"Why have you lost your job, Frau Rosenberg?"

They were talking over each other. There was no time for Margot to ponder her replies or even collect herself before answering.

"Some new law concerning my marriage," she tried to say over Goose's incessant barking.

It must have been getting on the senior Gestapo's nerves, for he pulled a gun out of his pocket and aimed it at the pup's head.

"Shut that mongrel up or I will."

Breaking into a cold sweat, Margot scooped the struggling Goose up and half-turned with her back to the men, her hand clasping the dog's snout in sheer desperation. "He's just a puppy! He doesn't know any better!"

Goose's barks turned to whines in Margot's hands, but she kept him pressed close to herself, shielding him from the muzzle of the gun.

"Where's your husband?"

Margot couldn't tell which one asked the question this time.

"I don't know. He comes and goes as he pleases." In spite of herself, Margot felt her entire body shaking. Not out of fear for herself—she didn't give a damn what they did to her—but for Jochen and Goose. "He doesn't do anything illegal."

"Except for coming up with all that suspicious cash."

"I told you, it's from my father."

"We'll have to question him about that. For now, we're confiscating it all. You'll sign the form and amount. Your lease is, naturally, terminated immediately."

Margot felt her head swim, cold waves of terror coursing through her veins at the prospect of losing all of their savings, drowning her in fear of what was yet to come. "Immediately? But where am I supposed to go? And what of all my furniture?"

"Frau Rosenberg, you ought to be grateful we're not arresting you. Where you go is no concern of ours."

"Well... can I have at least until tonight to move everything out? Please?" The last word tasted revolting in her mouth, but what choice did she have but to plead?

After releasing a dramatic sigh, the senior Gestapo waved his subordinate off. When the latter disappeared, leaving the unfinished form on the kitchen table, the senior Gestapo sat in the chair where Jochen had sat not an hour ago and began filling in the document. Without looking at her, he said, "Frau Rosenberg, put your dog away somewhere; lock him in the bathroom or a closet so we can talk."

Margot did as he requested, and then came and sat opposite him where he had indicated. He had finished filling out the form, and pushed the paper toward her. Her hand shook visibly as she signed her name next to his.

"Frau Rosenberg, you seem like a reasonable woman," he began, clasping his hands together. His tone was soft and conversational now, a far cry from the contemptuous barking he had employed before. "Don't you see all the trouble your husband is causing you? I'm the one who was tasked with assembling your file after the report we received. You were an excellent student at school; a very good athlete. Almost made it into a national gymnastics team but declined the offer in favor of a new one you received from the UFA."

"I played in theater before," Margot corrected him mechanically. "After finishing Max Reinhardt's acting school."

"Yes, you did. I apologize for omitting it."

Margot looked up at him incredulously.

"Don't look at me like I'm some sort of a monster. This is just a job and someone has to do it. And it's not a bad job, either; you have to understand. Is it a dirty one? To be sure. But we do it to protect you, our good Germans, from the harmful influence of Jews, Bolshevists, liberals, religious fanatics and such. You were on the verge of being discovered for the big screen." He paused for an emphasis. "Because of your husband, you lost that chance. Because of your husband, you lost your job as a seamstress and are unemployed now. Not even a productive member of society, and all because of him. It's because of him that you have just had to endure this humiliating search. Yes, I know just how humiliating it is; I can well imagine. Do you not think it's loathsome to me as well, having to subject you, a good woman, to such treatment? It's because of your husband that you're dangerously close to breaking the law. In fact, you *are* breaking it each time you allow him to touch you and thus defile our German race."

A big round teardrop landed on the document in front of Margot. She hadn't noticed when she began to cry. She couldn't hold it together any longer.

"Why do you all hate us so much?" She swiped at her face with the back of her hand. "Why don't you just let us live? What have we ever done to you?"

"Frau Rosenberg, you have done absolutely nothing to anyone." His comforting tone only made everything worse. Margot had almost preferred it when he was shouting. It was easier to withstand than this mock empathy. "It's your husband who has lured you into this marriage that goes again nature itself, and he won't content himself until he has ruined your life entirely. And then what do you think he will do? Find himself another victim to feed off. That's what they, Jews, do. They're parasites, plain and simple."

Margot held her hands in front of herself pleadingly. "All right. All right." She couldn't listen to this any longer. She knew it wasn't Jochen who had destroyed her life; it was blatant white nationalism and hatred for minorities, which had propelled Hitler to power and allowed him to pass all these laws that were slowly but surely turning their lives into a living hell, with no way out. But this Gestapo man would never see that, because he was a nationalist himself. What use was it to even try to convince him otherwise? Margot would have had better luck persuading a brick wall onto her side than him: a brainwashed, willful follower of Hitler's policies, who was so far gone that he was convinced he was doing her a favor, helping her open her eyes, see the error of her ways. For people like him, black was white and up was down as long as the Führer said so, and they called themselves patriots and waved their flags and talked about their proud history where the minorities didn't exist and blond German women only married blond German men. "If I promise to think about divorce, will you give me until tonight to move out?"

The Gestapo straightened slightly. A smile, genial this time, appeared on his face, still a bit uncertain though, as if he couldn't quite take it in, the swift effect his eloquence had produced. "I tell you what: I'll give you till the end of the week," he announced generously.

That was all Margot needed.

TWELVE

A single suitcase in hand—she didn't trust the Gestapo's promises as far as she could throw them and had packed only the essentials, along with documents and what little cash they had failed to discover—Margot paused in front of her mother's door and listened. Behind her, Jochen swapped Goose's leash from one hand to the other and cleared his throat.

"Shall I wait outside perhaps?" he asked quietly, still shell-shocked and blaming himself for everything, despite all of Margot's protests.

"No." Margot tossed her head. "All alone outside, with a suitcase, just waiting to be picked up...?" The thought of it turned her cold with horror. "No, you stay right here where I can see you."

Where I can protect you still.

"I don't think my sister is visiting," Margot whispered after some time, her ear against her mother's apartment's door. "Everything is quiet. Just the radio is on."

She gave a final tug to the belt of her overcoat to adjust it and rang the bell before she lost her resolve.

There was some shuffling inside and, finally, Maria's voice came amidst the working of the locks. "Gertrud, is that you?"

"No, Mother; it's me, Margot."

"Oh." The disappointment in Maria's voice was so palpable, Margot wondered if her mother would open the door at all.

She did, and swept her gaze over Margot, paused at the suitcase in her hands and narrowed her eyes first at Goose and then at Jochen and his felt fedora pressed against his chest in a gentlemanly manner.

"Good evening, Frau Kaltenbach."

Maria only pursed her lips. "What happened?" She turned to Margot, ignoring her son-in-law as if his very presence offended her. "You might as well come in. Not the dog though."

Margot wasn't sure if her mother meant Goose or Jochen. One could never tell with her.

"Jochen, tie him up to the banister, please," Margot instructed him softly. "Goose, stay. And be quiet." Goose released a soft whine but sat obediently, wrapping his tail around his paws. "There's a good dog."

It occurred to Margot that the reluctant invitation had more to do with her mother's concerns about nosy neighbors than with genuine hospitality.

As soon as they were inside and Maria had pulled the door closed, she resumed her position opposite the couple, hands crossed over her chest, seemingly blocking their way inside the living room.

"We need a place to stay," Margot said, without putting her suitcase down—she was in her childhood home and, yet, something prevented her from doing so. "Temporarily. Until we find an apartment."

"What happened to your old one?"

Her neck growing hot, Margot lowered her eyes. Not out of shame, but to conceal the defiance her mother, no doubt, would see there. "Someone reported us and they terminated our lease."

"Didn't I tell you that this was precisely what would happen if you kept playing around with the law?" Maria's tone betrayed just enough self-righteous gloating for Margot to grit her teeth together. "You may consider yourself fortunate they didn't arrest you both."

Once again, Margot said nothing. She swallowed the words that were about to burst out in an incensed stream and set everything on fire, burning whatever bridge remained between mother and daughter.

"Can we stay here?" she repeated instead, staring obstinately down; sounding like a broken record and hating herself for it, but having no other choice; not with Jochen hovering like a sad specter sentenced to eternal damnation just over her shoulder. "It's just for a few days. I'll start looking for an apartment first thing tomorrow morning."

"Tomorrow is Tuesday. You're not working on Tuesdays?" Maria looked suddenly suspicious.

"They don't need me there yet," Margot lied quickly. She had no desire to add yet another thing to the list of her failures—in her mother's eyes, that was. "I'm starting next week."

Maria released a tremendous breath. "Well, yes, of course you can stay here," she said, reaching for Margot's suitcase.

Margot was about to let go, regarding her mother's face in frank surprise. A small, hopeful smile began to grow on her face and, along with it, a vague feeling of shame for making her mother into a cold-hearted monster who would leave her own flesh and blood in the street when—

"You, not him though. And definitely not the dog."

With more strength than was necessary, Margot yanked her suitcase out of Maria's hands, causing her to jolt lightly forward and look at her daughter in surprise.

"Margot, come now. Don't look at me like I'm the enemy of the state."

"You're most certainly not, Mother." This time, Margot couldn't keep poison out of her voice.

"You know I can't have a Jew living under my roof." Maria whispered the word *Jew* in the same undertone of horror she would have used for a child killer the authorities were looking for. "Do you know what it would do to Kurt's career if people found out?"

"Kurt's career?" Margot repeated and broke into mirthless laughter. "No, we can't have that, of course. Kurt's career!"

"Yes, Kurt's career. You've always been selfish, Margot, always showed your character to me, even when you were a child."

Margot laughed louder, her free hand pressed against her forehead. She couldn't believe it. It was almost too much.

"But you can't keep thinking only about yourself. There are others to be considered."

"So why do you choose to consider Kurt and not Jochen?" Margot demanded abruptly.

Maria made no reply, only tilted her head to one side as if asking whether she had to spell it out.

"He has his own family, Margot," Maria finally said, more conciliatory this time. "He can stay with them while you're staying here and looking for an apartment."

"His family is in Königsberg. And, Mother, can you quit talking about my husband as though he's not in the room?" Margot snapped.

"Frau Kaltenbach is right, Margot," Jochen said in his mild voice, touching Margot's wrist but dropping his hand at once at Maria's disapproving glance. "I'll go to Königsberg for now, with Goose, while you stay here and—"

"Entirely out of the question." Margot turned to him. "Don't you see? That's what they all want: to separate us by any means. And where is the guarantee that they won't arrest you on the train?"

Jochen fell silent. There were no guarantees and they both knew it.

"No, Mother. Either it's two of us—" Margot tossed her head. "Three of us, I meant to say, because we're not leaving Goose either—or none at all. Now tell me: can the three of us stay here with you for a few days or not?"

"Where will you go, Margot?" Maria sighed, giving her daughter the same look she used to give her when Margot was a child. "Where will you live? In the streets?"

Margot nodded to herself. Something shifted in Maria's expression; some new alarm ignited in her eyes at the sight of her daughter's face slowly turning into a cold, expressionless mask.

"All right, Mother. It's a goodbye then. We won't bother you ever again."

"Now, Margot, stop it with your theatrics right this instant." A pleading note began to creep into Maria's voice. "It's not like I'm throwing you out in the street. I told you that you—*you*— can stay here for as long as you need."

But Margot was not interested any longer in what this woman she used to lovingly call *Mutti* had to say. Without a second glance, she pulled the door open and gestured for Jochen to follow. At the sight of her, Goose was instantly on his feet, licking his lips in his excitement and shifting from one paw to another as his tail thumped against the railing vigorously.

"Margarete, where are you going?" Maria called after her, this time genuinely alarmed.

Margot wouldn't grace the question with any response; she only bent to undo Goose's leash and patted him on his thigh for being a good boy.

"It's February outside! You'll freeze to death! They'll pick you up for being homeless! They'll put you in jail!"

"At least we'll be together," Margot muttered, more to herself than her mother. As she descended the stairs, an odd, lightheaded sensation came over her, of some inner cord being cut. "I'll never see her again," she said quietly to Jochen, her eyes strangely dry. "Today was the last time..."

"Of course you will," Jochen protested just as quietly, but there was no certainty in his voice. "She's your mother."

"No." Margot shook her head and stepped into the night. "You know how they say that one doesn't choose one's family? Rot. One chooses one's family all the time. She chose Gertrud and Kurt. I chose you and Goose. *Vati* chose Anastasia and us. We should have gone to them in the first place. I don't know what I was thinking coming here. I suppose I wanted to prove myself wrong, but instead..." Margot's voice trailed off as she looked at the indifferent dark sky above them.

Jochen took her hand in his and squeezed. In front of them, Goose was bouncing in and out of the fresh snowdrift.

"We'll pull through," Margot said and nodded to herself resolutely. "Together, we will."

Jochen brought her hand to his lips and kissed the back of it. Margot felt the wetness of his tears on her skin, but didn't say anything, not wanting to embarrass him by acknowledging it.

"Naturally, you can stay here, and particularly this handsome furry gentleman! What kind of question is that?"

Anastasia was squatting in front of Goose and making cooing noises at the pup as her dachshunds sniffed at their new pal excitedly.

Margot's father quietly and without any fuss took the suitcase and gripped Jochen's hand in his.

"Good to see you, my good fellow." Karl smiled warmly at his son-in-law. "Don't just stand there; take your coat off. It's hot as Hades here and Stasia positively refuses to open any windows." He shook his head in mock exasperation.

"It's February, if this notion is news to you," Anastasia countered without taking her face away from Goose's, who was busy lathering it with sloppy doggie kisses. "You Germans with your fresh air! If it was up to you, it would be as cold as an icebox in here."

"What kind of Russian are you, anyway, with your fear of cold?" Karl asked Anastasia playfully, helping Margot out of her coat.

"The kind who lived through too many subzero Russian winters to retain any semblance of fondness for them," came Anastasia's usual whip-smart reply.

Enveloped in her father's embrace and listening to the good-natured word-fencing between him and Anastasia, Margot felt instantly at home. Exchanging glances with Jochen, she saw that so was he. As for Goose, he was already sniffing around busily, his tail wagging ceaselessly.

They were ushered into the living room, where Anastasia, in her no-nonsense tone, ordered her guests to the sofa, poured them both stiff drinks—"Don't shake your heads at me; you both look like you could use some"—and disappeared into the kitchen, leaving Karl to the task of setting the table.

She would hear nothing before their bellies were full and their red-rimmed eyes had regained their luster. And even then, at the first signs of anxiety over their uncertain future returning to Margot's face, Anastasia herded her and Jochen into the guest bedroom with a gentle but firm motherly hand.

"You've had quite a day today. Go to sleep. Rest, and tomorrow we'll sit down right after breakfast and decide on an action plan. In Russia, we have a saying—something like, *morning is wiser than the evening*. You ought to sleep on it," she said, pulling fresh towels, bathrobes and extra blankets out of the dresser. "And I mean, sleep. Don't go tossing and turning on me, wondering if you'll end up homeless. As long as you have us, you'll never be homeless. You'll live with us until you find a new place to be—for as long as you wish."

Overcome with profound gratitude, Margot wrapped her arms around Anastasia, blankets, towels and all squeezed tight between them. "Thank you, Stasia. From both of us. Just... Thank you."

Anastasia only smiled and pinched Margot's cheek in a sisterly gesture. She had walked a few miles in Margot's shoes. A dark shadow of her turbulent past still passed over Anastasia's face whenever she mentioned it, before swiftly changing the subject. She knew precisely how it was, not knowing if she'd have a roof over her head the next day; she knew precisely how it felt, to be hunted and hated. Here, in the safety of her home, she made sure that those suffering persecution could forget, for a few precious minutes, hours, or days, that they were the hunted and hated, and find warmth, love and acceptance instead.

Margot had no blood relation to the woman who had broken her parents' marriage, according to her mother, but, as she settled down to sleep in the comfortable bed with her husband safely tucked in beside her, she suddenly discovered that she loved Anastasia, loved her with her whole heart.

THIRTEEN

The room was a square affair, tucked in between the landlady's bedroom and the kitchen, with faded yellow wallpaper of some unidentifiable pattern turned glossy-brown around the electric light switch and the doorframe. The door, painted white at one point, now also bore the marks of dirt and discoloration, with dried rivulets of spilt tea, or beer, or coffee—whatever it was— running along its bottom half. Moth-eaten drapes limply framed a window that was so cloudy, the sunny day outside appeared misty and dark. A black piano, just as dusty as the drapes, stood along the opposite wall, its three pedals sticking out like rotten teeth in a vagabond's mouth. Her eyes full of unspeakable torment, Margot looked up in the hope of a reprieve. There was none to be found there: the ceilings were high but stained with yellow along the multiple cracks.

"Is the roof leaking?" Margot asked, her doubtful gaze lingering on the stains.

"Freddy fixed it last spring," the landlady claimed in a tone of utter indifference and proceeded to inspect her little finger, with which she'd been digging in her ear not a minute ago.

In the kitchen, someone was cooking fish. Margot could

almost taste the stench of it, mixed with acrid frying oil, in the back of her throat.

"Is it possible to move this..." she hesitated, casting a look at a semblance of a sofa draped with some sort of a sheet, just as greasy and threadbare as everything else in this apartment, "... this bed somewhere? We have our own furniture."

The landlady stared at Margot as though she had said something incredibly idiotic. "The advert said it was a furnished room," she stated in her thick Berlin accent.

"Yes, I know." Margot was growing exasperated.

Ordinarily, she wouldn't have stayed in this sty for a minute. Everything inside of it—the communal kitchen and, a far more terrifying prospect, the communal bathroom—went against her obsessively neat nature. Just the prospect of having to take a shower—a bath was entirely out of the question—after one of the dubious-looking women in their grubby robes she'd seen in the building made Margot shudder in cold horror. Showering after any of the male tenants—one of whom was presently drinking his beer in the kitchen with the radio blaring, legs splayed, sweat-stained undershirt stretched over his enormous stomach—Margot didn't even wish to consider.

Ordinarily, she wouldn't have set foot inside these vermin-infested lodgings, but their Gestapo-ordered time was running out and no matter how accommodating Anastasia was, there was a *Blockleiter* in her building as well and he was growing more and more suspicious lately... More than anything, Margot didn't wish to cause Anastasia any trouble. She had been through her fair share already. It would be utterly selfish on Margot's part to bring the Gestapo to Anastasia's door just because she, Margot, was too squeamish and didn't want to move out until she found something more suitable. Not that there was anything more suitable to find. Not for a jobless, mixed couple with a dog, at any rate. Most landlords had already slammed their doors in her face after laughing at her derisively and calling her a few names, a "Jew-loving whore" being the nicest of them.

The time for being choosy had long gone. Setting her jaw, Margot swallowed her pride and managed a smile at the landlady. "I was just thinking that perhaps it might be possible to move it someplace... I'm not sure if you have a cellar perhaps?"

The landlady didn't react. "It'll rot in the cellar."

Margot looked at the sofa. Judging by the state of it, it was already halfway there.

"I'll pay you to get rid of the bed," Margot finally said. The shower was bad enough, but sleeping in someone's bed, infested with God knows what... Margot would rather sleep in the street, if she was entirely honest. "We'll bring our own bed."

"And what am I to do after you move out? Where will the new tenants sleep?"

Margot inhaled sharply. "We'll leave you our bed. It's a very good bed. Oak."

"What about the sheets?"

Margot gritted her teeth. "We'll leave you the sheets too. The pillows, the eiderdown blanket, the whole works."

The landlady shrugged. "Fine by me. But I can't move the piano."

"The piano is fine by us. My husband and I, we both play."

"It's out of tune."

"Jochen can tune it. He knows how."

"Of course he does." Margot scowled at the landlady's knowing smirk. "They're musical, the Jews, a'n't they?" the landlady finished in her thick Berlin drawl.

"What's so bad about being musical?" Margot retorted coolly.

"Noth'n. Is just, they like being better than common folk."

"No one stops *common folk* from learning music."

The landlady shrugged and yawned, already bored by the

conversation. "D'you want it or not? Eighty marks a month, one month upfront."

Margot paled in amazement at such blatant robbery. Their former apartment was a hundred. "It's a bit steep for a room," she said, trying to keep the indignation out of her voice.

From the landlady, another indifferent shrug. She didn't say anything, but her face did: whether Margot took the room or not made no difference to her. There were plenty of desperate Jews in Berlin. If she didn't take it, someone else would.

"We have a dog."

"You said that already. It's all the same to me. Just mind to keep 'im inside at all times and don't let 'im into the kitchen."

"Naturally."

With her heart heavy as a stone, Margot counted off the bills and handed them to the landlady. On the kitchen radio, Goebbels was ranting about Jews taking advantage of good, conscientious Germans. As Margot exited the room, the beer-drinking future neighbor of hers loudly belched his approval.

By the end of the week, Margot and Jochen had moved into their new room.

"Why... it's not that bad," Jochen said with a bright, artificial smile and looked about him, clearly in search of a place to hang his coat. Not finding it, he smiled sheepishly at Margot. "Other tenants use the communal rack in the hallway..."

Margot looked at Jochen's tailored gray overcoat. "No. We'll buy our own rack. Put it on the bed for now."

"Did the landlady say I couldn't use it?"

Margot felt a pinch in her chest at how resigned—almost nonchalant—he sounded; how used he had grown to being denied the most basic rights and privileges their "Aryan" compatriots took for granted.

"No, she didn't." That much wasn't a lie. The landlady,

indeed, didn't care one way or the other, but a group of the other tenants had cornered Margot when she had arrived two days earlier with a bucket filled with rags, lye and soap to scrub the room as best she could. In a no-nonsense tone, they had told her, "Keep your Jew husband to yourself if you know what's good for you." He mustn't set foot in the communal kitchen and Margot was to scrub the bathroom facilities clean each time after he used them. Margot had opened her mouth to ask if they would scrub the facilities clean after their own husbands used them, like the beer-guzzling hog she had had the doubtful pleasure to see in the kitchen, but ended up saying nothing at all.

She told Jochen, "I just don't trust those people. What if they steal it and sell it? The police will do nothing even if we file the report... No. It's best we keep to ourselves."

And so, they did.

Inadvertently, their neighbors made it easy, with the ever-growing list of their demands. When they insisted that Margot use the kitchen last, after all of the "Aryans" were done making and eating their breakfast, she began rising before the sun and making coffee and sandwiches for Jochen to take to work. When they began complaining that she was waking everyone up with her nocturnal clattering (despite Margot moving silently as a mouse—and just how much clattering could boiling coffee make?), Jochen bought them a small portable stove that ran on kerosene, thus reducing the need for Margot's loathsome trips to the kitchen dramatically. And when Jochen overheard one of the women tell Margot off for washing her Jew husband's dishes in the communal sink, he got dressed in complete silence, went out and returned with a big washbasin.

"That communal kitchen sink is awfully dirty," he said, deliberately loudly, ensuring that the busybodies in the kitchen along the corridor could hear him loud and clear. "We'll wash our dishes separately from now on."

That, and the indignant collective gasp from the kitchen, made Margot's chest swell with emotion.

And when the tenants began to grumble about Jochen throwing dirty dishwater out of the window and into an abandoned patch of garden outside, long overgrown with weeds, he listened to their complaints with a pleasant smile and inquired politely if they preferred he emptied the washbasin into the kitchen sink.

"Not the kitchen sink."

"The toilet then?"

"Not the toilet!"

"Certainly not the bathtub?" he asked then in mock horror.

Margot listened to him through the partially opened door and smiled softly to herself. She'd been mistaken when she thought that he had surrendered to them. He hadn't; Jochen had simply switched tactics. His resistance became a passive one. He was gradually wearing them down with logic and civility. All of their crude remarks broke against the impenetrable wall of his calm self-assuredness. All of their hateful glares drowned in the bottomless well of his bland smiles and mock compliancy. He nodded them to death and apologized himself out of their way until they grit their teeth in helpless ire. Absolutely nothing rattled him.

Soon, they began to lose interest, switching to Margot once again. She was more interesting to taunt: she still snarled back occasionally instead of rolling over and presenting her belly like that stupid dog of hers, tongue lolling to one side, all but asking for a kick.

However, all that came to a swift stop after one confrontation.

Margot was leading Goose along the corridor for his evening walk when one of the women—Margot never went to the trouble of learning their names—decided to descend upon the two easy victims. Her husband had come home drunk again and given her a couple of slaps after she "had the blasted nerve" to ask him where his monthly pay was; Margot and Jochen had heard them fighting despite the landlady's room separating their respective dwellings. The woman was in a foul mood and spoiling for a fight.

"Get that dog out of the way!"

Her shrill voice startled not only Margot, but Goose as well. He paused, his tail wagging hesitantly.

"Are you deaf or just daft?" the woman proceeded when Margot made no reply. "I said, get that damned Jew dog out of my way! Dirty mutt, spreading his fleas everywhere!"

The truth was, Margot was astonished by the attack, which came out of nowhere, and she simply couldn't gather how Goose, her sweet, gentle Goose, could be a bother to anyone.

"Well?! What are you staring at me for? I said, move that filthy dog."

The first shock gone, Margot's rage spiked, suddenly reaching boiling point. She bared her teeth, the lead tensing in her hands at once. "He's not filthy. Unlike you."

For an instant, the woman lost all faculty of speech. Then she whispered, "What did you say?"

"I said, you're a filthy sow, in a filthy robe you never wash; you stink to high heaven, just like your drunkard husband, and if anyone has fleas here, it's you two. Fleas and lice and bedbugs and roaches and God knows what else; crawling out of your room everywhere!" Margot was shouting too now, all of her good breeding suddenly forgotten.

A sudden silence fell in the building. Then Margot could hear hurried steps and doors being pulled open ever so slightly. Good; let them all listen. No matter how well it worked for Jochen, sometimes good breeding and charming smiles weren't enough. Some people only understood blunt force, and over the years, Margot had learned how to wield hers.

"Now, you get the hell out of my way before I set him on you, you big-mouthed bitch!"

Strangely enough, the woman moved out of her way and Margot marched resolutely past her, staring at her with her eyes burning with hellish fire.

"Jew-loving slut," the woman said uncertainly behind her back.

"Dumb, ugly sow!" Margot retorted loudly, not forgetting to slam the door after herself.

Inside the apartment, someone guffawed mutely. Margot thought she recognized the woman's drunk husband's laughter and smiled triumphantly to herself.

Later, Margot regretted her outburst—expected retaliation, harassment. She was constantly on guard, suspicious of everyone. But, contrary to her expectations, none followed. Perhaps, sometimes, blunt force was indeed what one needed to prove one's rightful place in the pecking order. Perhaps, sometimes one had to stand up for oneself, when passive silence and submission didn't produce any results.

FOURTEEN
OCTOBER 1938

Margot was cutting material in the middle of the floor when Jochen walked in, removed his hat and sat down on the bed heavily, all light seemingly gone out of his eyes. Officially unemployed, Margot had been taking on work from private clients who didn't care one way or the other if a Jew's wife was tailoring or altering their garments for half the usual asking price.

"Well," he began, crushing his hat in his hands and not even noticing Goose's wet nose as the dog nudged at him. "They've finally had enough. I suppose I should have seen it coming."

Scissors in hand, Margot remained on her knees but straightened up, preparing herself for another blow to follow.

The first one had landed in March, when Germany had walked into Austria as though into its own apartment and refused to leave, citing its southern "fellow German brethren's" will. Anastasia had been fuming about that "will" for the entirety of spring, marveling at how ordinarily welcoming Austrians had turned into mad fanatics seemingly overnight.

"You should have seen them, Margot!" she'd said, pacing her living room like a panther, eyes black as kohl. "Karl and I were having lunch at this inn we frequent whenever we go skiing. Such a quaint, Alpine place; such marvelous people there, so very friendly; and the hosts—the sweetest couple you could meet only in Austria! It has always been our respite from all this Nazi rot; our home away from home in the middle of the mountains. No politics, no racial hatred; just snow, crisp and clear air, and smiling faces everywhere. And suddenly, in the middle of the meal, the innkeeper calls out: 'Dear guests, our beloved Führer is about to make an announcement!' and puts that blabbering idiot on full blast through the loudspeakers. I almost choked on my soup! Your father's mouth was literally hanging open in amazement. And get this: all at once, all of those *marvelous people* leapt to their feet and raised their arms! I lost my appetite entirely. We left later that day, couldn't bear spending another moment there. I still can't fully fathom how Austrians could be so damn stupid. Frankly, I thought they were better than this."

It hadn't taken long for a second blow to land. This time, it was Sudetenland that Hitler had decided to "peacefully" incorporate into the Great German Reich, just as he'd done with Austria. And this time, Jochen had personally witnessed this "peaceful" incorporation, less than two weeks ago, on a gloomy Monday, when Hitler's Second Motorized Division sliced into the flood of evening traffic.

"Strangely, no one cheered them," he had told Margot later that evening. "On the contrary, people turned away, scattered into subways, cafés and stores; you could see their guarded faces peering out from behind the glass, checking when it was safe to come out again. Only a handful remained standing and watching and didn't even salute back when the soldiers were waving at them. I asked my taxicab driver what all that was about and he just said, *war*, and then removed his cap as if mourning all of those young soldiers going away... The entire scene had the feel of a nightmare about it."

"There won't be any war," Margot had told him then, though without much certainty in her voice. "People still remember the Great War. They won't welcome a new one."

"But all that business with Austria and Sudetenland..."

"That was—"

"What? Peaceful?" Jochen had mocked her, but without malice; only smiling sadly.

"Yes. Let's go with peaceful."

"The British and the French were none too happy about the Sudetenland. I imagine the Czechoslovaks, who weren't even invited for the talks about their own territory, weren't thrilled either."

"I don't know." Margot's voice had been full of doubt. "All of those Sudeten Germans went mad over Hitler, just as the Austrians did. They welcomed our troops as some sort of liberators."

"From what?"

"Beats me. Czech oppression, according to Goebbels?" Margot had glanced up from her work just to give Jochen an ironic look.

He had smiled at her arched brow, but there hadn't been much mirth in his expression. "I wonder what his Czech lady friend had to say about such oppression."

"Lida?"

"Yes."

Margot had been silent for some time. With her own troubles to worry about, she hadn't the time to worry about anyone else's. But now that Jochen had brought up Lida's name, Margot had suddenly begun to wonder just how well the actress was faring in the world of political intrigue, caught between two countries on the brink of war. Well, not war per se, but "special military operation," or whatever Hitler chose to call barging into independent countries under the pretext of protecting his

German citizens living there. "They'll probably make her an honorary Aryan or some such," she mused out loud.

"How can she stand him, I wonder?"

"She loves him."

"Do you think he loves her?"

Margot had said nothing for a very long time.

"I don't know. I want to hope so. Because if he doesn't..." She couldn't finish the sentence.

All that business with Czechoslovakia.

And now, as Margot searched her husband's ashen face, it dawned on her that all this concerned them as well; not just Lida and her high-ranking Nazi lover. "What? Jochen, what?"

He looked up finally, as though jerked out of his unhappy reverie. "Oh. Yes. John. He's leaving. And most of his friends. Almost all of the Americans still living in Berlin."

Almost all of the Americans, echoed in Margot's mind. *All of Jochen's customers.*

"They're moving their businesses elsewhere. The political situation is not too stable and..." Dropping his hat on the floor, he wiped his hands down his face with a moan. The expression of utter desperation on his face nearly tore Margot's heart to pieces. "They're certain there'll be a war, sooner or later."

The good dog that he was, Goose picked up Jochen's hat with the utmost care and deposited it into his master's lap. For some time, Jochen regarded it as a foreign object he didn't recognize.

"I'm officially out of work, Margot," he said after a pause, his voice full of desolate finality. "Officially out of work."

Margot felt all blood drain out of her extremities. Her head was suddenly very light and very cold. On shaky legs, she crawled toward her husband and lowered her head onto his lap as well, right next to Goose's. They remained seated like that for a very long time, Jochen's hands stroking them gently and absently, feeling like a family on an unmoored raft caught in the middle of a storm, who only had each other to rely on.

The office of Herr Stahl, the chairman of the Berlin Jewish Community, was small, poorly lit and wreathed with cigarette smoke. Countless butts littered the overflowing ashtray on Heinrich Stahl's desk and a fresh cigarette was already smoldering in his tobacco-stained fingers. He scratched his forehead pensively as he studied Jochen's papers—similar to those already stacked one upon another all around him. Even more binders and folders rose in miniature skyscrapers along the walls, creeping up to the barred window with its dusty glass, impossible to open, the locks painted shut. All of the shelves reserved for the binders originally had already been stuffed up to the ceiling.

Margot looked around her as Jochen sat next to her, ramrod straight and hardly breathing, his fingers clasped around his knee so tightly, his knuckles had turned white.

"Frankly speaking, there's not much I can do for you, Herr Rosenberg," Stahl said at long last, already passing the papers back to Jochen. "We have very limited resources that can only be spared on the members of the Berlin Jewish community."

Jochen blinked uncomprehendingly, making no move to pick up the papers. "But I am Jewish."

"It says here you're Protestant."

"Well, yes, I was baptized at birth, but—"

"So you're not Jewish."

"I am!" Pulling forward, Jochen opened his Kennkarte—identification card—and pointed his finger at the big red J stamped right next to his name. "I've been out of work for years now because I'm Jewish."

"Racially Jewish."

There was a pause.

"I don't understand," Jochen admitted at last.

Stahl sighed, removed his glasses and rubbed his eyes, red with exhaustion and cigarette smoke. To Margot, he suddenly looked very old and impossibly tired.

"I'll explain how it is to you then," Stahl said, placing his glasses back on the bridge of his nose and folding his hands upon Jochen's passport. "You're Jewish enough for the Nazis to take away your citizenship, but not Jewish enough for me to hire you in any capacity. The community has very strict guidelines, to which, as a chairman, I must adhere. We can only assist members of the community, that is, Jews who have been active in the community, who belong to a synagogue, who are married to other Jews, who raise their children in the Jewish faith. You're a Protestant who is married to a German and who, as far as I understand, has never set a foot inside a temple or held a Talmud in your hands." Stahl tilted his head to one side. There was genuine sympathy in his eyes. "It pains me to say this, but I'm afraid there's nothing I can do for you."

"So..." Jochen was looking at his papers, so carefully prepared and so very useless—his last hope, obliterated. "What am I to do now? Where am I to go?"

Stahl puffed out his cheeks, apparently raking his mind for options.

The secretary popped her head inside the office, but Stahl held up his finger in a sign for her to wait. All at once, Margot felt her chest fill with profound gratitude. The anteroom and the entire staircase leading up to his office were overflowing with people. Margot and Jochen had waited for their appointment for over three hours and yet, instead of sending them off on their merry way, he was still trying to help, genuinely trying. Just for that, she was eternally thankful.

"You could try the Protestant church," Stahl said at last. "I doubt they'll take the risk of assisting you though. The Party forced them to adopt their racial policies as well in exchange for sparing them the harassment, but you never know. Perhaps you'll find someone willing to risk his neck for you. Have you been active in your church at all?"

Jochen slowly shook his head, gathering his papers with hands that didn't seem to be obeying his commands.

"You could also try mixed businesses," Stahl suggested.

"Mixed businesses?"

"Yes. Those owned half and half, by a Jewish partner and a German one, and particularly if the Jewish partner is a foreign Jew."

"A foreign Jew," Jochen repeated.

"Yes. French or Dutch or American. They're still permitted to function here in Berlin. Who knows for how long, but it's worth a try. Though..."

"What?"

"You're a decorator by profession."

"Is that bad?"

"Not bad, but..." Stahl sighed. "Those are mostly textile businesses. Tailors and such. Can you sew at all?"

"I can sew!" Margot leaned forward at once. "I used to work as a seamstress for the UFA and have been taking private orders at home after... after they fired me. Do those co-owned businesses hire Germans married to Jews?"

"I can't imagine why they wouldn't," Stahl said, shrugging and smiling softly. "Try Schneller and Schmeider." Licking his finger, Stahl tore a page off his pad and began writing something. "Their office is on Königstraße, right next to Alexanderplatz. They're a leather clothing manufacturer. When you go there, ask for Herr Grohm and give him this note. Times are tough, but he owes me a favor." With that, Stahl handed the paper to Margot. "As for you," he said, turning to Jochen again, "if you can't find employment elsewhere, you could try selling goods door to door. Knives, colognes, perfumes, shaving creams, shoe polish. Anything that fits into a small suitcase."

"Isn't that illegal? For Jews, I mean?"

"It is," Stahl admitted calmly. "But what's not nowadays?"

"Get out of here! Well? Don't you understand German at all, you miserable oaf? I said, gather your little enterprise and get lost before I call the authorities on you!"

Caught between two men, Margot looked from her new boss, Herr Grohm in his outraged state, to the black-clad Orthodox Jewish man and back, at a loss.

In the past two weeks she'd been working at Schneller and Schmeider, she'd grown used to being dismissed early on Fridays, and the shorter the days were growing, the earlier Herr Grohm would close the shop, hide a black yarmulke under his stylish felt hat and set off in the direction of the nearest temple on foot, together with some of his workers.

After working on Lida Baarová's silk gowns, the tedious, menial task of sewing buttons to leather overcoats could have felt almost an insult, but Margot didn't complain. Work was work and, to be frank, her new workplace was a breath of fresh air after the UFA and the harassment that had felt never-ending by the time that she was fired. Here, Margot's new colleagues didn't care one whit whom she was married to and who she was herself. They bantered with her during lunch in the communal canteen as though she weren't a newcomer at all but a permanent fixture who'd been working alongside them for years, and they collectively cooed over Goose whenever Jochen came to meet her after work with the pup on the leash.

But today Jochen wasn't there; only this Orthodox man, in his long black coat, stooped and trembling openly before Herr Grohm's wrathful glare, his bony hands gathering cigarettes he must have been selling under the awning of Schneller and Schmeider before Herr Grohm had descended upon him like a hawk.

It was the first time that Margot had seen an Orthodox Jew up close. With the frank curiosity of a child, she stared at his sidelocks curled and tucked neatly behind his ears; at his graying beard; at the general "otherness" of him that was in his clothes and appearance.

He apologized to Herr Grohm softly in a language that could have been German but wasn't, but Margot understood it all the same, rather to her amazement.

"Don't speak Yiddish to me!" Grohm cut him off shrilly, his usually calm, intelligent eyes now bulging out of their sockets. "You're in Germany, so speak German!"

The man tried to explain that he was Polish and dropped another loose cigarette onto the ground.

"Do not even think of picking that up and selling it to a German," Grohm said very quietly.

Without turning around, Margot was becoming aware of several pairs of watchful eyes observing them closely.

The Orthodox man regarded the cigarette tragically but made no move to pick it up.

"It's all because of you," Grohm's voice was a mere whisper now. "All this trouble because of you. They began harassing *us* because of *you*; do you not understand this?"

The Orthodox man only bowed his head deeper, apologized several more times and set off in the direction of the Alexander-platz, along the road, avoiding the sidewalk that was for the Germans only.

Watching him go, Grohm released a heavy breath and turned to a man who worked in the accounting department, but whose name Margot couldn't recall with the best will in the world. "Next time you see him here, call the police."

"Maybe I'll just chase him off? Make a big scene for the public's benefit?"

"No. He'll be back again and someone will report that we allow him to use our business as a front for his little one and then..." His voice trailed off. He was gazing in the direction in which the Orthodox man had disappeared, looking as though the weight of the entire world lay on his shoulders. "We can't have that. They've spared us thus far, but we can't have that. You know that."

And suddenly, all of his desperate screaming and helpless rage made sense to Margot. He was afraid, mortally afraid for the business he was managing, for the people under his charge whose fates Grohm couldn't risk; afraid for himself and his own family, a Jewish family, one step away from God knew what horrors if Grohm wasn't diligent enough, if he didn't chase away the poor fellow Jew from the steps of his shop to save the others working under its roof. He must have felt disgusted with himself for it—and he looked it.

In a gesture of silent support, Margot offered him her hand and a smile. "Have a good Shabbos, Herr Grohm."

His lips quivered faintly when he nodded his gratitude at her.

FIFTEEN

NOVEMBER 1938

Margot arrived at work that Wednesday, she discovered the shop deathly still. Her colleagues were all there, but nobody was working. Instead, they were huddled in small groups in various corners, smoking a great deal and speaking in undertones, from time to time throwing frightened glances over their shoulders. From Herr Grohm's office, the unmistakable sound of Goebbels' voice carried long and far above the main floor of the shop. Otherwise, silence lay all about the machines and the workers alike, and it screamed volumes.

"Whatever is that lunatic raving about this time?" Margot also lowered her voice as she took her place at her workstation.

She was just about to arrange her handbag under her feet when she caught a warning glare from Emmi, also a German married to a Jewish man. Next to her, Lisl was staring into space with glassy eyes, her teeth biting into the already-raw skin around her nails relentlessly. Just like Jochen, Lisl was a baptized Jew. Just like Jochen, she had been married to a German; only, he had divorced her as soon as the marriage became an inconvenience to his career prospects.

"Some Polish idiot has gone and shot our German ambassador in Paris."

Margot turned around in her seat toward the voice. Johanna, another button-girl, was swinging her foot pensively, with her head half-turned toward Herr Grohm's office door.

"He wasn't an ambassador," Lisl said in a hollow voice, her eyes still staring, unseeing, into the void.

"Doesn't matter what he was," Johanna muttered, still listening closely to Goebbels' speech that was progressively growing in volume, threatening, stirring to action, calling for blood: *The Jews were to blame. The Jews were to pay!* "What matters is the Pole was a Jew and the fellow he shot was a German."

All at once, the radio died mid-word. With a sudden harsh screech, Herr Grohm's office door flew open, revealing Grohm himself, his face pinched into a frightful mask. "Everyone's dismissed for today."

When the workers exchanged uncertain looks but made no move to leave, Grohm bent over the railing separating the second floor where his office was situated and the first, where the workshop was set up.

"Go on. Well?!" He shouted at them, growing red in the face. "Are you waiting for the SA to barge in and escort you, what? I said, what!"

At the second *what*, wrenched out of Grohm's very gut from the desperate sound of it, they finally came out of their collective stunned state. The groups broke up; office workers poured out from their cubicles on the second floor, valises in hand, pulling their hats down on their faces. Workers began pulling on their overcoats, from time to time throwing looks at Grohm like sheep at their sheepdog.

Only the German workers remained by their stations, stealing glances at one another and thoroughly avoiding looking at their Jewish colleagues for some reason they all felt deep inside but couldn't quite explain rationally even to themselves.

"Herr Grohm." Emmi spoke up. "We can stay and work." She looked up at their immediate superior questioningly.

"Yes, we all can stay," another voice joined in, from a German apprentice working in the leather department this time. Emmi looked at him with gratitude. "Better than closing down the shop altogether."

"No." Grohm tossed his head categorically. "You heard what he was saying just now. If an enraged crowd breaks in, or worse, if the SA march in, they won't take their sweet time to check your papers. Everyone knows we're a partially Jewish business. They may attack you for working for us."

"Well, then we girls can stay; right, girls?" Emmi's gaze roved around as though searching for her fellow seamstresses' approval. "Surely they won't hurt women."

Judging by Grohm's expression, he wasn't convinced that this was the case. "Thank you, Emmi, but no. You all go. You have husbands at home. Go take care of them."

In any other case, Margot would take great offense at the statement, but at that moment, it had taken on an entirely different, terrifying meaning. She suddenly remembered that Jochen was somewhere out there, trudging through Berlin on foot with his small suitcase full of shoe polish, a walking target for anyone to report, place under civilian arrest for his illegal trading... or turn over to the SA.

"Huh, my husband is sitting at home, feet up in the air." Emmi waved Grohm off, unconcerned in the slightest. "Writing a book that will be a bestseller as soon as Hitler is dead." A few seamstresses broke into faint chuckles, grateful for the distraction. "I told him that it better be, or I'll personally take him to court for every single year during which I've supported his fat ass and make him pay back every single pfennig..."

Margot didn't hear Emmi's further plans. She was already

rushing for the door, ready to comb the entire city to find Jochen before it was too late.

In the streets, Goebbels' speech was pouring out from the loudspeakers mounted on almost every corner. Near the buildings with swastika banners hanging over their entrances, despite the early hour, the crowds were beginning to thicken.

The further the sun rolled toward the horizon, the deeper Margot's desperation grew. Out of breath, covered with sweat, the skin on her feet reduced to bloody blisters, she stumbled through the labyrinth of dingy alleyways and dilapidated buildings in the former "red" area of Berlin. By the bitter method of trial and error, Jochen had established this to be the safest one for his illegal trade. No one here slammed the door in his face, like the self-important maids of the affluent Grünewald villas; no one threatened to report, him like the *conscientious* middle-class Nazis from Charlottenburg; and no one cheated him out of his money by taking the product, advising him to piss off before they give him a good thrashing, laughing as they watched his humiliating descent down the stairs.

The former communists cared not for his racial status; only asked if the shoe polish was waterproof and paid without any fuss and in full. Some of them offered him leaflets, mimeographed and mortally dangerous; some—women mostly—pushed a sandwich wrapped in waxed paper into his hands and refused to take no for an answer. Jochen told Margot about them with warm fondness, and Margot saw his faith in humanity being slowly restored, even if only for a precious few moments.

Margot knocked on yet another door and received yet another sympathetic shake of the head. *The shoe polish fellow? No, he wasn't here today. Yes, they will tell him to go straight home if he appears. No worries. Good day to her too.* Margot crossed the entire building off her mind's map and proceeded to the next one, with the *Red Front* graffiti half-heartedly painted over with gray on its crumbling corner.

"Hello, forgive me please for bothering you," the words tumbled out of her mouth as the woman with a child screaming bloody murder on her hip opened the door to her incessant knocking. Margot couldn't recall how many times she had repeated the same words over the course of the day. "I'm looking for my husband. He sells shoe polish door to door."

"He was here last week," the woman replied, bouncing the red-faced child up and down. "Gave us a very good discount. Said he would be back in the beginning of December."

"Oh." Margot's entire face fell. "Thank you so much."

"Whatever for? I didn't help you any." The woman smiled against her child's screams in a way that suggested that she was indeed very sorry that she couldn't possibly do more.

"For buying from him," Margot clarified with a shadow of a smile.

The woman smiled bitterly and kindly at the same time. "You stay strong, dearie. We'll pull through and that's that."

Slipping in sleet mixed with refuse littering the streets, thinking of her husband's resilience, the way he'd accepted this work as simply what he had to do for the two of them to survive, Margot broke into a run, wiping the moisture off her cheeks. The darkness was falling. In the distance, a fire brigade's distinctive siren sliced into the dying day like a knife. Hurling herself into yet another dark building—the overhead lamp above the entrance broken and hanging crooked like a vulture's claw—Margot threw herself on the first door, knocking in desperation, swallowing tears and the thoughts of being too late, of not finding him in time, of never seeing that knowing grin of his, that arch of a lively brow as though in silent question, never feeling the warmth of his arms around her again.

"Good evening, forgive me please for bothering you—"—her

voice came out in helpless hiccups now—"but perhaps you've seen my husband? He sells shoe polish. His name is Joachim Rosenberg; tall, wears a gray coat and a matching fedora with a black ribbon…"

From inside the apartment, the smell of cooking wafted into the staircase and, all at once, Margot felt alone and without a home, abandoned by her people and God himself. In spite of herself, Margot broke into sobs in front of this stranger in a stained apron.

"You come in here, *Maus*." A pair of motherly, strong hands took her by the shoulders. "Look at yourself, all shivering. Come, I'll pour you something to restore your spirits."

Margot had long lost all power to protest. In the woman's firm embrace, she allowed herself to surrender, to be led into the warmth of a kitchen where a cat jumped on her lap and curled itself up, kneading its paws and purring louder than a pot on a stove. Without further ceremony, the woman poured her something clear and vicious-smelling into a cloudy glass, telling Margot to drink it in the same no-nonsense tone she must have used with her children, and hurled the window open.

"Otto!" Her voice echoed off the walls of the neighboring buildings. "Have you seen Herr Rosenberg today?"

"Who?"

"Don't be daft with me! Herr Rosenberg who sells shoe polish."

"Why?" the same child's voice inquired from the street below.

"I have business with him; that's why. Get your no-good gang together and go look for him."

"Why?"

With a huff, the woman shook her head. "So I don't give your fat behind a good hiding when you come back," she muttered under her breath. However, out loud she said something quite different: "So I can give you a few coins, you fox-faced market speculator!"

That must have got Otto's attention. In an instant, an exchange of whistles and excited shouts reverberated in the confines of dingy tenement quarters. The boys were on a mission.

With a surge of gratitude, Margot reached out for the woman's hand. "I'll give you the money to give them."

"Don't mention it, *Maus*." The woman regarded her with maternal solicitude. "He's Jewish, isn't he?"

Margot nodded; so did the woman, knowingly, sorrowfully.

"I heard what that sod Goebbels was saying this morning. Don't you fret; Otto knows his way around. His gang will find your husband in no time."

Warmed by the homemade vodka, the kitchen heat all around her and the cat in her lap, Margot sat quietly, grateful for the respite from her search, and soon nodded off without noticing it. When she opened her eyes, Jochen was standing in front of her like a vision from a dream, smiling and holding his hat against his chest, while behind his back, a young boy grinned widely, displaying the most adorable, mischievous gap between his two front teeth.

Otto's mother—named, fittingly in Margot's opinion, Angela—insisted on the couple staying for dinner. After they had shared it with Angela's husband, who had returned from his work at an armaments factory by then, and their four children, including the now-famous Otto, Angela sent them on their way with an escort of Otto Senior and his fellow factory workers.

In the streets, SA Brownshirts were already on the prowl, staring into everyone's face and smashing their batons into anyone looking remotely Jewish. Fires burned here and there, with police and fire brigades looking indifferently on. Margot looked around in horror at the broken glass of smashed windows that littered the ground and crunched underfoot, and the walls already defaced with anti-Semitic graffiti. But Margot's and Jochen's silent escort of hulking men in their workers' overalls marched on, challenging the violent mob with their heavy stares; cracking their knuckles in a subtle manner—a human shield against the Brownshirted darkness.

Not a single soul confronted them on their way home.

Nor would Otto Senior and his comrades accept a single Reichsmark for their help; they only shook Jochen's and Margot's hands.

"You have our address," Otto Senior said by way of good-bye. "Use it if you need it."

SIXTEEN

JANUARY 1939

With the new year came the snow flurries and a flurry of new laws, methodically listed on the front page of every newspaper. Hitler promised to return Berlin to Berliners, Germany to Germans, and the time to act, according to him, was now.

"Does this mean I have to apply for a new passport?" Jochen wondered out loud, stroking Goose's silky head absently.

Margot didn't want to talk about any of the new laws. They had only returned a few hours ago from Anastasia's, where they had celebrated New Year and where Margot had got uncharacteristically drunk on champagne, and later, Anastasia's cognac. All she wanted was to sleep—cover herself with the blanket entirely, head and all, and sleep through the whole of January, through the whole new year that had already begun rotten, through Hitler's entire reign—sleep through it and forget it like the nightmare that it was.

However, instead of burying her head in the metaphorical sand, Margot wormed her way out from under the blankets, took the paper out of Jochen's hands and squinted, through a pounding headache, at the column's tiny print with all its paragraphs and addendums.

"No. All we have to do is to go to a city magistrate and they will add the middle name *Israel* to your existing passport."

"We? I can go by myself."

"You're not going anywhere by yourself."

That had been the law of the Rosenberg household ever since the *Kristallnacht*—the night of the broken glass, broken bones, and broken lives. The Jews that had disappeared during it had, by now, returned from whatever hell they'd been through, eyes haunted, lips forever sealed, swastikas carved crudely into their foreheads. Those were the fortunate ones. The unfortunates had never been heard from since.

Jochen tried to protest, but Margot pulled her hair away from her forehead, revealing the patch where her blond hair had gone entirely white in the course of that one single day, and all his protests died on his lips.

"Will you have to take the middle name *Sarah* as well?" The disgust and horror at such a prospect was audible in Jochen's voice. He himself had long grown used to the abuse, the humiliation, but the thought of Margot going through it pained him to the marrow of his bones, Margot was well aware.

"No," she finally replied after studying all the nuances of the new law. There were several more next to it. Margot couldn't get to them just yet; not without Anastasia's cognac, she couldn't. "Only Jewish men, as in, Jews with two Jewish parents or three Jewish grandparents, are to take the middle name Israel; Sarah is for Jewish women of the same racial status. It doesn't say anything about German spouses of Jews."

An infinitely relieved and barely audible "thank God" broke from Jochen's lips. He exhaled visibly; even cracked a little smile, instantly mirrored by Goose's goofy grin.

With a nagging pain somewhere in the center of her chest, Margot thought of how attuned Goose had grown to the tense atmosphere all around them, as though he, too, felt unwelcome and constantly threatened. Instead of pulling on the lead and barking excitedly whenever Margot took him for a walk, Goose had learned to pad almost silently by her side, occupying as little space as possible, pressing himself into walls whenever a neighbor happened to pass them by in a narrow corridor. He never barked, never whined, never pawed or scratched at the door or the furniture when in distress; only crawled under the bed and stayed there, trembling with his entire body, when there was shooting outside or when the SA were rounding up more Jews, those no longer protected, those who didn't fit into Hitler's view of his new Germany.

"Margarete Rosenberg!" The landlady's booming voice behind their room's door tore Margot out of her unhappy musings. "Summons for you."

"Summons!" someone repeated gleefully in the kitchen and tittered, before being told to shut her beer trap in the landlady's no-nonsense tone.

Leaping to her feet, which brought a bout of nausea and another painful stab in her already throbbing temple, Margot turned the key in the door and pulled it open a notch.

"Happy New Year," the landlady muttered, not unsympathetically, and shuffled back to her room, leaving Margot staring at the paper bearing the Gestapo stamp with tired, black-rimmed eyes.

"What is it?" Jochen was on his feet as well, lingering just over her shoulder like a nervous, tortured specter.

"Don't know. Don't care."

With that, Margot slammed the paper on the small dining table and crawled back into their bed, which still bore the warmth of her body.

"Come under the blankets with me," she said, moving closer to the wall. "You too, Goosie. We'll handle it all later."

"Margot—"

"Later, Jochen. Not now. I just can't do it right now. I just can't..."

It was only January first and Margot had already had enough of this year. She didn't know how much more she could bear.

"Well, someone got themselves up swell," Margot muttered to Jochen, thrusting her chin at the magnificent four-story building housing the Gestapo headquarters at Prinz-Albrechtstraße 9.

For a while, they stood in front of it, Margot's arm threaded through the crook of her husband's, like two battle-weary comrades before the next phase of fighting.

"I wonder which Jew they commandeered it from," he replied just as quietly, nudging Margot in her side.

They exchanged glances and grins at the shared joke and then, on an impulse, kissed each other on the lips right in front of the enemy's windows just to prove to each other that love was still stronger than hate.

"You wait here," Margot said, wiping the smudge of her lipstick from Jochen's mouth with her thumb. "If I don't come out in two hours, go to Anastasia's and tell *Vati* about what happened. But do not, under any circumstance, go home; you understand?"

"What about Goose?"

"Anastasia will go get Goose. Do not go there alone."

"All right."

"Swear you won't."

"I solemnly swear," Jochen said, raising his hand in the air. Though, behind his theatrical seriousness, Margot still could see a glimpse of the very real human tragedy unfolding before their very eyes. How unfair it all was—scheming about possible escape routes when, just across the street, children in their winter *Jungvolk* uniforms were making a snowman as their mothers looked on adoringly. Their older counterparts from *Hitlerjugend* were already playing war in the park, with snowballs and snowdrift barricades, without a shadow of a suspicion that the man and woman passing by didn't know if they were about to look into each other's eyes for the last time or not. How damnably unfair, said the look in both Jochen and Margot's eyes.

At last, she let go of his hand. "Two hours."

"Yes."

"I love you."

"I love you more."

Margot nodded, swung sharply on her heel and crossed the street in a resolute, marching step before she lost her nerve.

Inside, a bored-looking official in an SS uniform checked her summons against his journal, marked something down and suppressed a yawn before motioning Margot toward the staircase. "Second floor. Room 12. Tell the secretary your name when you're there."

Margot told herself that she wasn't afraid as she mounted the carpeted stairs. She almost persuaded herself that she shivered because it was cold inside these stone bowels of the beast, so very cold, because the people who worked here were heartless and their blood was ice and all else was black and red; not because she was mortally afraid—not for herself, for Jochen. Hans-Joachim *Israel* Rosenberg.

The official's handwriting on Jochen's passport didn't match the original one and the name Israel stood out like a sore thumb, crooked and sloppy, between the calligraphic Hans-Joachim and Rosenberg. It spelled trouble, in dark blue ink next to the crimson of J, for Jew.

Jochen thought himself lucky. At least they hadn't carved a swastika into his forehead yet.

Yet.

Margot didn't think the joke was funny, at all.

The secretary took the summons from Margot indifferently and told her to wait in the anteroom with several other women, none of whom spoke, not even a whisper. They only had the same guarded eyes trained on the door swallowing and releasing more of them, one by one, some in tears and some pale as death, but just as silent as before.

Then, Margot's turn came; more waiting, this time inside the small room she was led to, with a table and two chairs and a window with bars on it, newly installed, judging by the look of them. Here, the air was chillier still, seeping in icy gusts through the cracks in the wooden window frame. The fact that they had found the money to install the bars but not to replace the old wood spoke volumes about the Gestapo's priorities. Terror was their first goal; not comfort.

Margot regarded, warily, the first official who entered the room and greeted her with an almost genuine smile—almost, but not quite. She'd seen her fair share of those well-rehearsed smiles, enough to instantly tell the difference between a genuinely good person and the actor merely playing one.

"Frau Rosenberg, you must be curious as to the reason we have summoned you here today."

"I must admit, it did come rather as a surprise," Margot allowed. "I don't recall breaking any major laws. Though, with all the new ones, it's difficult to keep track."

The Gestapo official chuckled at the joke. He was of her age, young and handsome in a glossy magazine way, with long fingers and neatly manicured nails. "No, you've been almost an exemplary citizen, Frau Rosenberg."

"Almost?" Margot arched a brow, feigning ignorance further, despite already knowing, sensing deep in her gut, why they'd sent this actor here first, why there was a long line of women outside, why the summons had come simultaneously with that new idiotic law about new Jewish names.

"There was that one issue with your apartment," the Gestapo explained, almost apologetically.

"*Ach,* yes, I remember."

"Is it all resolved now?"

"Oh, yes."

"So, you *are* divorced?"

Margot caught a glimpse of a predatory gleam in his smiling eyes, but it disappeared so swiftly, it could have been her imagination. Could have been, but wasn't.

"No. I meant, it's all resolved with the apartment. We're currently renting a room. But you know that much already. You did send me summons after all."

The official inclined his neatly coiffured head to one side, acknowledging the well-placed touché. For a few moments, the Gestapo's grin mirrored Margot's. Like a woman with all the time in the world, she crossed her legs and swung the tip of her boot in the air.

"All right." Much to her satisfaction, he surrendered first. "You're a smart woman, Frau Rosenberg. You must have guessed why we have summoned you here."

"You want me to divorce my husband." It wasn't a question.

"Yes," the Gestapo replied simply and benevolently. "You must have grown tired by now."

"Of my husband?" Margot couldn't help herself. The jab was out of her mouth before she could take hold of her tongue.

The Gestapo laughed again. He had a very good stage laugh; Margot remembered Wegener saying that a good stage laugh should carry far, whether in a theater or in front of a camera. The Gestapo had just that kind of a laugh. Very professional; perfectly mastered.

"Of your husband and all that comes with him. All the baggage, you understand?" He even winked at her. "It's a filthy area you live in."

"Well, you fellows chased me out of a nice apartment."

"Because of your husband." He spread his arms in a gesture of a professor, explaining the easiest solution to the problem his student kept failing to grasp. "If it weren't for him, you would have been living on the Kurfürstendamm, where you used to; you could have been a film star by now, who knows?"

"Like Lida Baarová?" Once again, Margot just couldn't resist the temptation.

Her smile slipped when she saw how the Gestapo's expression soured momentarily. He recovered himself in almost no time, but she had already noticed that something was amiss, suspected that something must be going on with his department and Lida. It had occurred to Margot that she hadn't seen Lida's name on any film posters lately. Neither was there any mention of her in the newspapers' gossip columns. It was as if the actress had suddenly vanished off the face of the earth.

Margot thought of asking whether Lida was in trouble of any kind, but then decided not to.

The Gestapo decided to forget the name also.

"At any rate," he began anew, clasping his fine hands atop the binder he'd brought, "you're a beautiful woman, Frau Rosenberg. Trust me when I say that I can understand... let's say... less fortunate-looking women staying married to Jews because they're afraid no German will marry them. But you, you must have admirers following you everywhere."

"I scarcely leave my room, *Herr Kommissar*." Margot herself decided on a term of address since he hadn't bothered to introduce himself. "I can't really go anywhere because my husband isn't allowed into theaters or into cinemas or even cafés, let alone restaurants. Not that we have money for eating out either, after the government took my husband's job and left me as a sole provider. And then took my job because I'm married to a Jew. If it weren't for another Jew who has thankfully given me a position, we would have starved by now."

"Do you see now how much trouble he's causing you?"

"No, I see how much trouble *the government* is causing *us*,"

Margot replied in a tone suggesting he'd just said something utterly idiotic, looking the Gestapo square in the eye.

His smile turned theatrically sorrowful. "It'll only get worse, Frau Rosenberg."

For the first time, Margot laughed openly, derisively. "Just how much worse can it possibly get?"

The Gestapo only looked at her a certain way and suddenly, in his dead, cold eyes, she read a death sentence to them all.

They learned soon enough how much worse it could get, just a few days later in fact, when yet another Gestapo official appeared at their door early in the morning, before Margot left for work, handed them a paper with a swastika stamp and declared that *the dirty Jews are to vacate the premises within three days*. Margot's question as to where they were supposed to go, he ignored with an icy indifference, as though explaining anything to the "dirty Jews" was far beneath his standing.

"You'll 'ave to find yourself a so-called Jewish house," the landlady explained after the man had left, handing Margot a newspaper with yet another new law laughing in her face with its black stubs of new Gothic font. Ordinarily, she wouldn't have been so obliging, but Margot had paid the January rent already, which she couldn't even consider asking for back. "An apartment owned by Jews. The Jewish council can assign one for you, from what I understand."

"And where will the owners of the apartment go?"

The landlady shrugged. "Nowhere. They'll stay there; it's just they'll have to take on tenants, is all."

With that, she was gone.

In the kitchen, someone suggested in jest that the new tenants would have to keep windows open for three days before moving in, to air out all the Jewish stench.

"I'd fumigate it," another voice joined in. "Who knows what vermin crawls there with that Jew dog of theirs and all of its fleas?"

Jochen had the suitcases packed by the time Margot returned from work. They left that very evening, without a single look back. It could only be better in a new place. At least there, everyone would be Jewish. At least there, they wouldn't have to listen to the insults all day long.

They stayed at Anastasia's for the time being, checking in daily with the Jewish Council on account of their new living arrangements. The line at the Council's headquarters snaked around several street corners, seemingly never diminishing in length despite the Council workers toiling at distributing living assignments from dawn till dusk. Those less fortunate, who had been kicked out of their lodging and didn't have anyone sympathetic to take them in, slept right in the street, with all of their belongings bundled up around them. At night, the entire area turned into a makeshift refugee camp, with small tarpaulin-covered tents serving as the only shield from the elements for those suddenly without a home, without a land to belong to.

It was during one such trip that Margot thought she saw a familiar face. Numb from cold, numb from the endless waiting, she pushed herself off the wall against which she was leaning, gloved hands jammed in pockets, and looked closer. To be sure, it couldn't have been her; Margot's vision must have been blurred, her eyes constantly tearing from the unforgiving gusts of wind. Even Jochen's tall frame wasn't enough to shield her from the elements. But then again, he'd lost so much weight; the coat all but hung on him now as though on a hanger...

"Lida?" Margot called, unsure, stepping out of the line and into the street.

The woman started visibly at the name. For an instant, their eyes locked and Margot saw that it was indeed her, Lida

Baarová, her magnetic dark eyes that used to hold entire Germany under their spell still recognizable despite being rimmed with black, sunken somewhat on her pale face, the lower part of which was hidden by a thick fur lined scarf.

Margot was about to raise her hand in greeting, but Lida, looking positively mortified, turned swiftly away and hastened her steps along the street on which Margot had never expected to see her.

Jochen called after her, but Margot only waved him off and hurried after the former celebrity, who, for some reason, looked as frightened and haunted as the crowd from which Margot had just separated herself. After a short chase through back alleys full of refuse and smelling sharply of urine, Margot caught up with Lida, not so much due to her own determination but because Lida had finally stopped under a torn awning of some *Lokal* that had long ago gone out of business.

"Forgive me for running," Lida said by way of greeting, her words forming small clouds of vapor above her scarf. "I couldn't risk being recognized. I'm not supposed to be in the streets. House arrest and all that business; you understand?"

Margot blinked at the actress incredulously. Lida was almost unrecognizable in a coat that was black and unremarkable, in boots splashed with mud and wet snow, her face paler and much narrower than Margot remembered, without even a trace of powder along her nose, which she kept tucking into the furry folds of her scarf. She looked resigned and infinitely tired, much like Margot looked on most days; only Margot was married to a Jew, whereas Lida was Minister Goebbels' mistress...

"House arrest?" Margot finally managed, the words turning heavy like rocks in her mouth. "Why on earth..."

Lida's pale, unpainted lips pulled to a faint smile just above her scarf—a smile that was forced and never reached her eyes; eyes full of shadows, without hope. "You warned me and I didn't want to listen," she responded simply and her lips trembled ever so slightly before disappearing behind the cover of her scarf.

"Did that odious serpent do that to you?" Margot demanded, her entire body shaking with sudden indignation.

They used to be, if not friends, comrades back in the day. Two "outsiders" in the world of immaculate Aryans. Margot was just as protective of Lida as she'd been during their Babelsberg days. Out of the entire set, it was Lida who had never turned on her and even tried to change her no-good lover into a semblance of a human being with a conscience—fat lot of good it did her.

"No." Lida shrugged her shoulders, either from the cold or disappointment, Margot couldn't quite tell. "He wanted to marry me. Even went to the Führer to ask for a divorce from his wife."

That was something new entirely. Margot had no insight into Goebbels' heart—if he had one, that was—but the gesture itself made her experience something akin to respect for the man. Frankly, she'd never expected him to do anything of the kind, but for Lida's sake, Margot kept her surprise to herself.

"What happened then?"

"What do you think happened?" Lida broke into mirthless laughter. "Hitler happened. Just as you said, Joseph may love me, but he'll always love his Führer more."

"Was it Hitler who ordered your arrest?"

Lida simply nodded.

"What are you doing here?" With a sweep of her hand, Margot indicated the area surrounding the Jewish Council.

Lida hesitated, but then suddenly dropped her guard, as though remembering that Margot herself was very much a persecuted minority. "I was meeting someone who promised to get me through the Czech border. They smuggle Jews the same way, so..."

Margot nodded several times. It all made sense now.

"Want to come along?" Lida asked and grinned, sincerely for the first time, her eyes igniting with a long-forgotten light at the shared joke.

"We have no money."

"No one has it nowadays. People who had it are all long gone—to Paris, to London, to New York, and good for them."

"We know no one in Czechoslovakia. Here, we at least have family," Margot explained, pushing her hands back into her pockets and shifting from one foot to the other. "And besides, we have a dog. Can't just abandon him."

"No, of course not," Lida agreed surprisingly easily and shivered as well. "It's getting cold, just standing like this. I should be going."

"So should I. Jochen must be wondering where I ran off to."

A shadow of something wistful and infinitely tender passed fleetingly over Lida's face, turning her eyes misty. "He's very lucky to have you," she finally uttered in a voice full of emotion.

Margot thought of reaching for Lida's arm, of telling her that it wasn't her, Lida's, fault, that Goebbels was a selfish and cowardly excuse of a man who wasn't worthy of her, that she would meet someone who would worship the very ground she walked on and laugh at her old self, far too young and naïve... But she ended up saying nothing at all.

Because there she was, standing by her Jewish husband when Goebbels didn't have the guts to stand up for his Czech beloved, the second most powerful man in Germany, and there wasn't a single thing that Margot could have uttered that would have changed that fact.

"Good luck to you, Lida."

"And to you, Margot. To you both. I hope we'll meet one day again."

"I hope so too."

The echo of Lida's steps had long turned into silence and

Margot still stood and gazed in the direction in which the actress had disappeared as the clouds were gathering overhead. She didn't need to look at the leaden sky to know that a storm was coming; a storm that not all of them would survive. Of that, Margot was also painfully aware.

SEVENTEEN

SEPTEMBER 1939

"Margot, wake up."

Margot stirred, mumbled something but made no motion to get up.

"Margot, we'll be late for our allotted bathroom time and will have to make do without a shower again."

"I don't care." Pulling the covers over her head, Margot turned toward the wall.

"You're planning to go to work dirty then?"

"Mhm."

"No, Margot, my love; we're having none of that." Despite all Margot's protests, Jochen was pulling the blankets off her head, scooping her into his embrace, kissing her awake. "You can sleep in the tub, while I'm washing your hair; how about that?" Without further ado, Jochen pulled her arms through the sleeves of her robe.

With the best will in the world, Margot couldn't bring herself to unglue her eyes. To be sure, it was early morning. In the kitchen, the Goldbergs were already making their breakfast —Margot could hear Frau Goldberg's exasperated pleas to her husband to *please get that cat; she keeps jumping on the sink near the stove and will surely singe her tail before long and set the entire building on fire*—but the morning had a quality of unreality to it. Time was all out of sync. Margot could swear she had just crawled into bed and forgotten herself in the sleep of the dead, without dreams, when one's eyelids are full of lead, and just a second later, Jochen was already shaking her awake, urging her to get up, because after the Goldbergs came the Rosenbergs' twenty minutes in the communal bathroom and after that the Greenblatts would occupy it. For that's how it was now in this new Jewish quarter, into which the remaining Jews of Berlin had been crammed, one family into each room, elderly, children, dogs, cats and fish alike.

Margot and Jochen were relatively fortunate: there were only two of them and their Goose. The Greenblatts numbered six, including the couple's two children and Frau Greenblatt's parents. There would have been eight, but Herr Greenblatt's parents had been dead for over six months.

Six months ago, there was still a chance to run for those with at least some means. Now, with the war in progress, even that last prospect was gone. They were cut off from the entire world, caught in the trap ready to snap closed, the noose tightening daily on their long-suffering necks. The only question that now remained was whether the Nazis would string them up or the rope would give in first, torn to shreds by the sheer willpower of people with nothing to lose.

The bathroom was still full of steam and pleasantly warm after the Goldbergs' use of it. Shedding her nightgown, Margot stepped into the tub, her eyes still half closed, and smiled in silent gratitude at the squeaky-clean surface under her feet. It was an unspoken rule among the tenants, cleaning after themselves each time they used the communal facilities—out of mutual respect for one another. There were no more "dirty Jews" and "clean Aryans" here. Everyone was equal. Everyone was family.

"Don't be stingy with that soap," Margot said as she watched her husband barely lather himself with a small bar smelling faintly of pine. To preserve hot water and time, most families showered together; those with children as well. What would have been considered inappropriate in any other time was suddenly the norm in this parallel new world of theirs. "I got us more. It's still in my handbag. I was so tired last night, I forgot to take it out."

Jochen widened his eyes at her, inclining his head in apparent admiration. "Who did you rob, *gnädige Frau*?"

Margot chuckled at the theatrically formal address —*Madame*—swiping at him with a wet washrag. The question wasn't without its merit: with the war had come ration cards. Everything was hard to come by now, unless one was a Golden Party Pheasant. The irony was, one of the biggest of the pheasants, Propaganda Minister Goebbels, insisted that the German people shouldn't mind one bit and should be happy to accept making sacrifices. Hadn't Poland fallen in a matter of weeks to their formidable war machine? What was a few less grams of meat if the Wehrmacht was fighting on the front line for their very future? Of course, Goebbels himself didn't have to sacrifice anything at all, unlike his former beloved, who'd been reduced to a fugitive overnight—hungry, hunted, betrayed.

"Anastasia got some from one of her connections."

"Black market?"

"What else? Oh, and Frau Goldberg got us some meat."

"No!" Jochen's hand, with the soap bar in it, froze midair. "Now, who did *she* rob?"

If regular German ration cards were a spit in the face from the Party, the Jewish ration cards were barely enough for survival. Jochen's ration card sheets were the same as Margot's, only his were stamped with a big yellow J, and all at once, *no meat or fish for you; no milk, no eggs, no white bread and*

certainly no cigarettes or coffee. The air and water are still free.
Take a sip and be grateful you're still breathing.

"Some unsuspecting grocer in Königs Wusterhausen,"
Margot explained with a laugh. "She'd been planning her
maneuver for quite some time. She purposely gathered all of
our, mixed families', ration cards—I gave her yours as well—and
went to the very outskirts of the city where there hadn't been
any Jews even before this whole Nazi business. So, she goes to
this grocer and puts all of our ration cards in front of him,
German on top, and demands meat for the exact number. The
poor devil starts counting them out, sees the yellow *J*—for the
first time in his life, apparently—and asks Frau Goldberg what it
means. *Jugend*, she says, *children*, without as much as moving a
brow. *Ach, children*, he says, and gives her all the meat she
wanted for her little ones." In spite of herself, Margot broke into
laughter. "I would love to see his face when he goes to exchange
those cards for money and discovers that he sold meat to Jews!"

Jochen, too, was wiping the corner of his eye. "Remind me
to shake her hand!"

"We decided to pool it together," Margot said. "I hope you
don't mind?"

"What? Meat?"

"Yes. Make one big dinner for everyone to enjoy."

"That sounds nice."

The smile he gave her reminded Margot of the times long
gone, and for one short instant, she forgot about the hostile
world around them and allowed herself to get lost in those beautiful warm eyes of his.

The moment of intimacy was interrupted by the creaking of
boards outside the bathroom. The Greenblatts were up, which
meant Margot and Jochen only had a few minutes left to finish
their mourning routine. State persecution left little time for
tender moments like this.

In spite of herself, Margot sighed at the injustice of it all. "Turn around; I'll scrub your back."

Jochen turned and Margot froze at the sight of an ugly red welt just under his left shoulder blade.

"What is this?"

"What?"

"The bruise on your back."

"Oh." His voice suddenly rose an octave, taking on that artificial cheerfulness Margot had grown to loathe ever since he'd been conscripted to the forced labor service for Jews a few weeks ago, at the beginning of the war. Now, day and night, he and his fellow former artists and intellectuals were working for the *Reichsbahn*, repairing the tracks, serving as bellboys for the arriving troops—and sometimes as punching bags for their superiors. "It's nothing. I was picking up luggage, was just about to straighten up and didn't notice a rod protruding from the train. You should have seen Adler! He slipped and came into a luggage-pulling cart face first. Still sporting a bump the size of a potato on his head, ha-ha!"

Margot looked at him without responding for a moment. She was already used to these denials—the excuses and hilarious anecdotes—*oh, you know us intellectuals, we're so clumsy, we stumble and fall all the time. Sometimes multiple times. Sometimes square on our faces.*

Sometimes Margot spared his pride and pretended to believe him.

Sometimes she felt hot, blinding rage build in her and rise to her very throat, and she had to clutch the pillow and scream into it, because if she didn't, that darkness within her would find an outlet, to be sure; someone drunk and in a uniform, whose skull she wouldn't mind bashing in in some dark alley with the first brick she could find—a vicious strike for each welt on her husband's body.

"Margot, don't look at me like that. It was an accident, I

promise." He turned away from her again, offering her his back —turned away from his wife in shame because some uniformed dungheap had hit him just because he could, just because he had a cane, just because it made his comrades laugh—seeing a Jew being hit.

"All right."

"It's true."

"I believe you." Margot knew how imperative it was for Jochen to preserve at least a fraction of his pride in front of her after just about everyone else had chipped away at it for years now. He couldn't hit back at them; he could only lower his head and apologize for being in their way. But, for his sake, she said the words he needed to hear.

"I'm glad to be back at work," Jochen continued. "I'm glad to be contributing. They even pay us. Eighty-eight marks is peanuts, of course, I'm well aware, but it's still something."

The lowest German worker received three hundred and twenty. Margot used to receive more, but ever since Schneller and Schmeider had been Aryanized last spring and turned into the Feodor Schmeider Company, Margot's salary had been reduced due to her marital status. To make up for the lost money, Margot had begun cleaning Grünewald villas three times a week after her shift at the leather shop. On Wednesdays, she passed by John's old mansion. It must have been Aryanized too: instead of the exotic ivy, two *Hakenkreuz* banners now decorated its walls.

"I rather preferred it when you contributed from within the house," Margot said quietly, careful not to touch the tender flesh as she lathered Jochen's back with soap.

"Miss my cooking?"

"I do, actually."

"Goose doesn't."

Margot smiled, grateful for the shower on her face now. When Jochen turned, he wouldn't see her tears.

EIGHTEEN

FEBRUARY 1940

Her shift at the leather shop had finished, and Margot was waiting for Jochen to finish his. It was Tuesday, no cleaning work for her today, no Grünewald and no ice-cold marble floors scuffed by the multiple jackboots of their uniformed inhabitants; only a *Bahnhof* near Alexanderplatz, open to the elements and the self-imposed watch Margot would carry for as long as needed.

Just two weeks ago, she would have been at the grocer's at this time, waiting in a long line for her meager share of eggs (if any were left), meat or poultry (it was mostly poultry these days) and whatever preserves of the day were available. Then, she would take a train home, kiss Goose on his wet, happy snout and chat with Frau Goldberg as they shared the kitchen and, most of the time, whatever delicacies one of them had managed to procure that day.

But two weeks ago, Herr Greenblatt had wandered into the apartment white as chalk, dropped into a chair in the kitchen without removing his coat or even hat, and began mumbling something that made absolutely no sense—something about luggage that had arrived by itself, all marked with Jewish last names and the departure point—Stettin, just an hour away from Berlin—but no Jewish passengers themselves; only the SS opening that luggage and sorting through the belongings, people's personal belongings—imagine that?

He'd grown silent after that, the suspicion of something dreadful hanging in the air. No one had said anything for a very long time, as though putting their worst fears into words would somehow make them real. But then the weekend edition of the *Beobachter* had arrived and, with it, the proud announcement of Schwede-Coburg, the *Gauleiter* of Stettin, that his *Gau* was the first one in the entire Reich to be completely *Judenfrei*—Jew-free—an Aryan paradise, a Germany for Germans—Hitler's dream wrapped with a bow, from Schwede-Coburg, with love.

"It says here that they deported Germans married to Jews as well." Frau Greenblatt's gaze had roved around their small communal kitchen, the paper rustling softly in her unsteady hands. "Deported to some ghetto in Poland."

Since then, Margot kept her daily vigil by Jochen's workplace, in subzero temperatures, in blizzards and wind, her eyes trained on her husband's gray figure with fierce, protective light in them. She couldn't care less if they deported them both; that was fine by her. But no one was coming and taking her husband away; over her dead body, SS or not. She'd lunge at their throats with her bare hands; she'd gouge their eyes; she'd bite and kick and scream and raise hell on earth, but one thing she would never do was go down without a fight.

A seemingly endless freight train pulled in to the station, its tail all but lost in the gathering storm. A few Wehrmacht soldiers disembarked and were stretching their legs on the platform where Margot stood, while the forced laborers' foreman was shouting his orders at the men running about and slipping in sleet and icy patches in their civilian half-boots, made to work in the open, while the civilians and the troops warmed themselves under the steel hood of the station. The laborers tried holding onto their fedoras that the wind—and the foreman —kept knocking off their heads, and stumbling in the folds of their overcoats as they struggled with the latches on the freight train's doors; former Jewish intelligentsia turned into slaves. It would almost be comical, had it not been so tragic.

"Move your fat tails, you lazy scum! Well?! Get on with it; we don't have all day!"

Through the intensifying blizzard, Margot could barely see the ant-like, busy figures of the forced laborers, bent and stumbling under the load of luggage and crates bigger than them that they were carrying and stacking onto the edge of the platform. One of the laborers, an elderly man judging by his stooped posture and the stiff manner in which he moved—with this weather, his arthritis must be acting up, Margot thought— strained under the weight of the crate the foreman had dropped unceremoniously onto his narrow shoulders from inside the train car, lost his footing and would have most certainly fallen had not Jochen, beside him, caught him midair, and steadied the man before taking the unbearable load off his shoulders.

"Careful with that, you feebleminded swine!" the foreman bellowed, outraged. "That's French cognac! It costs more than your life, you pair of muttons!"

Next to Margot, one of the Wehrmacht men stopped his leisurely pacing and stiffened visibly.

"Leave them alone." His voice carried far and loud along the platform. It was the voice of a man used to giving commands and having those commands obeyed. "Harassing one's workers never made them any more productive. Have you heard of leading by example?"

To Margot's great satisfaction, the foreman's expression quickly changed from wrathful and authoritarian to confused, before becoming the picture of servitude.

"Apparently not," the Wehrmacht officer concluded, clasping his gloved hands behind his back. "Else, you would have been in the army instead of harassing these poor devils. Take that crate yourself and show them how it's done. Well?"

After a moment of hesitation, during which the foreman was trying to decipher whether the Wehrmacht officer was joking or not, he climbed down from his perch and approached Jochen. After another glance in the officer's direction, the foreman heaved the crate onto his own shoulders, instantly bending almost in half under its weight, and stumbled in the direction of the sorting station.

"Thank you, *Herr Offizier*," Margot whispered with all the gratitude she felt for the man at that moment.

He looked confused. "Are you waiting for someone here?" he asked against the howling wind.

"My husband is there." Margot motioned toward the slave laborers.

"Jewish?"

"Yes."

The officer nodded several times. "I had a brilliant young man serving in my company. Also Jewish. Well... half-Jewish, a *Mischling*. A Jewish father, who must also be toiling somewhere..." He made an annoyed half-gesture with his hand toward the train, but dropped it helplessly by his side. "Brave, smart, such a good comrade—the entire company loved him. Went through Poland and the whole of Europe with me, that boy. Would have been promoted three times already, would have been an officer himself, but..." Another sigh, much more telling than a thousand words would be. "I kept him in my troop even after the decree came out, releasing all the *Mischlinge* from military service. But then some SS halfwit from the political department reported me and I received the direct order from the OKW, the Wehrmacht High Command itself." His gray eyes stared hard into the snow. "Damn rotten business."

"Yes."

"But your husband is a very lucky man."

"No." Margot shook her head with a faint, half-frozen smile. "I'm a very lucky woman."

AUTUMN 1940

The U-Bahn train's lights blinked once, twice. On cue, honed by months of the relentless British campaign, the commuters' eyes glanced up at the ceiling. The train took a sharp turn, screeched to a careful halt and shuddered suddenly. Somewhere overhead, a muted echo of an explosion spread through the tunnel's walls. Margot felt as though her very bones absorbed the sound.

The lights blinked one last time and went out altogether. In the darkness, someone cursed the head of the Luftwaffe, Göring, quietly but viciously.

"How long has it been since that self-important fathead declared that we may all start calling him Meyer if only one bomb falls on Berlin?"

"And whatever happened to our brave Luftwaffe bombing those Brits into oblivion?" Someone else gave his voice, making use of the gloom.

With their faces hidden, everyone was brave. All of a sudden, everyone had an opinion.

"Oh, shut your traps!" A woman bristled somewhere near the back of the train car. "Just a year ago, all of you were cheering the undefeated German army and pledging your allegiance to your beloved Führer."

With a threatening hiss, the doors sighed and pulled open, allowing faint wafts of cool air mixed with track grease and crumbling plaster inside the car. Somewhere outside, still too far ahead to make out his exact words, the train conductor was moving along the tracks, repeating the same command.

Another series of explosions broke overhead, much closer this time, making the wooden seats under their coats sing with tension. Margot felt Jochen's fingers search for her hand and close around it.

On one of the opposite seats, a child began to wail.

Suddenly, a voice said, "Does anyone else smell rubber burning?"

A wave of panic swept over the commuters. Everyone began sniffing at the air, sticking their heads out the opened doors.

"Quit causing panic! Nothing is burning!" Despite the sentiment behind the words, the voice that uttered them sounded close to hysterics.

"It is, too! I'm an electrician. I know what an electric fire smells like."

"*Frauen* and *Herren*—"

"Must be the conductor," Jochen whispered into Margot's ear.

"According to the air warden's regulations," the conductor's voice boomed from the speakers, "everyone must vacate the car and proceed to the nearest air-raid shelter. Please, walk along the tracks following your fellow commuters who have already left their respective cars. Move in a single file, and mind the distance between you and the commuter ahead of you to avoid a stampede. Once you're outside, the policeman on duty will direct you to the closest air-raid shelter."

"Isn't it safer to stay inside the train rather than venture outside and try to make it to the shelter?" someone asked doubtfully.

The rest of the commuters were already pushing their way toward the doors.

"Stay inside and get electrocuted for all we care," another voice called in response.

"No, it has to do with the underground tunnel walls; they aren't reinforced. They may collapse."

"What are you talking about? The walls inside the U-Bahn tunnel are more reinforced than any shelter!"

The bickering went on for some time, first inside the car, then outside in the tunnel, until it died completely somewhere in the distance.

Margot couldn't help but chuckle when Jochen released a breath of obvious relief and stretched his legs all the way out in front of himself.

"*Ach*, at last. The whole car to ourselves. What do you say to that, Margarete?"

"I say, it's much better than any shelter."

"We're like royalty here."

"To be sure."

Something heavy dropped overhead. Then, after an instant of silence, the air itself appeared to explode, sending their ears ringing and eyes smarting with the sheer pressure of it. All at once, the temperature appeared to be rising, sucking all the oxygen out of the air. Shedding her coat, Margot wiped at the thin film of sweat that had broken out on her temples and forehead. Somewhere a few meters above them, more bombs continued to explode.

"Can the air spontaneously combust from the blasts?" Margot asked in a carefully controlled voice.

"No, I don't think it can. Not inside here, at any rate." Jochen, too, was shrugging his way out of his coat.

"But outside?"

"Maybe outside, just around the explosion site. Or maybe it's the bomb itself that does it. I'm not a specialist in bombs, you know."

Margot thought she heard him laugh and laughed in response, hoping that he'd hear feigned mirth in her voice as well. "No. But you're a specialist in surviving. That's why I'm asking."

A sharp blade of light sliced the darkness around them.

Momentarily blinded, they couldn't make out the source of it until a voice, full of stunned amazement, called out to them.

"What in Hades are you two still doing here? Didn't you hear me call to everyone to leave the car?"

"Which station have you directed them to, Herr Conductor?" Jochen asked the man, shielding his face from the bright yellow glare of his torchlight.

"The Zoo; where else? It's the nearest one."

"Are there any Jewish shelters there then?"

"No, of course not!" The man sounded annoyed. "There are no Jews there and certainly no Jewish shelters."

"That's what we assumed," Jochen replied, as unrattled as before. "There would be no point in us trying to make it inside. They wouldn't have let us in at any rate."

"Why wouldn't they—" the conductor began to ask, and then choked on the words as it finally dawned on him. Slowly, he lowered his torchlight. There was nothing else for him to say.

By now, as the "brilliant" Luftwaffe's campaign against the British RAF had first come to a stalemate at around July and soon turned against Germany altogether, more and more people spent their nights in various reinforced cellars and very few of them wanted to have anything to do with the remaining Jews also seeking shelter from the RAF bombs. No one cared to reinforce the cellars in the Jewish tenements. The fewer Jews survived the blasts, the better—this was the popular sentiment among the officials whom those Jews, Margot and Jochen included, had petitioned. There were only "Aryan" shelters near their building, and even those were streets away, and to reach them took more than fifteen minutes of brisk running with their valuables and papers stuffed into sacks they had to haul on their backs as they tried to outrun British bombs. But even then, one "Aryan" building superintendent or another would block their way with his arms stretched wide and wild eyes.

"A Jew?" he would bellow as he looked at Jochen's identification papers. "Are you quite mad? Do you wish for those people down there to breathe in the same air you're breathing out? Have you completely gone off your head?"

Margot, with her German passport, he would admit, relenting after Jochen's desperate pleas. But Margot wouldn't go down without her husband, and so, they returned to their apartment and played cards while the fire and death itself rained outside, and told each other anti-Hitler jokes they overheard on the BBC radio the Greenblatts kept concealed in their apartment and took out only in the evenings for everyone to gather round and listen to with a renewed hope lighting gradually in their eyes. And the Grim Reaper himself, who had cut at the heating pipe with his scythe in one of the "Aryan" shelters Margot and Jochen had been turned away from and scalded all the people inside to death, would turn his sightless eye sockets away from the couple, because even he couldn't bring himself to do to them what their fellow Germans were ready to do.

"Well... stay here then, I suppose," the conductor said at last, averting his gaze and carrying the light away with him. "They'll restore the regular service soon enough. We should start moving within an hour, if nothing is damaged on the line."

He went away, but something of the light didn't. It remained inside the train car, because the hearts of two people inside it were enough to carry it through the darkness.

NINETEEN

SEPTEMBER 1941

"Have you heard the news?" Herr Brandt, the shop's new foreman, announced, sauntering out of the office formerly occupied by Herr Grohm.

Herr Grohm himself had long been gone, since the Aryanization of the business, just like the rest of the Jews—and where to was anyone's guess. Unlike Grohm, the new foreman had little experience in leather manufacturing, but he strutted around in a Party brown uniform and was loyal to Hitler like a dog and that was all that his new bosses needed to know. Now, in place of elegant, tailored civilian jackets and coats, Luftwaffe bomber jackets and long SS overcoats lined the workstations as far as the eye could see. As for Margot herself, she'd been promoted from the button-girl to the gloves and belts department. It went without saying that the gloves and the belts were for the army also. German civilians would just have to make do without and be happy to make the sacrifice in the name of the Reich's glory.

"Have we taken Moscow at last?" Herr Schneider, Margot's immediate supervisor, looked up from the shop's floor to the second-floor railing, on which Herr Brandt was resting his white, pudgy hands.

To Margot's subtle satisfaction, Herr Brandt's expression momentarily soured. Despite all the propaganda pouring from the shop's loudspeakers on a daily basis, it was no secret that the Russian campaign wasn't quite going according to the German High Command's plans. After attacking the Soviet Union in late June, despite the non-aggression pact between the two countries, the German army had been about to hold victory parades in both Leningrad and Moscow. Respective medals for taking the cities were issued; speeches prepared. But something had gone wrong—what precisely, no one could quite tell, not even the Greenblatts' BBC—but the fact remained: unconquerable Wehrmacht was presently fighting the blasted Bolshevists for every obscure village long burned down by the Bolshevists themselves, instead of touring the Kremlin and drinking victory champagne at the Hermitage.

"No, not yet," he allowed, adding, "though I'm certain that our victory is imminent."

Brandt recovered himself quickly, Margot had to give him that.

"It is only matter of time," Schneider agreed, inclining his head subserviently.

"A new decree has just been issued," Brandt announced triumphantly, his white fingers clasping at the railing like the claws of a vulture. "From today, every remaining Jew in Germany over the age of six must wear a distinguishing mark, the yellow Star of David, on the left side of his breast, sewn onto all of his outer clothing."

Margot's hand, with a ruler in it, froze over the leather strip that would soon be an overcoat's belt. There was a heap of them on her worktable, of different lengths and shapes—the sliced remains of leather overcoats and military jackets. But all at once, they weren't simple leather cuts anymore. They were the hides of skinned cows and lambs and pigs, the physical remains of a heap of corpses—animal corpses for now, but how long would it be before it was human corpses, brutally murdered and skinned; how long would it be before one SS sadist or another would wear gloves made of human skin—

Dropping the ruler onto the table, Margot pressed her ice-cold fingertips to her temples, squeezing her eyes shut, forcing the vision out of her mind. *What a terrible, terrible image. What had possessed her?*

"Now we shall know for sure who's a Jew and who's not."

A new wave of nausea swept over Margot. She clenched her teeth until her jaws ached, silently begging whatever higher power there was for Brandt to just shut his mug and let her work in silence.

"It will certainly make it easier to get rid of them now," Schneider added, almost gaily.

"Mhm. Send the trucks onto the streets and collect them all like the garbage that they are."

"And dump them behind the city limits where they belong."

"Nah, they're like roaches, they'll just crawl right back."

"Well, I say dump them and burn them then. That should solve the problem."

Suddenly, the entire shop was noisy with laughter. Only Margot didn't laugh. With her glazed-over eyes, she was staring deep into the heap of skins, seeing the future, and it was worse than Dante's purgatory.

"I'm supposed to pay for this travesty?!"

Jochen's voice boomed around the Jewish Community office.

The clerk behind the glass looked up, startled by the shout, and pointed a helpless pen in the direction of the price list. One Star of David—twenty pfennig.

"I can read!" Jochen bellowed, his entire body trembling with indignation. "I'm asking you what sort of a mockery this is, making us purchase these atrocities against our will?"

Margot placed a hand on his back, where all the muscles were strained like strings about to snap. Not to comfort him; there was nothing that she could do to comfort him at this point, but just to show that she was still there, still with him, and would forever be by his side, until death, if it came to that.

Jochen swung round, searched her face in desperation and swallowed once, twice, before turning back to the clerk.

"We wouldn't have charged you at all, *mein Herr*," the clerk tried to reassure him, his voice wavering. "But the flag manufacturing plant that's producing these things needs to be paid for their troubles. Trust me, we're only charging you the production cost; nothing else..."

It was then that Jochen must have noticed the clerk's Star of David sewn neatly over his jacket. Margot saw her husband looking at it for some time before releasing a breath of utter dejection and surrendering his sixty pfennig for the hateful things. "Three, please."

That evening, Margot sewed them on his suit jacket, his overcoat and his sweater—tightly, as the regulations prescribed, just like the clerk's wife must have sewn it for him.

"I'm not going outside except for work. Never again," Jochen declared that night, staring grimly at the bright yellow patch—*Jude*—marring his only good jacket. "Frankly, even going to work... I can't imagine what that'll be like now."

Neither could Margot. All at once, the last protective shield of invisibility was gone. The last Jews of Germany had been marked for everyone to see; vulnerable prey for the predators in leather coats.

"It's all right. We take the train together to Alexanderplatz. I'll just walk you to work from now on. I'm already meeting you after." Margot tried to smile, but her lips quivered and curled into a grimace.

But it wasn't all right. Nothing would ever be all right, ever again, it occurred to Margot the next morning, when they stepped out into the street and were met with hostile looks, jeers and outright taunts from the people who wouldn't have paid them any heed just twenty-four hours ago.

"Shame on you, German woman, for that Jew!" a well-dressed man called out and spat on the ground, dangerously close to Margot's shoes.

"Dirty Jew-loving tramp," a woman commented from the steps of a milkman's shop.

At the entrance to the U-Bahn, a newspaper seller leaned out of the window of his kiosk and made an indecent gesture, asking Margot if she preferred her liverwurst circumcised.

Holding her head high, Margot ignored him, just like she ignored the policeman who approached the couple on the platform and tried to wiggle his pencil in between the cloth and the star on Jochen's left breast. Much to the crowd's disappointment, it was sewn on tight. No fines for this particular Jew, it seemed.

In the distance, the train was approaching. Someone voiced the idea of pushing the Jew under it.

"Let's push them both," another voice called out.

There were a few mortified exclamations, but many more approving guffaws. Looking ash-white, like a man who'd been mortally wounded, Jochen let go of Margot's hand all of a sudden and began excusing his way to the other end of the platform. Stunned and unable to move, Margot watched him enter a different car and she allowed the crowd to carry her into the closest one. As though by magic, everything changed. No one looked up from the papers they were reading. No *Hitlerjugend-*

attired boy began to taunt her to impress his blond comrades with his witticisms. Even those hurling abuse at her at the platform now ignored her entirely, as if not having a Jewish husband attached to her somehow restored her public image.

Margot rode the train in that blissful silence for four minutes exactly, until the next stop. As soon as the train slowed down, she made her way to the car where Jochen was, smiled when she saw him standing in the corner just beside the sign that read *Seating reserved for Aryans only*, walked resolutely over to him, looking so surprised and visibly startled, and kissed him loudly on his cheek.

"And there you were, imagining that you'd gotten rid of your old ball and chain, eh, Herr Rosenberg?" Margot pinched him playfully on his cheek and circled her arm through the crook of his, while the rest of the car gaped at them in stunned amazement. "I regret to inform you, that is not going to happen."

"Margot," he whispered into her hair, pleadingly.

But Margot would have none of that self-sacrificial nonsense. "It's not going to happen, I said."

With a rush of infinite affection, she felt him circle his arm around her waist and pull her tightly against himself, against his chest where his heart was beating for her only, under the yellow star with the word *Jude* on it.

TWENTY

MAY 1942

"Who died?" The question flew off Margot's lips before she could stop herself.

In her defense, the question was more than appropriate. What else was she to think when she entered their communal apartment, weighed down with enough groceries to last for a week, and discovered all the families huddled together in the Greenblatts' room, sobbing inconsolably. Even Herr Greenblatt himself was wiping his eyes, his lips trembling around the pipe he was sucking on—the sole means of distraction he had left. Surrounded by her children, Frau Greenblatt had her face hidden entirely in the fur of their Persian cat Snowflake. In the corner, Herr Goldberg was staring pensively into the cage of his wife's beloved canaries. Even they were uncharacteristically silent, as though sensing something vaguely dangerous in the air, much like their ancestors sensed death in the miners' oxygen-deprived tunnels.

Instead of a reply, Frau Goldberg, with her handkerchief also pressed against her swollen red nose, handed Margot the only paper Berlin Jews were allowed to read after all other subscriptions had been cancelled for them: *Jüdische Nachricht-*

enblatt. In it, as was always the case with the "Jewish" newspa-per, the latest decree was published—and this one was one of the most cold-blooded and cruelest yet. As Margot read it, she felt her heart turn to stone.

> *As of Monday of the following week, all Jewish households, including intermarried couples, are to destroy their pets, including dogs, cats, birds, rodents, rabbits, etc., either by employing the services of the Animal Protection Association or a private veterinarian. Certificates confirming the destruction of the animals are to be submitted to your local Gestapo office.*

"What..." Margot tried to swallow once, twice, but her mouth had gone suddenly dry. "Why... why on earth...?" With the best will in the world, she couldn't finish the sentence. The words simply wouldn't come. Groping for a chair behind her, Margot dropped into it heavily, feeling as though a fist had just punched her—straight in her gut, which she was pressing now with one hand.

"The logic behind this new decree is that apparently the pets are better off dead than being looked after by Jews," Frau Goldberg explained. Her voice was hollow and emotionless. In her lap, her long-haired dachshund softly whined. The sound nearly tore Margot's heart in pieces.

"Goose," she whispered and dashed into the hallway, groceries lying scattered where she'd dropped them when she stepped forward to take the paper.

As soon as she tore open the door to her and Jochen's room, Goose broke out of Jochen's embrace and leapt happily at Margot, licking her hands and face and nuzzling her with his wet nose, as she fell in a heap in the threshold. She didn't see Jochen approach; only felt his arms around her and Goose and his chest heaving with silent sobs against her shoulder. Never before had she seen her husband cry this way. The sight of it terrified her worse than anything.

And then she was livid, burning with hatred and anger of an overpowering force that Margot had never felt before. She had thought she was mad with fury when that vile former neighbor of theirs had called Goose a flea-ridden Jew dog. But that couldn't compare to the homicidal fury raging in Margot's chest now.

"We're not doing it; you hear me?" Her teeth clenched tight, Margot felt her entire body ringing with nerves, with some newfound strength. They could only push her so far before she would start shoving back. "I'll rip their hearts out with my bare hands before they come for Goosie. Goosie's going to live. He's going to live and he's going to survive this war and I'll person-ally walk him over the ground where the Nazis will lie their heads like they deserve and make him piss all over them!"

Suddenly on her feet, Margot grabbed Goose's leash from the hook by the door and attached it to his collar. Swiping at her face, she took the tag with Goose's name on one side and Margot and Jochen's current address on the other and pressed it into Jochen's hand.

"Where are you taking him?"

Jochen was still on the floor, stroking Goose's silky head and paws and back.

"To Anastasia's."

"You think she'll take him? She already has two dogs of her own."

"If there's one person in Berlin who will have him, it's her."

With a final parting kiss, Margot left her husband where he still sat slumped on the floor and headed for the former living room, now the Greenblatts' room, where the rest of their adopted family was mourning their pets.

"Give me Hazel's leash." Margot held out her hand to a

stunned Frau Goldberg. "Well? We don't have much time. And take her tag off."

"No!" Misinterpreting the gesture, Frau Goldberg pressed the dachshund against her chest, half averting her body from Margot. "I'll take her myself tomorrow. The law goes into effect tomorrow. There's still a few hours left—"

"I'm not taking her to the veterinarian to get killed, for God's sake! What sort of monster do you take me for? I'm taking her to my... stepmother. And father. They're both Aryan. I'm taking Goose there too."

All at once, all eyes were on Margot. Silence fell over the room. It lingered there for a few moments, until little Sonja Greenblatt's soft voice broke it, wavering and full of hopes the nine-year-old girl had already grown to see being broken:

"Frau Rosenberg, could you please take Snowflake too?"

Her eyes full of inner torment, Margot looked at the beautiful cat Frau Goldberg always chastised for walking around the stove and nearly setting the tenement on fire, but never, not once, chasing away, for everyone loved that cat. Even the canaries did. Even Goose, who got smacked by the cat's fluffy paw quite often on his curious snout, after nosing about too close to Snowflake's business. Sometimes Snowflake wandered into Margot's room and sat square in the middle of her sewing, twitching her tail at all Margot's half-serious requests to get her bushy-tailed behind off her work, only to end up letting Snowflake onto her lap. And for a time, with a purring cat curled on her, she would feel as though everything was as it should have been; feeling warm and at home and so very loved, forgetting about the bombs exploding outside and the hatred directed at them from all over.

She looked at the cat and nodded slowly, deliberately. "Not right now—two dogs already—but I'll ask Anastasia. I promise, I'll ask. Even if she can't take her, she'll find someone who will. She always comes through. She will this time, I know it.

Just... let me take these two pups to her first, all right? And then I'll come back for Snowflake."

Sonja nodded readily, her entire face transformed, lit up from the inside.

Before long, her mother was kissing Snowflake all over. "You hear that, old girl?" Frau Greenblatt asked the cat. "You have just been granted pardon! You'll live, you nosy little arsonist-to-be. You'll live!"

"Frau Rosenberg." It was Herr Goldberg this time. His hand, with the pipe in it, hung by his side, before he gestured with it uncertainly toward the canary cage. "Do you think it's possible..." His voice trailed off before he could finish. He, too, had long ago forgotten how to believe in miracles.

"I'll ask." Margot nodded again and took Hazel's leash out of Frau Goldberg's hands.

Both dogs were already pulling in the direction of the front door, anticipating a walk. Frau Goldberg and her husband had to catch squirming Hazel to kiss her on her head one last time. They told her to be a good girl and promised her that they would come and get her as soon as this all was over, for surely such a madness couldn't possibly last long.

Margot didn't expect to see a line outside the premises of Dr. Leib, their local veterinarian, but here they were, men and women, entire families, with their pets on leashes or in their hands or in carriers or cages. There was a curfew for the Jews and many of them were forced labor workers. It made sense that Sunday was the only day when they could take care of the whole damned business before the Gestapo would come and tear the animals straight out of their hands and slap a fine into their empty palms instead—for dragging out the affair for longer than necessary and not complying with the order when they were told. Against an obscenely bright-blue sky stood a column of the condemned, a menacing prediction of what could be to come. Margot tried hard not to hear their desperate cries: barking, meowing, chirping and whining, replete with human sobbing and children's pleas. In her entire life, Margot hadn't seen a sadder sight.

She tried to hasten her steps, to pass the heart-rending scene that would be emblazoned into her mind for as long as she would live, but suddenly there were rushed steps behind her and a woman's hushed voice and fingers reached out for Margot's sleeve but fell short of catching it. In her other hand, the woman held a leash with two spaniels the same color as Goose.

"*Gnädige Frau—*"

Margot was walking faster, shaking her head, trying to ignore the woman and her tear-stricken face and her dogs that looked like miniature versions of her own.

"I saw your coat. You're not Jewish—"

"I can't," Margot hissed back, searching the streets around for the telling ill-fitting suits. They were patrolling more often than not now, checking the papers of everyone without a yellow star and conducting random searches whenever the fancy took them. Margot did not need their attention on her now.

"Could you please take my babies? They're all I have left. They killed my husband during the Soviet Paradise reprisals—"

Margot winced at the reminder of how the Gestapo had swept through the neighborhood and grabbed the first random hundred Jews they saw to be hanged, because some other Jews —Margot thought they were called the Blum group by the papers, but who could tell if this was even their real name and whether the so-called terrorists were indeed Jews?—had set off a bomb at Goebbels' love child: a tremendous exhibit of the so-called Soviet Paradise. The aim of the exhibition was to terrify the German population by showing them what life under the Bolshevists was like so that they would cough up more donations for the German army and not grumble so loudly when their rations cards were reduced even more. What it had achieved, though, was skepticism at best, and at worst, a shower of anti-government leaflets listing a number of the Nazi Paradise specifics mockingly similar to the Soviet ones; comparing the German Gestapo to the Soviet NKVD, the German camps to Soviet camps, German Hitler to their Stalin, and the inevitable death sentence as soon as someone said a word against either...

"My father is dead as well." The woman's shaking voice brought Margot back to reality. "He was at the Jewish hospital with cancer, but then they discharged him because there were only so many beds left and there was nothing else they could do for him at any rate. My mother was looking after him, but then the deportations started last fall and they received their papers for resettlement. I tried to get him an exemption; they tell us they send Jews to the east to work on farms, but what sort of worker would he make with his cancer? But the Gestapo came all the same and dragged him out of his bed and down the stairs, just like that, by the legs, and then my mother, she opened the gas while I was at work and by the time I got home, she was dead too and—"

That was more than Margot could bear. Without any regard for the Gestapo possibly lurking in the shadows, she reached for the woman's hand and silently took the leashes into hers, adding two more dogs to her growing pack.

The woman's teary thanks and hushed laughter full of wonder and disbelief and grief all mixed in one rang in Margot's ears long after she had left the Jewish quarter.

Anastasia opened the door in one of her Japanese kimonos stained with paint and did a double take at the sight of a veritable dog show on her doorstep.

"Good to see you, Margot, love, and... whoever all of these four-legged friends of yours are?" She arched her brow but stepped aside all the same, motioning the dog gang inside. Anastasia's dachshunds were also already welcoming the newcomers with excited barking, sniffing at their tails and nosing around their wet snouts.

Margot hesitated where she stood, regarding Anastasia's immaculate light beige runner. "Anastasia, I have a huge favor to ask."

"Oh no." Anastasia's eyes fell tellingly on the dogs.

"Yes. I'm afraid so. If you don't take them or find a home for them, they will all be destroyed. A new decree has just come out that all Jewish households, including the mixed ones, are not allowed to have pets and that they must all be destroyed—"

"Those bastards are killing animals now?" Anastasia's nostrils flared, and she sounded just as mad as Margot was. "Don't just stand there like a poor relative, come on in... Dogs, too. Who do we have here? Hello, Goosie! Remember me?"

He clearly did, judging by his excited whines and all the dog kisses he bestowed upon Auntie Stasia, as she preferred to be addressed in her fur-nephew's presence.

"And who are these fellows?" Anastasia asked, holding her hand out to the rest of Margot's pack.

"The dachshund is called Hazel. She's our neighbors' dog. And these two, I don't even know. Some woman begged me to take them near the vet's office and I—"

"You couldn't say no." Anastasia gave her a knowing grin.

Margot only shrugged helplessly.

"You're lucky, because neither can I. I'll definitely take my Goosie and his little lady friend since they already know each other. As for these two young fellows..." She kneeled down and lifted each dog's hind leg. "I beg your pardon, a young fellow and his lady friend—or sister—most likely sister, judging by their coats? I'll find them good homes too. Don't fret. If no one takes them, I'll just keep them myself."

"Oh, Anastasia, you're a lifesaver!" Tangling herself in leashes and dogs, Margot was hugging and kissing Anastasia on her paint-sprinkled cheeks and hair. "I don't know how to thank you!" And then she remembered, and bit her lip.

Anastasia stopped petting Goose and looked at her, then tilted her head to one side with a theatrical sigh. "What now?"

"There's also a cat."

"A cat?"

"And canaries." Margot grimaced.

Anastasia only rolled her eyes, moaning. "You're killing me. You're positively slaughtering me!"

"I know, I know..."

"The canaries, your mother will just have to take the canaries. I'll tell Karl to take them there next time he goes to pay that woman's bills. It's only fair that she should contribute for all the money she's getting from him. No offense, but that woman is a leech."

"None taken, and she is." It came as a surprise to Margot, the fact that she scarcely felt anything at all at the mention of her mother's name. Perhaps it was better this way, keeping Maria in the furthest, cobwebbed corner of her mind, tucked away neatly with all the hurtful childhood memories, looks of disappointment and judgement that had never ceased. Why pick at the old scab? Margot felt it wiser to let it heal, form a neat scar tissue that would no longer hurt when prodded.

"Good. That's settled then. As for the cat... I'll figure something out."

"Can I bring her here later today then?"

"Yes, bring her. What the hell. At this rate, four legs more, four legs less..." Anastasia waved her hand, with the cigarette in it, in the air.

"I love you, Anastasia. You know that, don't you?"

"Don't forget that when the Bolsheviks come to Berlin."

For an instant, Margot forgot all about the furry bodies squirming around them and sniffing at the walls and the rug. "Do you think they will?"

Anastasia shrugged pensively. "They will, sooner or later. And with the United States at war with Germany too, with them and the British supplying the Soviets with all sorts of food and weapons, I think it's only a matter of time. Germany is still holding strong. It'll hold out for some time, but it has stretched itself too thin. They can't hang onto all of the occupied territories. Numerically, it's not possible."

"Will you be in danger then?"

"Being a former aristocrat and half-German on top of it? What do you think?" Anastasia laughed mirthlessly, but then waved away the future with yet another negligent sweep of her hand. "Don't worry your head about me. I'm a survivor. It's your husband who you should worry about. When a nation begins to kill off defenseless animals, it's only a matter of time before they move on to their owners."

TWENTY-ONE

BERLIN. FEBRUARY 27, 1943

Something was terribly wrong. With her hand pressed against her chest, Margot watched the trucks pull to a stop along their narrow street, virtually sealing it. Through the fog of her breath on the glass, she saw the gray figures of SS men descend upon the snow-covered cobbles, slamming their jackboots onto the stones with blood-chilling finality. Moments later, they were inside the entrance to the building, their feet banging on the wooden stairs, their fists smashing into apartment doors.

Margot jumped at the sound of hissing behind her back—vicious, viper-like.

"Blast," she cursed quietly under her breath, groping for the burning ersatz coffee she had left on the stove. She grasped the handle with her bare hand and froze where she stood as the thunderous blows came again—raining on the front door of her apartment, this time.

"SS! Open up!"

Stunned and half-paralyzed, Margot wasn't aware of metal burning her skin until the pain caused her to scream and release her fingers. Hot liquid scalded the skin of her bare legs at the exact same time the butt of a rifle crashed into the lock of the front door.

"I'm coming!" Jumping over the puddle and waving her burned hand in the air, Margot rushed toward the door before they could break in and shoot her for not opening it fast enough. They'd done it to one of their neighbors already, during one of the previous round-ups, releasing a machine-gun round into her body right in the tub where she was showering, in front of her children.

"Aryan! Aryan!!" Margot shouted at the top of her lungs as she leapt away from the door, which was kicked open by the SS jackboot. She hastily took her identification paper from her pocket and held it up for the SS man to see.

Snatching it from her, he perused the document carefully, checked the name against the list and hurled it back into Margot's face. Any respect for a German woman flew out the window when the German woman was married to a Jew. This was nothing new. In the ten years that she and Jochen had been married, Margot had grown used to such attitudes. She caught her identification paper and stepped back, making way for more SS men flooding the apartment.

"There's no one home," she said before they could start tearing the place apart in their search for inhabitants. "I'm alone here."

"Where's your husband?" the SS with the list demanded.

Margot looked at him. In his eyes was nothing but ice and death, and it occurred to Margot that only she stood between her husband and the man's machine gun.

"He went to the police headquarters to renew his pass for taking public transportation to work." There was no point in lying. Jochen was an exemplary citizen, always following the rules, never breaking any laws. *Fat lot of good it did him*; the grim thought occurred to Margot before she chased it away. "The Greenblatts are at work, both husband and wife, and their children are at the Jewish school, the one on Auguststraße... No, I'm sorry." Margot tossed her head. "I'm forgetting; today's Saturday, so they must be at the synagogue. They're being watched over there while their parents are at work."

"Which one?"

The question wasn't without its merit. Only a few synagogues had survived the fires of the Kristallnacht back in 1938.

"Heidereuter synagogue, near Rosenstraße."

The SS man nodded, visibly satisfied.

"What of the Goldbergs?"

"Herr Goldberg is at—"

"*Jew* Goldberg," the SS man corrected her coldly. "There are no *Herren* among Jews."

"He's at work as well," Margot said, lowering her eyes—not out of deference of any sort but to conceal the sheer, cold hatred the SS would most certainly see in them had she not done so. "He's with the same forced labor unit as my husband, with the *Reichsbahn*. They work at the Lehrter Bahnhof. And Frau Goldberg..." Margot purposely paused, but the SS issued no correction this time. Frau Goldberg was Aryan, just like Margot. She was still addressed with respect, even if she wasn't treated with any. "Went to get groceries. She has just gone, so I'm not expecting her back anytime soon."

"We don't need her." The SS with the list was already waving his hand for his underlings to follow him out.

When they'd gone, Margot returned to the kitchen window, where she could see the SS were already herding the Jewish Quarter inhabitants into their trucks with curses and the butts of their rifles. Then they slammed the doors and drove away. The street was quiet again, as though nothing had transpired mere minutes ago.

In Margot's ears, the sudden silence rang ominously. In a puddle by her feet, the spilt coffee looked like dried blood.

. . .

"Should I have lied to them?" Margot asked for the third time in five minutes.

It was quarter past two. Frau Goldberg had just returned from her grocery-hunting, boasting about the pig hooves she'd procured for all of them to share. Forgotten, the hooves lay in a heap by the sink, together with the peach preserves and bottles of milk, their necks poking through the holes of net bags. Frau Goldberg herself sat on a small rickety stool with her coat unbuttoned, staring at the patch of linoleum Margot was gradually wearing out with her pacing.

"Should I have?" Margot repeated.

"No." As though coming out from under a spell, Frau Goldberg slowly shook her head. "No. Why would you do that? Lying wouldn't do anyone any good. With those lists of theirs, they know where every single Jew is anyway. They've been assembling those lists for years now."

"I told them where Jochen was." Once again, Margot looked at the clock. He should have been back by now. "Should I go and look for him?"

"To the police headquarters?"

"Yes."

"There's probably a line there. You know how it is."

"The longest it usually takes him is five hours. He went there early, by seven. He should have been back by now."

"They won't do anything to him. He's married to a German. Just like my Rudi. They're rounding up Jewish families only. We're mixed."

"Why were they asking about him then? And about you and your husband?"

"Just checking." Frau Goldberg shrugged. "You know how they are."

Frau Goldberg desperately tried to sound nonchalant, but behind her seemingly offhand comments, Margot detected the same worry that had been nagging her for hours now. Otherwise, she would have taken her coat off and gone about her cooking as she always did, cursing at the cat that was no longer there out of habit and singing anti-government songs she'd overheard on the Greenblatts' radio.

"I should go and look for him," Margot repeated, a veritable broken record.

"What if he returns and you're not home?"

"You'll be home. You'll tell him where I went."

Frau Goldberg looked at her for a very long time before nodding slowly. Margot was already at the door when her neighbor's voice reached her from the kitchen where she still sat. "Frau Rosenberg?"

"Yes?"

A pause, louder than a thousand words. "Could you also go to Alexanderplatz and see where Rudi is?"

For a moment, Margot wished she hadn't heard. If the undefeatable Frau Goldberg, who wasn't afraid to trick grocers into accepting Jewish ration cards, was losing heart, the situation was going to the devil.

"Of course I will," Margot said quietly and pulled the front door closed behind her.

On the stairs, just one flight down, a torn teddy bear missing a button of an eye was lying, bearing the imprint of an SS jackboot.

At the police headquarters, they told Margot that yes, Jew Rosenberg had come over to prolong his pass, but they had handed him over to the SS as per their instructions.

"What instructions?" Margot's voice broke into a pitiful half-shriek mid-word. Down her back, cold, sticky sweat was snaking in rivulets.

"The latest ones, from yesterday."

"But he's in a mixed marriage. I'm his wife. I'm Aryan! He's exempt from any round-ups."

The policeman behind the reception glass shrugged, suppressed a yawn and returned to the crossword puzzle at the back of his newspaper.

For some time, Margot stood in front of his window, watching him fill out the little white squares with his pencil.

"Do you know where they could have taken him?"

"Outside Berlin," came the indifferent reply.

"Where exactly?!" Margot shouted this time and slammed her open palm on the limestone counter.

The policeman looked up, startled.

Shaking all over with helpless wrath, Margot leaned forward, her jaws clenched tightly together. She had nothing to lose any longer. She'd continue screaming and staging the most frightful scene until they told her where her husband was. They would have to arrest her before she'd shut up.

"Where exactly?" she repeated very quietly, ready to raise hell if he continued to ignore her.

There was something in her voice that made the policeman lose interest in his crossword puzzles.

"Hey, Kapke!" he called over his shoulder, without averting his watchful eyes from Margot. Judging by his look, he wouldn't put it past her to jump over the counter and grab him by his neck. "Where did the SS take the Jews?"

"Which ones?" came the reply from the office right next to the reception.

"The ones they grabbed from here, the intermarried ones."

"Rosenstraße, I think. The Jewish community center, or a synagogue or some such."

"Not the Luftwaffe barracks?"

"No, those are different Jews. Regular ones, without German spouses."

Kapke was still saying something, but Margot had already turned on her heel and was out of the door.

Hopping on the first streetcar, she rode the entire way to Alexanderplatz near the steps and leapt off before the streetcar had a chance to stop completely. On her way to the Lehrter Bahnhof, she pushed and shoved through the thickening after-work crowd, which, much to Margot's annoyance, went about its business as though the lives of thousands of people weren't hanging by a thread this very moment. To be sure, most restaurants had remained closed after Goebbels' Total War call—*no more idle dining and bourgeois entertainment, ladies and gentlemen; everything for the front and everyone to the factories*—but street vendors still sold pretzels near the U-Bahn entrances and from the loudspeakers near the train station itself poured something much too brassy and cheerful.

On the tracks, there was the usual commotion: trains hissing and spitting smoke, soldiers unloading their injured, Red Cross nurses handing out hot soup and ersatz coffee to the bandaged warriors who had fared better than their stretcher-bound comrades and still had both hands with which to hold the mugs. But there were no Jewish slave workers to help them carry those stretchers this time. Margot thought that they'd been moved further away, perhaps, to the outside, to the tracks themselves. She hastened her steps when she saw a small group of workers digging at the ground around the tracks, but they weren't the familiar Berlin Jews. Instead of well-worn but still elegant coats, begrimed rags covered their skeletal frames, and instead of yellow stars, red crosses marked their backs.

"The Soviets," said a soft voice.

Margot turned sharply toward the voice that had startled her despite its gentleness, and came face to face with a man bearing the uniform of the *Reichsbahn*. She'd known him; he sold tickets in a booth near which Margot carried her nightly vigil waiting for her husband to be released from his slave-labor duties. The futility of her efforts tasted of tears and bitter disappointment on her tongue.

The ticket seller nodded his acknowledgment and motioned Margot discreetly after himself.

"The SS took them all this morning and not twenty minutes later brought these poor devils," he said quietly, stealing a glance right and left, handing Margot a small bundle through the door of his booth. "You know Herr Goldberg, correct? I saw you with his wife here a few times. Here, take his things. His overcoat and wallet. He didn't want the SS to have it."

Margot nodded, whispered her thanks and stood for a very long time in the middle of the platform, staring at Rudolf Goldberg's overcoat and wondering how it was possible that a human life could have been reduced to a pile of clothes overnight.

A pile of clothes and a torn teddy bear.

Then, willing herself into motion, Margot burst into a run once again, and then it was all bustling U-Bahn, a bus, a streetcar, empty streets in the Jewish Quarter, and Frau Goldberg's drawn, pallid face and a cigarette trembling in her hand, as she stared at her husband's overcoat with eyes full of disbelief and inhuman torment. Besides her, the communal apartment stood empty. The Greenblatts had never come home, just like their neighbors from upstairs, downstairs, the tenement building opposite them. All around the street, the dark windows of the Jewish communal living quarters stared back at the women like empty eye sockets.

In silence, they made their way through the labyrinth of the streets until they reached the familiar Jewish bakeries and small shops, now also dark and deathly quiet. They knew that they had reached the right place when a small crowd—women mostly—came into view near the former Jewish center. They were relatively quiet still, shifting from foot to foot in the gathering snow, blowing on their hands and asking questions in the general direction of the guards, all of which were unanswered.

Margot and Frau Goldberg tried their luck with the guards as well, and were also ignored, with typical SS arrogance. But as the night gathered around them, the crowd began to thicken, swelling with sheer numbers and growing indignation. Now, instead of polite questions, demands and protests were being hurled at the guards.

The curfew time had come and gone. One Gestapo official or another came out of the Burgstraße's Jewish Desk headquarters—an inconspicuous affair of concrete gray with mold-stained stairs and bird-stained sills—and tried to shout something about everyone being arrested if they didn't disperse immediately, only to be called a Nazi swine and have a snowball hurled at him, narrowly missing him.

"We're not going anywhere until you release our men!" someone shouted from the thick of the crowd.

"Suit yourselves! I'm calling for reinforcements."

This time it was a rock that crashed into the wall dangerously close to his head. The Gestapo ducked, slammed the door after himself and left the guards alone with the women.

"You, ladies, better scram before you get shipped off to the east along with your husbands," one of them advised, trying to sound threatening.

But not a single woman moved. There was only one door to the building. No one was getting out—or sneaking anyone out for that matter—without going through the German wives first.

TWENTY-TWO

Overnight, the size of the small crowd doubled. Now, there were quite a few men among them too; Aryan men, eyes ringed with black shadows, shouting their wives' names into the detention center's dark windows. Across the street, in the Gestapo quarters, overhead lamps blinked to life as the new day dawned and the blackout curtains got dutifully pulled away by secretaries' nimble fingers. The lamps were just as sickly yellow as the faded circle of the sun that hung limply in the sky before drowning in the dirty, soaked cotton of clouds completely. From the roofs, moisture dripped incessantly onto women's upturned faces. It seemed the world itself was crying along with them.

Margot had long lost count of the circles she made around the building, shouting Jochen's name until her voice had grown hoarse. Frau Goldberg had no better luck locating her Rudi. She, too, was struggling to stay on her frozen feet, full of nerves and exhaustion.

"They must be there," Margot kept repeating with a stubbornness that refused to see any reason. "They must be."

By mid-morning, a few more tarpaulin-covered trucks

pulled up next to the entrance just to be swarmed by the desperate mob.

"Back! Get back right this instant or we'll shoot!" the SS bellowed in the women's faces, stopping short of shoving them away with the butts of their rifles.

Jochen couldn't be on those trucks, but Margot still searched the star-marked human cargo that was spilling into a narrow corridor made by the SS, just wide enough to smuggle them into the detention center. There were children among them this time, wide-eyed and screaming for their mothers, some clutching small wooden shovels in their mittens crusted with frozen snow.

"They're snatching children from the streets now, the beasts!" someone shouted in utter outrage.

"What?" someone called from the back.

"The children!" another voice from the front row echoed the first. "They were clearly playing outside when these fiends grabbed them!"

From her position near the front, Margot saw two SS men exchange nervous glances. As though propelled to action by such unimaginable cruelty, the crowd began pushing forward once again, murmuring its fury louder and louder. Margot felt herself being pushed forward; now she was pressing against the backs of the women in the front rows; could see clearly the faces of the detainees, lined with worry and fear.

"Joachim Rosenberg!" Her voice joined the chorus of her fellow protesters. "Has anyone seen Joachim Rosenberg?"

"Rudolf Goldberg! I'm looking for Rudolf Goldberg!"

"Julius Siegler!"

"Rachel Heller!"

"Martin Lewine!"

"Back, I said!"

A single shot fired in the air silenced the crowd for an instant. Drawing her eyes to the top of one of the trucks, Margot saw an SS commander standing on the roof of its cabin, his hand with a service pistol in it. Following another command of his, the SS on the ground assumed their usual parade-crowd-containing formation. They were a human chain now—two men facing the detainees pouring into the building and one clasping his comrades' belts and facing the crowd.

Frightened momentarily by the shot, the crowd shifted around Margot; shifted, but didn't scatter, much to the SS commander's annoyance. Now, it was she who stood in the front row, face to face with one of the SS men, just a little taller than her in his helmet.

For an interminable moment, their eyes bore into each other. He tried to press his mouth into a severe line, tried to knit his brows into a menacing grimace, but instead of feeling intimidated in the slightest, Margot felt her lips twitch in a mocking sneer. The SS man wavered, clasped the belts of his comrades tighter, as though in search of support, but Margot had already opened her mouth and bellowed, louder than the SS commander before her, in her hoarse voice that somehow carried more power in it than ten SS commanders put together:

"Joachim Rosenberg! Jochen Rosenberg! I'm here, Jochen, and I'm not going anywhere until they release you! You hear me?"

This was the battle call that the crowd seemed to have been waiting for. Before the SS could take charge of the situation, the mob surged forward once again, screaming their spouses' names into their frankly frightened faces, shaking their fists in the air and even making a grab for one or other of the Jews.

"Write to us what you need!"

"Press a list to the window so we can see."

"Make a list of names once you're inside, will you?"

Suddenly, emboldened by such unexpected support when they had little to hope for, the Jewish detainees began shouting their names into the crowd.

"I'm Werner Bergmann! Could you please tell my wife I'm here?"

"Werner Bergmann," Margot repeated loudly enough for the man to hear her, seek her out of the crowd and nod his gratitude before he was shoved unceremoniously inside, with an SS boot to his behind. "Does anyone have a notebook and a pencil I can use? Anyone? I want to make a list."

She waved her hand in the air. Before she could repeat her request, a few notebooks began being passed over the heads covered with fancy hats and old kerchiefs. In another moment, Margot had a notebook in her hands, which were frozen to the bone but still functioning somehow, and now her entire body was buzzing with some strange, powerful energy, Margot searched around herself for a place to press the notebook against, met the eyes of the SS man again, grinned sweetly and savagely and slammed the notebook square against his chest. As he looked on in indignant, helpless ire, she wrote the very first name out of many that would soon fill every last page—Werner Bergmann—and spelled it out loud, right into the SS man's mouth for him to choke on it.

"I'm going to faint if we keep at it."

Margot nodded at Frau Goldberg's words without moving away from the wall against which she was leaning. It was Sunday evening; they hadn't slept a wink since Friday morning, carrying on their watch, sustained by nothing at all but the sheer power of their love.

The SS had come and gone with their trucks. Now, there were only four members of the Tall Guys Club, as they were mockingly called by Berliners, guarding the entrance, sullen and black like ravens in their *Leibstandarte*-issued overcoats. Not long after the sunset, the temperature had plummeted once again and if it hadn't been for a thermos with hot coffee in it that Marthe, one of the wives also looking for her Jewish husband, had shared with Margot and Frau Goldberg, they would have suffered from hypothermia; of that much Margot was certain.

"We should make a system of some sort. Carry out our watch in shifts. There's about a hundred of us here—enough of us to do so," Margot suggested, rubbing her eyes, which kept closing despite all of her efforts to keep them open. "Otherwise we'll all fall asleep right here and they'll smuggle our men out from under our noses."

"She's not wrong." Greta, another wife from their small circle of activists, nodded knowingly. "There's a reason they haven't called a police squad on us yet. They're counting on wearing us out this way; then, they won't have to bother with arresting us all."

"No, it's not that," Frau Goldberg protested, lighting her cigarette and offering her almost depleted pack around. A few women gratefully took whatever was left. They shared everything now—coffee, cigarettes, biscuits and grief. But they also shared hope and that was all that mattered to their men locked inside. "Don't forget, after we lost Stalingrad and the entire Army Group there, they called up whoever was left here on civilian jobs. There's only so many slave workers they can bring here, and those are all half-starved and don't work well enough to fill their production quotas. So, first they close all restaurants and entertainment centers to free up waiters and the rest of the staff for the factories. But then they see that their number is so measly, they have to resort to the help of the ones they'd been keeping barefoot and pregnant in their kitchens—us women. How many of you received summons to the factories?"

A murmur of confirmation was her response.

"I got out of it fast." Marthe laughed. "I'm married to a Jew. I'm politically unreliable."

"I know many women married to Germans who got out of it

too, out of personal convictions," Greta said, cupping her hands around the match Frau Goldberg was holding for her. "Almost every family has lost someone to this blasted war already. No one wants to contribute any more to prolonging it."

"Those four do," someone sniggered with a nod toward the SS guards. They stood, still like statues, thoroughly ignoring the taunts as if such remarks were below their dignity. Only on the youngest one's face, red splotches were slowly breaking through his impenetrable mask, betraying his emotion—shame or anger, Margot couldn't quite tell.

"Well, let them go and win it single-handedly instead of standing here like statues," Marthe shouted.

"Some brave soldiers, guarding helpless civilians inside!" someone else called out from the crowd.

Margot chuckled softly. "The system, ladies. Before we all drop with exhaustion right where we stand."

"You two have been here the longest," Greta said, pulling on her cigarette. "Go home for tonight and we'll stay here and guard the men."

"All right. Tomorrow we'll bring the supplies," Margot agreed, pushing off the wall against which she was leaning. It was almost astounding how much effort it took her to do so. "We'll bring whatever we have for the men too. Those four won't stay here forever either, so maybe someone more agreeable will come along. We'll try to bribe them then."

"Do you have any money?" Greta asked.

"I have some, but I also have someone who can lend me more, in case I need it."

"Get as much as you can, will you?" Marthe pleaded. "And we'll bring more when we switch shifts Monday evening."

"I'll leave the notebook here with you. Guard it as you would your life."

Both women nodded solemnly, taking the book carefully out of Margot's hands.

"We will. Go now, and sleep. And don't fret. No one will leave this building while we're here."

With hearts that were just a little lighter, Margot and Frau Goldberg set off in the direction of their street. They would sleep the sleep of the dead that night. With their new comrades, they had nothing to fear.

Without their husbands' voices, the apartment seemed deathly still, robbed of something precious. Out of habit, they made dinner for four, and stared in silence at one another as they realized their mistake. All at once, roast potatoes with precious bits of blood sausage mixed in tasted of ash in their mouths, much too difficult to swallow due to the lumps that had lodged themselves in their throats.

Out of desperation, just to fill the intolerable silence, Frau Goldberg tried to make conversation—something that Margot couldn't even concentrate on—but receded slowly, lost track of her own words and pushed the last piece of a potato around her plate.

Margot, too, sat without movement for a long time. Then, as though emerging from a daze, she lifted a silver fork in the air and held it in front of her black-rimmed eyes almost with accusation. "Frau Goldberg, see this?" When her neighbor acknowledged her with a mystified nod, Margot continued, an embittered grin creasing her pale lips, "Do you know how many times I scolded Jochen for using that fork for roasting blood sausage over the gas? He loved the damned thing, roasted just so, but he blackened the silver in the process and I was so mad at him because we couldn't afford baking soda any longer to clean it." There was a long pause and then, Margot's sharp intake of breath, eyes drawn to the ceiling so that the tears wouldn't spill, treacherous, along her drawn cheeks. "God, what I wouldn't give now just to watch him roast the damned sausage over the gas! Why did I care about the blasted silver in the first place? What do I need it for, without him—"

A sob escaped her lips and then all she could feel was Frau Goldberg's arms around her shoulders. With one cheek pressed against the other, they could no longer tell whose tears dropped on the blackened silver Margot would purposely never clean again.

"The train will not stop at Bahnhof Börse. I repeat, the train will not stop—"

"They closed Rosenstraße's U-Bahn station." Margot spoke over the conductor's voice, looking at Frau Goldberg in alarm. "Those bastards have closed the damned station!"

"That's fine." Frau Goldberg was already pushing her way through the morning commuters to the train car's doors. "That's just fine. We'll walk then. They can't have closed the streets, can they?"

But the question wasn't really rhetorical. Through the windows fogged with breath and patched with old advertisement stickers, Margot tried to steal a glimpse into the streets below. From the train's elevated position, she could see the smoke rising from the chimneys on the roofs, anti-air-raid floodlights and guns gleaming dully in the sun, polished to a bright shine by the personnel manning them for the occasion—it was March first, the official Luftwaffe Day. She could see bicycles moving along the elevated train tracks and a rare car—one Nazi bigwig or another's; the rest had long been requisitioned from the general population—but no tarpaulin-covered trucks this time and no SS, thankfully.

But then again, they preferred to move under the cover of the night or in the early hours of the morning, to spare the general population the unseemly sight of them hurling an old Jewish grandmother onto a truck as if she were a log, or dealing a small yellow-star-marked child a swift backhand slap if he just wouldn't cease crying for his mother.

The streets were quiet as Margot and Frau Goldberg descended the stairs—one train station early, but this would just have to do. However, as they approached the familiar street corner behind which the detention center and the Gestapo headquarters lay, they recognized the unmistakable echo of raised voices, female mostly, mixing with the sounds of a city stirring to life.

"They must have been at it all night." Margot hastened her steps, a smile growing on her drawn face in spite of herself.

"Good." Frau Goldberg picked up her pace too, passing her arm through the crook of Margot's. "If we women can't sleep because they took our husbands, let those Gestapo muttons stay up all night too."

"Pardon me, are you going to Rosenstraße too?"

Startled by the voice just behind their backs, Margot and Frau Goldberg turned abruptly on their heels and fell into amazed silence at the sight that presented itself in front of their stunned eyes.

In their excitement, they had failed to notice that they weren't alone running down the stairs of the U-Bahn station. They were only the first ones. Behind them, a small group of women, some holding young children by their hands, was following closely, all dressed warmly, some carrying thermoses and net bags stuffed with goods and clothes and even folding chairs. They had come to stay. And they wouldn't leave until their men were released; Margot saw it written clear on their resolute faces.

"Yes," she replied, taking the glorious view in, drinking it like liquor that warmed her instantly and went straight to her head. "Yes, we are. Follow us."

The women followed.

.   .   .

After releasing Greta and Marthe from their overnight watch, Margot began making her rounds through the newcomers, taking names and marking down the ones who had been found. Somehow, their ingenious men had procured scraps of paper and cardboard, managing to press them against the glass for the women outside to see. They wrote their names there and right under, *I love you with all my heart! Fear nothing, my dove...* The most fortunate ones had even held their palms against their husbands', separated by glass only; they even heard muted reports through the glass ("They fed us chopped cabbage," "No, no bedding inside, just some straw on the floor,") and assurances that everything would certainly be all right, as long as they had each other. It seemed that the policeman who had replaced the SS guards and stood watch through the night deliberately looked the other way while families made contact with each other. Hearing this, Margot's heart sang with gratitude, for remaining a human being in a world of heartless beasts.

She was leafing through the notebook when her heart dropped deep into her stomach and froze there, too fearful to beat, at the sight of his name—the most important name in the entire world—scrawled by an unfamiliar hand on the last page.

Hans-Joachim Rosenberg, married to Margarete Rosenberg, maiden name Kaltenbach; no children; good health.

Rudi was there too, but his name was already swimming before Margot's eyes as she turned to Frau Goldberg and gathered her in an embrace that only sisters could share; sisters who had been through hell and back and held each other's hand throughout their journey.

By noon, more women had poured into the narrow street. There must have been over two hundred of them now, stomping their feet in comradely fashion and unraveling their own handwritten banners for the Gestapo to grind their teeth over. But when Margot went to take their names, they only grinned at her knowingly.

"No, we don't have anyone there, love."

"We came purely out of solidarity."

"Not right for those skull-heads to separate families."

"Family business ain't no government business. Why should they care who we choose to sleep with?"

Margot guessed that that last statement was a particularly sore subject for Edna, who had uttered the words in visible indignation. She was here with Erna, and it was Margot's suspicion that they weren't simple flatmates as they claimed.

Edna had a bakery, but she hadn't opened it that Monday. "Let's see how those Grünewald Golden Pheasants—or their housekeepers, I should say—will like their breakfast without fresh rolls."

Erna, too, was keeping her laundry and dry-cleaning store closed that day. "And I won't open it until they let everyone go," she declared, puffing on a cigarette she had rolled herself. "Let them strut around in dirty uniforms and unstarched shirts; see if I care."

Some of the older newcomers were former suffragists who had dusted off their warriors' spirit still smoldering inside them from the old Weimar days. Some were former social-democrats who had just had enough of that Nazi rot. Some were underground communists; Margot even recognized a few familiar faces from the time she had prowled their quarter in search of her husband, on the eve of the Kristallnacht.

It wasn't only unfortunate wives married to even more unfortunate Jewish men's business. The protest was growing and so was the number of voices within it.

By two o'clock, an already illegal gathering had become a veritable protest.

"Release our men! Release our men!"

Women weren't pleading any longer. They began to shout, to demand. Fists pumped the air.

"Bring back our children! Bring back our husbands!"

Heels stomped the cobbled street as those husbands looked on from behind the glass, misty-eyed.

As darkness enveloped the city, the Gestapo officials from the Jewish Desk stalked out into the street again. There were three of them this time, visibly annoyed by the noise they'd been forced to endure. For some time, they stood, barely illuminated by the light coming out of the door they'd left open. Otherwise, the building itself, just like the streets around, was dark as pitch, following the blackout regulations.

"Have you no shame at all?" the tallest one shouted, hoping to out-scream the women who paid no heed to him and his small delegation whatsoever. "They can hear you at Reichsmarschall Göring's Luftwaffe headquarters!"

"Good!" came the prompt reply, followed by sniggers.

"Of all the days, you have to parade here and annoy our good airmen on their special day."

"You want us to shut our traps?" one of the women called back to them, emboldened by the darkness. The Gestapo made no reply. The question was rhetorical. "All you have to do is release our men."

"You know perfectly well that we can't do that."

"Why not?"

"We have orders."

"Whose orders? Reichsmarschall Göring's? It's fitting that he celebrates his brave Luftwaffe with our screeching in the background then."

The bickering went on for some time until suddenly an air-raid siren cut it short. Its wailing grew in volume until it was joined by others, to the north of Berlin and then to the east as well, until the entire city was immersed in one endless cry, like a child caught in between two warring parents, unable to endure any more emotional torture.

All eyes were drawn to the skies now, which were being probed by searchlights like the backdrop to some grotesque horror show. It was a cloudless night, the air crisp and clear—the bombers' perfect weather. Just like the women around her, Margot stood with her head slightly cocked and listened. *No anti-aircraft guns' muted booming yet; not even in the north.* But time was scarce; she could all but feel precious seconds seeping through her fingers like sand.

The Gestapo felt it too. Their leader paused for a fraction of a moment, regarded the women with malicious triumph and swiftly dove inside, motioning both of his orderlies to follow him —into the safety of a reinforced cellar, no doubt.

"Wait!" Margot didn't recognize her voice as she burst into a run after them. There was something wild, primal in it. "You can't just leave them there! You can't!" She slammed the weight of her entire body into the door, but it was locked fast. Not even a thin sliver of light seeped from behind it. "This is slaughter! Outright slaughter!"

"Go down to the nearest shelter then; no one is holding you," a muted voice answered from behind the door, already receding. The rats were running down to their hiding place and laughing at her desperation.

"It's not me I'm worried about, you scum! You're human scum; you're lower than that, you soulless serpents!" She could scarcely hear herself over the mournful wailing of the siren; only felt that her face was all wet now and the wind was biting into it relentlessly. In the distance, still very far away, the first few fiery flowers blossomed in the sky, but the echo of the explosions reverberated through the ground; traveled up their legs and creeped into their very stomachs.

Everyone froze where they stood, their frightened eyes

darting between approaching death and the small building where life's flame was still burning. So much innocent life, stuffed into small, narrow rooms, waiting to be extinguished, obliterated into dust and ash.

Then, a new sound mixed with the cacophony of the night. At first, Margot couldn't tell what it was, if it was happening at all; this odd song of sheer terror and desperation; if she weren't imagining it all, sleep-deprived and driven to half-madness by the events of the past few days. But slowly, one by one, the women's heads began to turn toward the holding center. There, men were banging on the glass, pleading with the women—not to do something about them as one would imagine, but to run, run as fast as they could, save themselves while there was a chance for them, for the bombs were falling closer now, covering entire streets with a carpet of liquid fire, sending waves of heat in the air, warming the icy March night with its ghastly breath.

From the roof of the Luftwaffe headquarters, several flak guns began to bark. The searchlights were approaching a dark patch of sky above their narrow little street now. As though hypnotized, Margot watched them catch an enemy flyer in the crisscross of their columns of light, following the progress of the deadly cargo it unloaded straight from its steel belly, spilling fire-charged loads so closely now, she could hear them hiss as they charged toward the ground.

The series of explosions stunned them momentarily. Deafened and dazed, a few women opened their mouths in silent shrieks—Margot couldn't hear anything at all, besides those ear-splitting blasts and the frantic beating of her own heart—and then they began to scramble in different directions, some running toward the explosions against all reason. But the fire was everywhere now. The air was suddenly too hot to inhale. It singed the lungs and dried her tears before they could spill anew, and yet, Margot made no move to escape it.

Instead, she pressed her back against the wall of the detention center and sat on the ground, trembling under her as though ready to open and swallow them all—those who ran and those who hadn't; who stayed despite it all and were content to die this way, burned alive or torn to bits or buried under the crumbling walls of concrete and metal as long as their loved ones were in the same purgatory, just inches away, close enough to touch in the last moments of their life.

TWENTY-THREE

The bombing ended as abruptly as it had begun, and now, silence was somehow even louder than the hellish hour they'd lived through. *How could it be just one hour?* Margot wondered, listening to the clock striking eight in the distance.

They'd lived; the realization of it dawned on them as they slowly rose off the ground, dusted themselves off and touched their limbs in disbelief. All around them, fires burned; against the indigo sky, the Luftwaffe headquarters was missing a chunk of one of its wings; the entire stretch of Königstraße was ablaze, and yet, the flimsy detention center, with all of its inhabitants, stood perfectly untouched, as though some higher power had covered it with a protective, impenetrable dome that was now lifted. Instead of bombs, gray ashes were now falling all around, turning the women's uncovered heads prematurely gray.

"How are you? All right?" Margot asked Frau Goldberg, also visibly shaken but unhurt.

"My ears are ringing something frightful, but all my limbs are still about me, so that's good, I suppose," Frau Goldberg replied with a wavering smile and patted Margot over in search of injuries. "How are you? Hurt?"

"No. Just shell-shocked a bit."

One by one, they helped each other to their feet. Before long, they began knocking on the windows.

"Everyone all right there? Anyone injured?"

No one was.

The SS arrived an hour later; regarding—visibly dumb-founded—the only uninjured building in the vicinity and the defiant women covered with ash from head to toe, disappearing again without uttering a single word.

Some forty minutes later, a car with tiny yellow slits for headlights pulled up at the entrance, spitting out an SS official and his adjutant holding a stack of papers and a flashlight in his gloved hands. Silently, the adjutant opened the door to the holding center and disappeared inside. Several minutes passed, and then, to the women's astonishment, stunned men began to emerge from inside, holding small square papers in their hands.

"Martin!" A shriek broke from the crowd, and in an instant, a woman hurled herself on one of the men's necks.

"All men from privileged intermarriages, those with their children baptized in a Christian church, may consider them-selves free," the SS official announced to the crowd and climbed back into his car.

All around, in stunned silence, women watched this miracle unraveling before their eyes. For a few moments, not a whisper was exchanged, as though they feared to jinx their good fortune. But as more men spilled from the detention center's entrance, hope began to ignite in the shell-shocked crowd, sending waves of hushed speculation through its rows.

It was the first night that they saw that their actions could actually lead to victory.

It was the first night that they dared to believe that love was more powerful than death itself.

· · ·

Margot didn't hear the knock at first. Forgotten in a blissful dream—the first after countless nightmarish nights, in which Jochen came out of the holding center's doors and right into her awaiting arms—Margot swatted at the insistent banging on her door as one would at a fly. But when a hoarse voice that only the nastiest types of government officials appeared to have called her name, Margot threw the covers off herself in an instant, immediately fully awake, heart pounding like a drum—a demented alarm honed by the years of the Nazi-Party-instilled instinct.

Just as drilled by constant harassment and searches as Margot, Frau Goldberg stood on high alert at the entrance of her room's door, her hand holding the ends of her frayed robe together. On her way to the front door, Margot caught a silent thrust of her chin—*Who's that?*—and responded with a just-as-puzzled shrug of her own—*Damned if I know.*

Margot's relief must have been palpable when the official at the door turned out to be an ordinary postlady, for the postlady smirked as she handed Margot an official notice for which she was to sign.

"Sleeping late, eh? Keep sleeping. You'll have nothing else to do now anyway."

With that gleeful remark, she was gone.

Margot opened the notice, which wasn't sealed but simply creased shut for all curious eyes to see, and felt nothing at all at the words that would have sent her reeling for days on end in the not-so-distant past.

"Anything important?" Frau Goldberg called from the safety of the apartment.

...and therefore your employment has been terminated as of...

The words scattered and fell onto the floor together with the notice. Margot stepped on it as she turned on her heel to lock the door after herself.

"No. Nothing at all."

.   .   .

For the next two days, Margot arrived at Rosenstraße with small
parcels under her arm, searching for a friendly face among the
police guards to take pity on her and take the packages inside to
her husband. More times than not, they cringed, cursed under
their breaths, but accepted the parcels nevertheless. Seeing
them disappear inside the door and emerge a few minutes later
with a reassuring nod in her direction sent her spirits soaring.

"The police, they're not SS," a barmaid from the café
across the street commented as she polished a glass with a dubious-looking off-white towel. Sympathetic to the women's
plight, the café owner kept it open for them from the early
morning till the very beginning of the evening curfew and
never chased a single one of them off, even when they had no
money or ration cards to give him business. The barmaid, with
a Berlin accent just as thick as the owner's, also didn't mind
them warming themselves up at her bar and always had a fresh
pot of chicory coffee brewing, even for the ones who couldn't
afford it. "Most of them are old guard, Weimar Social-Democrats. They don't fancy all this rotten business any more than
we do."

Margot nodded and cupped her coffee with both hands,
giving herself into the blissful sensation of warmth seeping into
fingers that had been frozen stiff.

"I got fired today," she said, surprising herself with how
calm her voice remained.

"How do you know?" The barmaid—Lisl—checked the
glass against the light and, satisfied with her efforts, placed it
under the counter.

It was no secret that while some women still went to work
just to reappear at Rosenstraße in the evening, the other half
didn't bother with such trifles at all any longer. It was that
second half that had become Lisl's regulars, like Margot, who

spent all of her remaining ration cards on Lisl's coffee and warm soup.

"The postlady brought me a notice of my termination this morning." With a vacant look about her, Margot took the paper out of her pocket, regarded it indifferently and crumpled it with a small shrug.

"You don't seem to be too upset about it, dove."

"I'm not. Just a few weeks ago, losing my job was my biggest fear. You lose your job, you lose your ration coupons. And I had Jochen to feed; his rations wouldn't suffice to feed even our dog, back when we still had him. And now..." She shrugged again. "I thought I knew fear when I was afraid to lose my job." *But nothing compared to the cold terror of losing someone who was the center of her very existence.* Margot didn't have to finish the sentence. Her silence did it for her, and Lisl nodded, poured more fresh coffee into Margot's cup and patted her arm with maternal affection.

"I can't say that I understand, because I don't. My husband is not Jewish. But I sympathize because I love that bastard with all my might, even when he comes home drunk and falls asleep in the bathtub, or serenades at the top of his lungs and the neighbors begin banging on pipes—I still love him even when I curse at him and deal his fat tail a couple of smacks. I look at you all and can't fathom what you girls are going through. As I said, my husband is not Jewish, but if he were, I would be right there with you. I might tell him he's a no-good scoundrel, but he's my scoundrel and I would blacken the eye of the first Gestapo who tried to take him away from me."

"I considered the idea," Margot admitted. "It would certainly give me great pleasure, but then they'd arrest me too, and then who would try to sneak sandwiches and blankets for my Jochen?"

"That friend of yours."

"Hedwig?"

Sometime between the bombings and sleeping next to each other to share body heat—the heating system in their tenement was now *kaput*—Frau Goldberg had ceased to be Frau Goldberg and become Hedwig, just as Margot was now Margot, instead of Frau Rosenberg. Margot had learned that Hedwig had a sister, who wished to have nothing to do with her whatsoever, just as Margot's sister Gertrud had cut ties with her after Margot had—in her view—chosen Jochen over her. The truth was, neither Margot nor Hedwig had chosen anyone over their immediate family. All they wanted was to live and be left in peace, but some people just couldn't have that. Some people's very insides churned when they saw an Aryan woman hand in hand with a Jewish husband. Some people would have refused to buy from Erna knowing that she shared her bed with Edna. Some people had so much hatred stored inside them, they just had to spill it onto everyone else, so that everyone else would be just as miserable as they were. For happy people don't know hate; don't carry it in their hearts. Happy people want others to be happy. They share their light, just as Anastasia did, just like Lisl, just like the policeman who had smuggled Margot's small parcel to Jochen only a few hours ago, returning with words of gratitude and encouragement: *He says not to worry about him. He's in good health and high spirits. He says he loves you very much and misses you dearly. You and some goose, whatever that means.*

"Where is your friend, by the way?"

Margot blinked a few times, Lisl's words dispersing the clouds of her thoughts.

"Hedwig? Oh... She went to the Clou, I think."

"The entertainment center?"

"The very same."

"I thought it was closed. Total War and what have you."

"The SS turned it into a holding center."

"More Jews?"

"Who else?" Margot sighed tiredly. "Rudi's sister and her family are there. But they're not from a mixed marriage like him. They're all Jewish. Hedwig went to check on them."

"I never knew we had so many Jews in Berlin." Lisl chuckled good-naturedly.

Margot didn't join in with her laughter this time. Staring in the mirror past Lisl's shoulder—the mirror reflecting the café and the women in the street outside—she felt a terrible pinch of foreboding deep in her gut. This couldn't go on for much longer. Either the Nazis would back down and release them or they would deport the men.

Then, there wouldn't be any Jews left in Berlin.

No Jews, and no reason for Margot to live.

With grim finality, Margot downed her coffee, wishing it were something much stronger. She headed outside, to look at the windows that were nailed shut and hope to catch a glimpse of the one for whom her heart was beating, while she still could.

Something dreadful had happened. As soon as she left the safe harbor of the café, Margot saw the traces of terror etched into Hedwig's face before Hedwig could utter a single word as she approached the crowd.

"What? Hedwig, what?"

Margot had to give her a prod before Hedwig seemed to come out of the dreadful state of her dark reverie, swallowing hard, once, twice.

"Do you have a cigarette?"

They were standing outside, among the familiar crowd, all the women's concerned, searching eyes trained on the newcomer like they always were whenever someone arrived with news.

"Thank you," Hedwig rasped, cupping her shaking hands around a cigarette and the match that a helpful hand offered. As she did so, Margot noticed an angry red welt peeking from under Hedwig's cuff and stretching across the back of her entire right hand. "They took them all. They're all gone from Clou. I was there... I tried to help..."

She stared at her injured hand in disbelief, as though seeing it for the first time. It occurred to Margot that Hedwig was still much too stunned to process it all; too dumbfounded to believe that this was truly happening, a nightmare unraveling before her very eyes.

"There was a man there, with a horsewhip," she continued hoarsely. "He wore a pinstriped suit with a flower in his lapel, dressed as though for some celebration. But he must have been SS, for all the uniformed men, they listened to his orders. And he lashed and lashed everyone, men and women and children—it made no difference to him—and he screamed something frightful... They drove them all into the trucks and the SS, they were beating the elderly who couldn't climb inside fast enough." Without her noticing, Hedwig's free hand was rubbing at her chest, at the heart that was bleeding inside it from the orgy of violence she had witnessed. "I tried to help one elderly gentleman up and—"

She lifted her hand up, her face crumpling into a grimace of helpless suffering. A collective groan issued from the crowd.

"I tried to ask where they were heading," Hedwig continued, tears spilling freely onto her cheeks. "One of the policemen later told me that they took them to the freight station on Quitzowstraße. And from there, east. He didn't know where exactly, just east."

In utter silence, Margot stared at that red mark on Hedwig's hand and saw a death sentence written there, in blood. Countless rows of monstrous what-ifs began their relentless march across her mind, pounding nightmarish scenarios deep into the folds of her consciousness.

What if they grabbed her Jochen next?

What if they shoved him into the freight car, worse than branded cows, straight for slaughter?

What if the east meant certain death?

What if he disappeared without a trace and even if she followed him, she'd never reunite with him, not even for the slightest fraction of a second, not even to say goodbye?

What if…

What if…

What if…

Among the blood-colored clouds, the sun was rolling westward when the Gestapo came. There wasn't a pinstriped suit among them, but their faces were set as though they'd come prepared for battle. In one hand, one of them was holding a note.

"*Down with the Nazis!* Someone has thrown this out of the window," he declared to the crowd from the steps of the holding center.

Women eyed him with great suspicion, particularly on account of the truck from which he and his cronies had climbed out. Its tarpaulined top gleamed ominously in the rays of the setting sun.

"We've been lenient enough with you," he continued, clearly reassured by the silence. "But for our goodwill, we've been repaid with malice instead of gratitude. This is a highly treasonous affair"—he waved the note in the air—"and measures must be taken to punish the guilty."

"What are you talking about?" Margot didn't recognize her voice as it carried long and far above the women's heads. "All the windows in the holding center are nailed shut!"

As though her remark was the signal they'd all been waiting for, the women joined in with their protests. Some began shaking fists in the air, visibly outraged.

The Gestapo surveyed them for some time with his eyes slightly narrowed, reminding Margot of a scientist holding a scalpel to a frog.

"Then someone must have smuggled it from the inside." He changed his tactic, realizing his mistake. "Either way, it was delivered to us from here."

But it was too late for him to silence the women. The timing was all wrong. There were too many of them surrounding the detention center; even the ones who had left for work every morning had returned to carry out their nightly watch. And they weren't ignorant any longer either. Hedwig had opened even the most unbelieving eyes to the fate that awaited their spouses if they weren't firm enough in their desire to protect them.

"Now, we shall go inside and ask the guilty party to come forward of their own volition," the Gestapo continued.

But Margot wasn't going to be fooled, and nor were the women all around her. The Gestapo never announced their plans or reasoning to anyone, and especially not in such detail. They came and went and did whatever they pleased, thoroughly ignoring regular civilians; they strutted about with an air of superiority, demigods with the power to decide who was to live and who to die. So, why this speech now?

"They're lying," Hedwig declared as soon as the Gestapo disappeared inside Rosenstraße 2–4. "No one inside would write any treasonous notes."

"That's right," Marthe joined in. "They only write notes to us, asking us for supplies or sending their love."

"It's a test of some sort," Margot said very quietly, more to herself than to anyone in particular. All the women's heads turned to her in rapt attention. "They're testing waters after the Clou. They want to see if they can get away with it."

"Get away with what?" Someone asked what needn't be asked.

"Taking our men away," Margot responded darkly, feeling a sudden rush of adrenaline surging though her veins.

She had already begun making her way toward the stairs to

occupy a strategic position, to throw herself at the Gestapo if they tried to lead Jochen through those doors, when the officers reappeared.

But when they returned, they had six women with them. Six Jewish women, deathly pale and trembling in the grip of gloved hands that held them firmly by their forearms. Once again, the leading Gestapo scanned the crowd. Surprised at such a turn of events, the crowd of women quieted themselves momentarily. A hint of a satisfied smile appeared fleetingly on his face but was gone before anyone could be certain that it was there.

"These are the perpetrators," the Gestapo announced, lightly pushing the woman he was holding to the front. Thin, long-limbed, with high cheekbones and wide-set, brown liquid eyes, she reminded Margot of a fawn, an innocent and trembling creature with a hunter's knife already at her throat. With frantic eyes, she was searching the crowd, her mouth forming the name of the one whom she desperately hoped to see, but no sound came out. He wasn't there. "We shall be taking them with us for an interrogation and immediate deportation right after they sign their confessions."

"You will do no such thing!" bellowed a man's voice.

All the heads twisted around, turning to the tall man making his way forward from the thick of the crowd.

"You have arrested my wife, who has never said a word against our government," the man continued, now standing in front of the steps. He was dressed in an elegant overcoat and held a briefcase in one of his hands; not battered, but rather new, with a shiny buckle and corners that were still sharp. A brown felt fedora partially concealed the wrathful expression on his handsome, intelligent face. "Whoever reported her involvement must have been lying. I'm one of the chief supervisors at the Krupp factory here in Berlin and I can vouch for my wife's innocence in written form if needed, just like my supe-riors who've known her for a long time—"

The Gestapo lifted a conciliatory hand in the air, inter-rupting the husband. "Which one is your wife, Herr...?"

"My name is Spitznagel. There she is, in the red coat." He pointed at one of the women, the smallest one in stature.

Without further ado, the Gestapo motioned to one of his orderlies to return her inside.

"No need for any written statements. Your word is enough for us, Herr Spitznagel. Whoever identified her as a perpetrator must have been mistaken. Now"—once again, the Gestapo's hawkish gaze roved around the crowd—"can anyone else vouch for these five?"

There was a moment of silence.

Desperately, the condemned women searched the crowd for their husbands' faces. They weren't there to stand up for them.

"I'm quite certain that if you call their spouses for interroga-tion, you'll be able to clear their names as well," Spitznagel began saying, but the Gestapo silenced him with his raised hand.

"These women are no concern of yours, Herr Spitznagel. We shall take them into custody and sort it all out later."

With that, the Gestapo man made his way through the crowd that—powerless to stop them—parted just enough for him and his underlings to pass, with their victims in tow.

With hot acid that such an act of injustice sent surging through her veins, Margot tried to catch at least one of the women's eyes, just to show that they weren't alone, that the women of Rosenstraße would be back for them as soon as they sorted their own men out, but all of them only looked down at their feet—resigned to their fate, one foot in a metaphorical grave. The image of them going forever singed itself into Margot's already bleeding heart like a scar that would never heal.

Only after they were gone did the meaning of it all dawn on Margot.

"They're taking the ones who have no one to defend them," she said, sharing a comradely cigarette with her fellow protesters. "Jewish families at the Clou; these women, whose husbands weren't here to speak up for them... They tried to take Frau Spitznagel, but as soon as they heard that that fellow worked at Krupp's..." Once again, her voice trailed off, her mind feverishly at work. "But that's good. It means they're still afraid of public outrage. They're still afraid of *us*."

This was war, their personal war, and the enemy was formidable and armed. But as long as they had courage, as long as they refused to surrender, as long as they stood up for the ones without a voice, there could be hope.

TWENTY-FOUR

The fifth day of March dawned bitterly cold. Margot's breath froze over the layers of her scarf in droplets of crystal. But the women were here all the same, feet stomping, hands clapping to keep them warm in the subzero temperatures. Just a couple more hours and Edna and Erna would arrive in their beat-up bakery truck, spared from being requisitioned only because it limped and shook on the cobbles something frightful and issued rounds from its exhaust worse than any flak could. And then, it would be fresh bread rolls for everyone, still warm and all but melting on their tongues despite being a wartime, watered-down version of regular bread. But it was baked with so much love, it made up for the strictly rationed, and therefore lacking in taste, ingredients. Lisl would brew her vicious chicory coffee; the red-mustached policeman would swap with the SS on their post, the one who pretended not to see when women smuggled parcels for their husbands through a Jewish orderly, and the morning would grow a little warmer, with a promise of hope in the air.

"A fine friend you are, nothing to say! Keeping to yourself in the moment of crisis."

A familiar voice, accompanied by excited dog's whining, broke through the morning fog of Margot's reverie. In disbelief, she rubbed her eyes with her mittens, tried to blink Anastasia and Goose's image from her sleep-deprived eyelids—but she was still there, marching toward Margot and her comrades-in-arms with Goose straining on his leash.

"Cat got your tongue?" Anastasia teased by means of greeting, that good-humored smirk Margot had grown to know so well playing on her full lips painted burgundy-red.

All at once, a rush of such inexplicable affection and gratitude surged through Margot's suffering heart, and she broke from the crowd and hurled herself at Anastasia's neck, burying her face in the layers of scarf and fur and signature French perfume. "Anastasia... Goosie!" Margot scooped the dog up and held him tight while he went frantic, squirming with his entire body in her arms and licking the tears off Margot's face. "You're here, you're really here!"

"Naturally, we are." Anastasia's eyes narrowed, shining darkly as she surveyed the surroundings: the SS in their post, the plaque of the Gestapo's Jewish Desk office on the opposite side of the street. "You thought you would just protest here all by yourself and not invite me?"

She was all playfulness and irony as always, but Margot caught a dangerous undertone in Anastasia's voice. She stared the SS down from under her thick black lashes, and her nostrils twitched and flared. Her entire body, hidden under layers of fur and wool, moved with the fluidity of an animal as she stalked her way closer and closer to the entrance.

Margot blocked her path, putting Goose's goofy grin before Anastasia's face, trying to distract her before she pounced on the guards like she'd pounced on John at the party that seemed to have happened a lifetime ago.

"I didn't want to say anything, Anastasia. You've already done so much for us and there's nothing that you can do now at any rate." Margot tried to reason with her, tried to push Goose into her arms, but Anastasia made no motion to take him. Her eyes were on the guards still, staring, black as coals. "You'll only get yourself in trouble. Don't start anything, I beg you. You're an immigrant yourself, and half-Russian on top of it. They'll hurl you away together with them," Margot motioned her head toward the holding center, "and ship you east."

"The east doesn't frighten me." There was steel in Anastasia's voice. "I came from the east. Hey!" Before Margot could stop her, Anastasia called out to the SS on guard. "You! Yes, you, the Tall Guys Club. What are your names and ranks?"

With an air of someone who had every right to be there, Anastasia produced a small notebook and a pencil from her pockets.

"Are you a journalist, or what?" one of them called back, suddenly suspicious.

"What if I am?"

"Do you have permission to be here?"

"Do you?"

The SS bristled. "Get lost before we arrest you."

"Why would you arrest me? Are you doing anything illegal? Is that why you don't want to give me your names?"

The air was growing thicker and chillier by the moment. Holding her breath along with the rest of the women, Margot had just opened her mouth to implore Anastasia to stop it right this instant before she got herself arrested as an enemy of the state, but then she saw something in that mad half-Russian's eyes and kept quiet.

There was no fear of arrest or even execution there. There was only fierce love and willingness to put her head under the ax for the right cause—because she'd seen persecution first-hand, she'd seen martial law before it had come into existence in Nazi Germany, she had been in Jochen's place—not on racial grounds but on class ones—and she would die before she'd let the same thing happen to anyone else.

And so, Margot stepped away and, instead of blocking Anastasia's path, linked arms with her—the woman who had become family to her.

"You know what? Never mind the names. I'm not a journalist. I'm an artist and so..." Anastasia didn't finish; she only flashed the SS that feral grin of hers and, stuffing the notebook into her pocket, produced a sketchbook from under her fur coat and began sketching the men's faces in it with almost photographic precision.

As soon as it dawned on the SS what it was precisely that she was doing, their leader leapt down from the stairs and was upon her in a second. But Anastasia was faster than him. Dodging his hands, she threw the album over her shoulder and into the crowd, where it disappeared instantaneously, and, when he made another grab for her, shoved a small white card into his face.

"I would like to make a call to your superior, who just happens to be my son-in-law. Would you be so kind as to accompany me and listen to what he has to say?"

With cold sweat breaking out on her temples, Margot made out Kurt's name and rank on the business card embossed in black, with two lightning bolts of the SS marking its corner. Her sister Gertrud's husband, Sturmbannführer Kurt, whose house Margot had personally promised to burn to the ground during their meeting at the Olympic stadium.

"Anastasia," Margot mouthed, shaking her head.

The rank on the card produced a certain impression. The SS hesitated but took it from Anastasia's hands all the same, eyeing her the entire time like a poisonous snake.

While he was preoccupied with the calling card, Margot leaned closer to Anastasia and began whispering in her ear:

"What are you doing? He won't help. He'll only be glad if Jochen disappears—"

"Margot," Anastasia purred back without taking her eyes off the SS, "what will happen to his career if they find out that his brother-in-law is a Jew?"

Margot pulled back in stunned disbelief. Coming out here to protest was one thing, but threatening a high-ranking SS man with outright blackmail was a whole different business entirely. A game of Russian roulette, and Anastasia had just loaded a single bullet into the gun.

The words froze on Margot's lips, and the SS man, huffing and puffing in visible discontent, began motioning Anastasia after himself and into the Gestapo headquarters.

"Hold Goosie for now, will you?" were the last words Margot heard from her, thrown with wonderful nonchalance over Anastasia's shoulder. "I'll call your father first. He'll be here shortly and will take Goose from you."

If I don't come back, her heart racing, Margot finished mentally for her, the woman who didn't have to lift a finger for Margot's family, but who put her very life on the line just because it was the right thing to do.

An hour passed, and Anastasia still didn't come out. Margot's father appeared from around the corner instead, half-trotting, holding onto his hat, out of breath and pale with fright. He scooped Margot up and hushed her as soon as she tried to explain, in a voice strangled with sobs, about Jochen and Anastasia and her entire life that was about to go to pieces.

"It's all right, *Maus*." Karl called her by her childhood nickname—*little mouse*—and all at once, Margot felt soothed by his protective embrace. "I'm sorry that I haven't been there for you as much as I should have, but I'm here now. And together, we'll pull through. You'll see that we will."

"I should have stopped Anastasia. It was idiotic, the entire plan of hers; it will never work; I see it now. It'll only anger him more—"

"Hush, *Maus*. There's nothing you could have done. Stasia is a force of her own. Once she gets something into that obstinate head of hers, an entire army wouldn't be strong enough to deter her."

It sounded very much like a eulogy. Margot looked at her father. There was mist in his eyes, but unmistakable pride in his voice. Karl threw a gaze full of infinite longing at the locked door of the Gestapo headquarters and pursed his lips so they wouldn't tremble.

"I have filed for divorce," he said suddenly, his eyes still on the door behind which the one he loved was being held.

"Good for you, *Vati*." Her chin resting on his shoulder, Margot was looking in the opposite direction, at the doors of the holding center.

"You're not mad, are you?"

"No. You should have done it a long time ago."

"Gertrud doesn't think so."

"Gertrud has Mother and Kurt. The three of them will be very happy together." With the best will in the world, Margot couldn't keep the bitterness out of her voice.

How sad it was, having a government so divisive that even members of the same family now belonged to two opposite camps, waging a partisan war on each other.

"They keep giving me trouble though," Karl said softly and resentfully.

"Mother and Gertrud?"

"Your mother did throw a right fit, but, no, I'm talking about the magistrates. They keep asking me for better grounds for divorce. As if not living with one's spouse for years and having nothing in common with her isn't good enough."

"They would have granted you divorce if Mother was

Jewish. In a split second."

"I know. Pathetic, isn't it?"

At their feet, Goose whined softly. Even he appeared to agree.

Soon after, Edna and Erna arrived with the day's bread, but it just didn't taste the same. Margot found she had no appetite at all. Instead, she marched back and forth in between the holding center and the Gestapo office and chanted, together with her father, until their voices grew hoarse, "Reunite. Families. Now! Reunite. Families. Now!"

And along with them, women marched as well, the women and the few men there were, and children and one mahogany-colored dog barking his solidarity as the Gestapo looked on from above at windows fogged with breath and helpless fury.

The Gestapo remained there, behind the limestone barricade of their office, when a newcomer arrived and positioned herself on its steps, holding a small postcard in her hand for everyone to see. Margot took in her lavender coat, her blond locks pinned in an obvious rush and already coming undone, her bright pink cheeks, the face of a porcelain doll, and her stance of a warrior ready to die, and thought it to be the most wonderful contrast she'd ever seen.

"Where have you sent my husband, you brutes?" In the crisp air, her voice rang high and clear above the crowd. "*Stay strong, my love. God willing, we'll meet again! My heart is forever with you, no matter the distance.* This was sent from some town in Poland. My husband managed to throw it from the train's window. A cattle train. The kind Polish farmer who'd seen it happen picked it up and mailed it to me, explained it in his letter."

A communal gasp turned into silence, growing more outraged and ominous by the moment.

"Told you they were shipping them east," Hedwig hissed under her breath.

Margot saw her father turn to her, looking alarmed. In the couple of hours that he'd spent there, he had come to know these women in person—Hedwig and Marthe and Edna and Lisl—and their battles were his battles too now; for the Gestapo could ship the woman he loved east as well, just as they'd done to these women's husbands.

Margot's frozen lips, pale-purple in the bitter cold, pressed into an even harder line as she listened closely.

"Where is he?!" The new woman's voice broke, turned into an anguished cry as tears poured from her eyes. "Where is he, you murderers?"

"And where are the women you took?" Marthe shouted, her hands framing her mouth to amplify her voice.

The tables were turning slowly, deliberately. The crowd was pushing forward now, a wave gathering new force, ready to sweep everything out of its way.

"Where are those people from the Clou?" Hedwig shouted next to Margot.

Only Margot didn't scream anything. She felt lightheaded, frozen stiff and half-starved, but this wasn't the reason why she hadn't budged even when the crowd began slamming their fists into the Gestapo headquarters doors. Some terrible transformation was occurring in her as she watched a Gestapo official appear on the doorstep and, instead of giving an explanation, demand the name of the person who had sent the postcard.

The gall of that swine... Margot's lips moved but she couldn't tell whether she uttered the words or only thought them.

"*People* sent it! Human beings!" the widow—she must have been a widow by now; everyone was just as certain of it as the woman herself—cried into the Gestapo's face. There was no deluding them any longer. The fate of the Jews was death, imminent and brutally swift—the Nazis had made it abundantly clear.

The Gestapo recoiled from the unexpected attack; tried to collect himself and put on a mask of indignation. "So, you're saying we're not human?" But the mask didn't fit him properly. To her horror, Margot could swear she saw it crumble and fall off him in pieces, revealing some nightmarish creature underneath—not quite human, but something vile, crawling with maggots, a half-rotten corpse in an ill-fitting uniform. That, too, was disintegrating, just like the entire façade of the organization he served, the government he had pledged his allegiance to, uncovering their true faces they'd been successfully hiding behind the masks of the people's "servants."

"You're not human. You're murderers." Margot's voice came out flat and emotionless in a moment of sudden silence. The Gestapo met her eyes; paled slightly, visibly. It wasn't a heated accusation this time; not just some exaggerated term thrown at his face. She was stating a simple fact. "Murderers."

He pulled himself up, made an about-face and retreated behind the door.

"Murderers!" the crowd hissed after him. Hissed, then murmured, then began to scream. They were a mob now, uncontrollable, fired up with outrage and suffering that had lasted far too long—not just a few days here in the wind and snow, but years before that. Years of deprivation, discrimination, persecution and sheer hatred directed at them for loving those they weren't supposed to.

And in the middle of it, Margot stood, sick to her stomach with the hateful policies and false pretenses that this was all for their own good. She felt it harden on her like plaster—this exhaustion and the constant fear and abuse—turning her into something more than a woman. It turned her into a warrior who refused to budge even when an open military vehicle arrived with SS men sitting there, all steel and weapons and not a single heart among the four of them.

The Gestapo must have made a call, begging for reinforcements against the unarmed women. It was almost amusing, the fear that women's rage instilled in those supposedly powerful men, now cowering behind bolted doors and hoping for the SS to sort "those mad broads" out. A dark shadow of a smirk began to form on Margot's lips, mirrored by those of her sisters-in-arms. Yes, they must have been mad to fight guns with sheer rage, but that madness was righteous. They had been pushed for far too long. Now, it was their turn to shove back and, by God, Margot would see to it that they remembered that shove for centuries to come.

The truck kept driving on, guns trained on the women's chests. The sun tore through the clouds and in its sudden blinding light, Margot recognized Kurt as the SS squad's commander. He recognized her as well; she saw it in the slits of his cruel eyes. So, it was personal now. Not just a German against a German, but family against family. Here, something much bigger was at stake. Here, in the small street of Rosen-straße, good itself battled evil, and no matter the outcome, Margot felt at peace with herself, knowing precisely on which side she was fighting.

"Disperse right this instant or we shall ram through this illegal gathering!" Kurt bellowed above the growling of the truck's engine.

Margot met his stare with her own and stepped forward just when he expected her to back down. "So, ram."

"Do not force my hand, woman!" Kurt waved his machine gun in the air. It was meant to be a show of force, which, for some utterly inexplicable reason, didn't impress anyone in the slightest.

"You still don't understand, do you?" Margot cocked her head at him, almost pitifully. "We're not going anywhere. You'll have to either release our men or kill us all. But you won't frighten us into submission. Not anymore."

Kurt's angered face turned to the color of ash. Never before had his authority been challenged in such a manner. Margot saw muscles working near his set jaws; all the while the crowd calmly looked on.

"Ram them!" He had finally lost it.

The driver of the truck looked from his commander to Margot and back, his gloved hands uncertain on the wheel.

Kurt grasped him by the collar like a dog. "Mow them down or I'll have you shot for insubordination! And what are you waiting for?" Whipping round, he stared at his men, looking just as dubious as the driver. "Shoot them!"

Reluctantly, the SS leveled their machine guns at the women's chests. They were used to flexing their muscles at the communists and Jews, but these were women, their German women, certainly not the enemy but young, pretty faces and bright coats and stockings and heels... They began to shoot, but visibly at the cobbles at the women's feet, at the already pock-marked walls, at the sun itself bathing the women's heads in its golden light like the saints with halos in ancient paintings.

With Kurt's fist on his collar, the driver accelerated hard, right toward Margot, who simply refused to move. Her father and her fellow comrades linking arms, meeting steel with unprotected flesh, drawing strength not from the machine guns that were blasting all around them, but from their hearts that beat for the men and women they refused to abandon.

"Stop right this instant!" Karl was screaming in a voice full of rage and righteous fury. "You're shooting at the people you're pretending to protect, you murderers!"

In sickness and health.

"You're a murderer, Kurt, you hear me? A murderer and a criminal and you shall bear this guilt for the rest of time—"

Until death do us part.

"Jochen," Margot whispered with a last longing look at the holding center's windows, closing her eyes against the blinding light of the military car speeding head-on toward her.

EPILOGUE

November was unseasonably cold the year when the war
ended. By the North Sea, it was colder still, with harsh, unforgiving gusts of wind tearing into the clothes of the crowd of
refugees waiting to be admitted onto a ship sailing for New
York. The sky hung low and leaden above the waters smashing
into the iron side of the beast that resembled a battleship much
more than a passenger one. Perhaps it used to be at one point or
another. Perhaps it still carried some of its guns on its deck.
They said some Nazi submarines still roamed the dark waters of
the Atlantic in search of vulnerable prey. They said half of the
criminals who should have been tried at Nuremberg, together
with the meager bunch the Allies had captured, were missing.
They said a lot of things these days.

"Is that all your luggage?"

Margot hid a smile at the dubious look an American
serviceman gave the small suitcase she held in her hand.
Around the wrist of her other hand, a frayed rope was tied—
Goose's leash that had seen him through years of bombard-
ments, daily walks among the rubble, lines for water and, later,
for ration cards, and at last, an intolerably long trek to the North

Sea, half on foot and half on trains that were only just now resuming their service. He looked like a junkyard dog, all skin and bones, fur covered with the dust of the roads he had trotted on, but his silly doggie grin was still in place, as though he, too, sensed a new beginning as he sniffed at the air around the great ship.

Margot's suitcase itself, just like the few clothes in it, had come from the Red Cross. Besides her wedding ring and the clothes on her back, Margot didn't have anything left of her former life. Whatever she hadn't sold on the black market in the last couple of years of the war, the bombs had claimed. Not that she minded all that much. Margot preferred to have a fresh start, without a single reminder of the nightmarish past.

"Do you get a lot of refugees overburdened with luggage?" she asked, only half in jest.

"You'd be surprised. Some helped themselves to whatever was left of the Nazi bigwigs' fortunes. As reimbursement of sorts." With that explanation, the American marked Margot's suitcase with chalk and motioned her and her four-legged companion toward the ship's deck.

However, instead of climbing the wide ramp, Margot paused at the bottom, squinting against the salty droplets hurled at her face by the relentless wind, and turned to watch the American, now staring at a worn backpack, handsewn and patched at the seams—a typical refugee affair that had survived the persecution, bombing and the war itself.

"Shall I ask?" The serviceman had trouble finding a spot to mark on that grubby item.

"You can, but I fear it'll take too long to explain."

Margot couldn't help but give the smile of a conspirator to her husband, who winked at her over the serviceman's shoulder. Jochen hadn't fared any better than Goose—Margot couldn't stop giggling at the thought of when the couple had been trying their best to put themselves into a presentable state the day before boarding. There was only one cracked mirror for a few hundred of them in a former sports center turned refugee center and Jochen had laughed incessantly as he ran a comb borrowed from a fellow traveler through his closely cropped hair. Goose had fleas and he had lice. Goose's "coat" had turned into an atrocity and so had Jochen's, but what was one to do if there wasn't enough water to drink at the end of the war, let alone wash an overcoat and a dog on top? They were both half-starved, but, just like Goose, Jochen wouldn't stop grinning ever since they'd reached the port town of Wesermünde. He, too, must have smelled freedom in the air.

"Jewish?" the American asked sympathetically, just now noticing the outline of a yellow star that was no longer there, burned out by the sun over the years, on Jochen's gray overcoat.

"Yes."

"From the camps?"

"No. From Berlin."

The American straightened up, staring at the man in front of him in utter amazement. "How did you manage to survive, buddy?" In his voice was barely concealed wonder.

Jochen's grin grew on his emaciated face, turning almost mischievous as he regarded Margot. Catching onto something, the American shifted his eyes from the man in front of him to the woman he had just checked, and back.

"My wife wouldn't let Berlin's Gestapo take me," Jochen replied at last. "We were locked in a Rosenstraße holding center for a week. The SS were getting ready to ship us east as soon as they were done shipping other Berlin Jews. The SS were already preparing us for cattle trains: we had only straw to sleep on and a bucket in a corner of each room to relieve ourselves. Scarcely any food or even water. But then our wives found out where we were being held and, from that moment on, the SS didn't have a chance. They challenged them openly; wouldn't disperse even when threatened with machine guns. In the end, that's what saved us. The power of their love that was stronger than any threat, any bullet. They physically blocked the SS truck with their bodies. The SS splattered the ground and walls around them with bullets, accelerated towards them trying to frighten them into leaving, but our wives stood their ground until the victorious end. After the SS realized that our obstinate ladies wouldn't budge or see reason, there was nothing left for them to do but release us. After all, executing German women in cold blood or even arresting them all en masse wouldn't sit well with the general public. Ordinary Germans, they didn't care much for us Jews, but when it came to German women, that was a different subject entirely. Not even Hitler would approve of something of that sort, and that should tell you something."

"You're pulling my leg," the serviceman said, an uncertain smile playing on his clean-shaven, youthful face.

"I'm standing in front of you, aren't I?" Jochen beamed once again and motioned at the people waiting in line and also smiling the same mysterious smiles. "We all are. Because our women didn't give up on us."

Somewhere in the crowd, Margot's father also stood, his hand most likely circling his new wife's waist. The Nazis wouldn't let him marry an enemy of the state and a foreigner, but the officials from the American sector of Berlin had been only too glad to permit the victim of Nazi persecution and former political prisoner Anastasia Kasdorf to become the new Frau Kaltenbach. Convicted of taking part in illegal gathering and treasonous activities in the time of war, Anastasia had spent the last few years of the war locked in Spandau prison, her life hanging in a delicate balance that could have been tipped by any official's whim. Anastasia herself claimed that it was pure luck that, too preoccupied with a failing war effort, the SS somehow neglected to execute her as they'd been promising her they would for quite some time. It was further sheer fortune

that her file had been destroyed during one of the bombard-
ments and therefore, to the Soviet SMERSH agents, she was
simply a political prisoner, a victim of fascism, whom they
released without further ado. The Americans, in their turn, had
promptly issued refugee visas for both couples. Margot remembered how, upon her release from Spandau prison, Karl had
asked Anastasia if she wished to go back to France perhaps, but
Anastasia had declared, in her no-nonsense voice that had lost
nothing of its confidence while in captivity, that she had had
enough of Europe and the further she could get away from it,
the sounder she would sleep.

Apparently, Margot's brother-in-law, Kurt, shared Anastasia's opinion, as he'd run from Berlin in civilian clothes with
forged documents just before the Soviet forces encircled the
capital, leaving his wife, Gertrud, and mother-in-law, Maria,
behind, much to their dismay. Margot had learned of their
predicament from the letter they'd sent through the Red Cross,
using their endless refugee lists to seek her out. Margot had
considered crumpling the letter in her fist and hurling it out into
the street, but she was much too kind of a soul for her own good
(Anastasia's words, accompanied by a shake of a stubborn head
full of black hair now streaked visibly with gray). Through the
same American agency, she had tried to appeal to the authorities on her mother and sister's behalf as they stood, miserable
and reduced to nothing overnight, behind her. However, despite
all of her requests, the Americans refused to have anything to
do with supporters of Nazism and, instead of issuing them visas,
ordered them both to the denazification program.

"You ought to be grateful we don't arrest you for your
husband's crimes," an American official had grumbled when
Gertrud had tried to protest, and slammed the stamp onto her
papers. "Report to the indicated headquarters for lectures. Go
learn what your husband was up to."

Margot hadn't seen either of the women since.

Somewhere in that crowd, Margot's former sisters-in-arms stood with their husbands in tow—Hedwig and her Rudi, Greta and her Fritz, Marthe and her Otto—the past behind them, left somewhere among the ruins of Berlin where it belonged. In front of them, across the stormy Atlantic, lay the future, unknown and slightly terrifying. They would scatter across the states and learn a new language and try to live a life that was alien and not quite their own, but they had proved that they were survivors, that they could make it through anything as long as they had each other.

Their love was their guiding compass. All they had to do was follow its call.

A LETTER FROM ELLIE

Dear reader,

I want to say a huge thank you for choosing to read *The Wife Who Risked Everything*. If you did enjoy it, and want to keep up to date with all my latest releases, just sign up at the following link. Your email address will never be shared and you can unsubscribe at any time.

www.bookouture.com/ellie-midwood

Thank you so much for reading Margot and Jochen's story! Even though both of them are fictional characters, they have been inspired by very real people who lived in Berlin during the Nazi rule, namely Charlotte and Julius Israel, Elsa and Rudi Holzer, Wally and Günter Grodka, and also Werner Goldberg —a *Mischling* (a degrading term for so-called "half-bloods" with one Jewish and one Aryan parent) whose picture was posted in *Berliner Tagesblatt* with a caption reading "The Ideal German Soldier."

All of the anti-Semitic laws and their timeframe are also true to historical fact, just like the fictional consequences Margot and Jochen had to suffer as their result. Fictional events involving certain historical figures mentioned in the novel are also based on true events. For instance, Josef Goebbels indeed intended to leave his wife for Czech actress Lida Baarová until Hitler interfered, at which point Lida's very life was threatened.

With her former high-ranking lover offering her no protection, she had to escape Nazi Germany in secret, which was no easy feat given the fact that the Gestapo were following her closely. I thought that Goebbels abandoning the woman he claimed he loved more than anything represented quite a contrast to the devotion "Aryan" wives displayed toward their Jewish husbands, and so, I decided to include it in the novel to show once again the hypocrisy of Nazi leadership and the bravery and selflessness of regular German citizens who would stop at nothing to save their persecuted spouses.

When describing the climatic events of the novel—the Rosenstraße protests themselves—I tried to stick to the real timeline of the events as closely as possible to preserve historical accuracy. All of the events shown through fictional Margot's eyes indeed happened and were later recounted by women taking part in those protests. The bombings, the sympathetic bar owner across the street, the police passing parcels with food and items of personal hygiene for the men and women detained in the holding center, and even the SS charging at the crowd with their armored vehicle and shooting at the protesters with their machine guns, are also based on the first-hand accounts of the survivors.

In my research of the protests, besides the surviving historical documents, I relied heavily on a truly outstanding historical study that I highly recommend to everyone interested in reading the real accounts of these few couples that inspired Margot and Jochen—*Resistance of the Heart* by Nathan Stoltzfus.

Thank you so much for reading! By doing so and by spreading the word, you ensure that the actions of these brave women and men will be known to future generations and hopefully help to prevent the horrific events of the past ever being repeated. Out of the entire Jewish population of Nazi Germany, the overwhelming number of Jews who were fortunate to survive the Holocaust were mostly Berlin Jews. It is my —and most historians'—profound conviction that they would have most certainly been deported and murdered if it weren't for the brave actions of their spouses, who risked their own lives to stand up for their loved ones and went down in history as heroes who led the only successful protest in Nazi Germany. Thank you for taking interest in their story and thus keeping their memory alive.

Never forget.
Never again.

www.elliemidwood.com

 facebook.com/EllieMidwood

ACKNOWLEDGMENTS

First and foremost, I want to thank the wonderful Bookouture family for helping me bring the Rosenstraße protests' story to light. It wouldn't be possible without the help and guidance of my incredible editor Christina Demosthenous, whose insights truly bring my characters to life and whose support and encouragement make me strive to work even harder on my novels and become a better writer. Thank you, Bookouture family, for all your help and support throughout the years. It's been a true pleasure working with all of you and I already can't wait to create more projects under your guidance.

Huge thanks to my family for believing in me and showing such enthusiasm for each one of my new book babies. Thank you for raising me a free spirit, for letting me choose my own way and supporting me on every step—I am where I am now thanks to your unconditional love and unwavering faith in me and my abilities. Love you to death.

A special thanks to my fiancé and two besties (sisters from other misters, as I call them) for their love, support and understanding when it comes to missed dinners and lunches because of my deadlines—I promise, I'll make it up to you!

Huge thanks to all of my fellow authors whom I got to know through social media and who became my very close friends—you all are such an inspiration! I consider you all a family.

And, of course, huge thanks to my readers for patiently waiting for new releases, for celebrating cover reveals together with me, for reading ARCs and sending me those absolutely amazing   I-stayed-up-till-3am-last-night-because-I-just-had-to-finish-your-wonderful-book messages, for your reviews that always make my day, and for falling in love with my characters just as much as I do. You are the reason why I write. Thank you so much for reading my stories.

And, finally, I owe my biggest thanks to all the brave people who continue to inspire my novels. Some of you survived the Holocaust and the Second World War, some of you perished, but it's your incredible courage, resilience and self-sacrifice that will live on in our hearts. Your example will always inspire us to be better people, to stand up for what is right, to give a voice to the ones who have been silenced, to protect the ones who cannot protect themselves. You all are true heroes. Thank you.

Printed in the USA
CPSIA information can be obtained
at www.ICGtesting.com
LVHW090811070424
776674LV00039B/1119